THE BUDAPEST CONNECTION

ADVANCE PRAISE

"Dr. Henry Lee is writing novels in his spare time! Whether he is recollecting, creating, or fantasizing, *The Budapest Connection* is an exciting, educational, interesting, and suspenseful read!"

—Harry Lee
Sheriff, Jefferson Parish, Harvey, Louisiana

"Drs. Lee and Labriola have created a winner, a novel filled with murder and international intrigue."

—Ursula McCafferty
Author of *Home Is the Sailor, Home from the Sea*

"This story is a master of intrigue that reflects the abilities and experiences of the authors. It is a terrific blend of mystery fiction and real forensic science. Dr. Lee is a mentor to forensic scientists and Dr. Labriola is a mentor to mystery writers."

—Dan Uitti
President, Connecticut Authors & Publishers Association

DR. HENRY C. LEE

& JERRY LABRIOLA, MD

THE BUDAPEST CONNECTION

a novel

Prometheus Books
59 John Glenn Drive
Amherst, New York 14228-2197

Published 2006 by Prometheus Books

Inquiries should be addressed to
Prometheus Books
59 John Glenn Drive
Amherst, New York 14228–2197
VOICE: 716–691–0133, ext. 207
FAX: 716–564–2711
WWW.PROMETHEUSBOOKS.COM

10 09 08 07 06 5 4 3 2 1

Library of Congress Cataloging-in-Publication Data

Lee, Henry C.
The Budapest connection / by Henry Lee and Jerry Labriola.
p. cm.
ISBN-13: 979–1–59102–465–1 (alk. paper)
ISBN-10: 1–59102–465–X (alk. paper)
1. Forensic scientists—Fiction. I. Labriola, Jerry. II. Title.

PS3612.E34287B83 2006
813'.6—dc22

2006020171

Printed in the United States of America on acid-free paper

PROLOGUE

Both Interpol at the international level and SWAT teams at the local level have been successful tools in handling emergency situations and helping to combat crime. Interpol's official name is the International Criminal Police Organization. A voluntary law enforcement entity, it involves 179 member nations. SWAT stands for Special Weapons and Tactics; teams with this designation have become an integral part of contemporary special police forces.

Why not then have a single highly specialized coalition to help handle emergency situations and solve crimes, one that includes internationally recognized forensic scientists? They might be dispatched anywhere in the world at a moment's notice, travel as a unit in their private jet, and gather information at "hot case" crime scenes whose integrity has been maintained, or at "cold case" scenes where reconstruction of the crime would take place.

Such a team—five in number—forms the backdrop for this mystery novel. The group is known as the Global Interactive Forensics Team, or GIFT. In a field with burgeoning forensic technologies, GIFT was conceived as a means of pooling global experience and expertise.

Dr. Henry Lee
Dr. Jerry Labriola

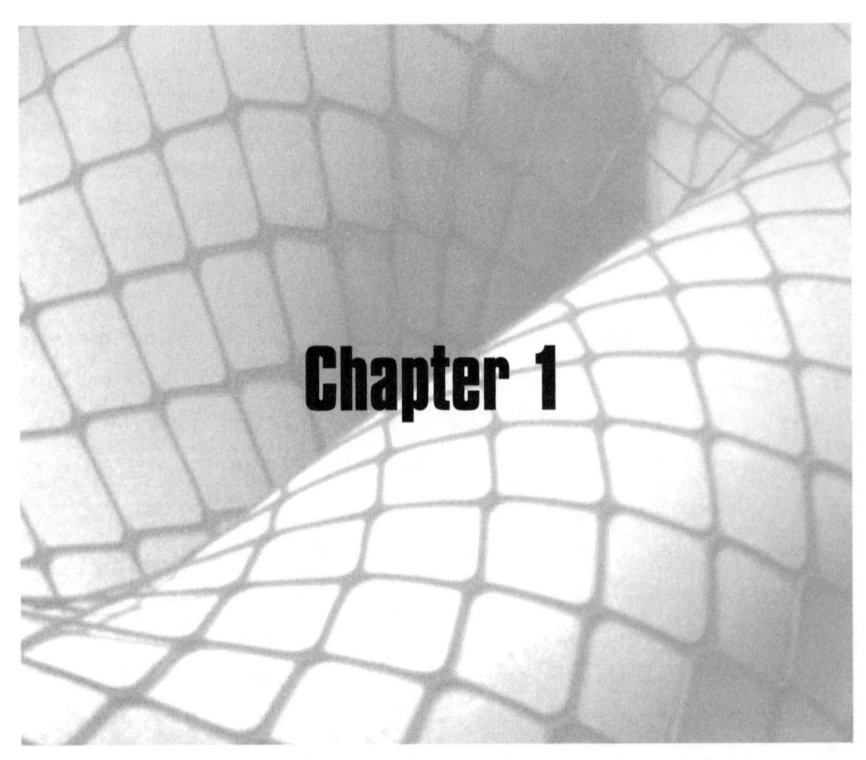

Chapter 1

WEDNESDAY, OCTOBER 16
8 PM

Dr. Henry Liu had never seen anything like it. Three nude dead bodies arranged into the shape of a perfect triangle. All white female. All young. All in their late teens. They lay face-up, each with one eye open, one closed. He spotted a single gunshot wound at each girl's left temple.

Dr. George Silvain, a noted forensic pathologist from New York City's east side, had been summoned to the crime scene at the edge of the Brooklyn Marine Terminal, a complex running two miles along the waterfront. Surveying the bodies, he in turn requested the assistance of the other four members of GIFT, the Global Interactive Forensics Team. They had been winding down their regular monthly meeting at Baderro's, a four-star restaurant in midtown Manhattan.

"They're like winks," George said. "The killer's scoffing, don't you think?"

"No, they have more meaning than that," Henry replied, peering down at the women. "Even the triangle does." He walked carefully around the bodies, his hands clasped behind his back, conscious of the "give" in the wooden dock. "How about it, Ed? Rings a bell?"

Ed Blegan, a state police sergeant, had driven him to the scene. Ed looked at the bodies. "Don't tell me the Triads?" he whispered. "We were just talking about them last week."

"Uh-huh," Henry said, his attention divided. He glanced back at their car, then to the right toward a short wooden jetty. There, he couldn't account for twin shadows that swept over the open water and dissolved into the blackness beyond. Or, in a fleeting moment, another shadow he caught in the corner of his eye; it disappeared behind the nearest harbor building.

"The handiwork of the Chinese Mafia?" Silvain finally interjected.

"Maybe I'll explain later," Henry replied. "Ed, do me a favor. Get the camera. Take a distant shot of the full bodies from right here. Then a closer shot of each one and a close-up of their faces."

The sergeant left for the parking lot. Henry shouted, "And bring some gloves."

Since the inception of GIFT, Ed was a bodyguard to the group when assembled and to Henry in particular. He became Henry's side-kick, confidant, and most reliable sounding board. Barely forty—at six foot four and 250 pounds with probing eyes and hollow cheeks—he was a remarkable Clint Eastwood look-alike, except a bit heavier. And Henry reminded him of it regularly.

"Does that make your day?" Ed would ask and he'd laugh at his own comment as if he never made it before.

"But wouldn't it *really* make your day if you could squeeze into your uniform?" Henry once teased.

"Why should I?"

"Why shouldn't you?"

"Because Eastwood never shows his muscles."

The sky was overcast, the moon pale. To the far left, the sign for Pier 6 could be made out on a stanchion. Its light cut through wisps of vapor usually seen at daybreak. Several cargo ships lay moored nearby, dockside cranes with dangling nets silhouetted above their poles. The combined sounds of a distant foghorn and barking dog seemed rehearsed. There was no fishy smell, which Henry would have expected on such an unseasonably warm night, and no stevedores around, which he wouldn't have. Back in the adjacent lot, six blue and white police cruisers were angled haphazardly, their strobe lights still flashing, doors open, radio transmissions spewing police-code jargon. Several nondescript cars were grouped alongside. Thirty feet from the bodies, a mobile unit of lights flooded the area like a highway construction site at midnight. Half a dozen uniformed police officers stood at attention along a strip of yellow tape that formed a wide cordon at the periphery, while a handful of plainclothes detectives quietly milled about its center, not far from Henry. Twice as many news reporters craned over the tape.

"No picture taking, folks," a police lieutenant exclaimed, "or we confiscate your cameras."

A short, bald detective, Harold Latimore, eased up to Henry. They had worked together before. "What do you think, doc? Any ideas?"

"Hal, you know my stock answer at this stage of the game. . . . So, who found the bodies?"

"Two of our men were cruising the area and they saw a car speeding away. It shot right out of the rear driveway of the parking lot. Out of sight like *that*," he said, snapping his fingers. "They thought they'd better investigate rather than chase after the car."

Henry looked back. "One driveway," he said. "Two parking lots. The one we all parked in, and over the scrub brush to the right of that, probably one for overflow. Did the officers say they saw the car leave from one of the lots or just from the driveway?"

"From the lot, as a matter of fact."

"Which one?"

"Overflow."

"I see," Henry said, running a finger over his lower lip. "Could they identify the make of the car?"

"No, too far away, but they said it was a sedan. Dark color."

"So they searched the area, saw the bodies, and radioed in?"

"Correct. Then we dispatched our uniform and detective divisions. I.D. should be here any minute."

Henry nodded politely. He signaled George over and said, "The police called you directly?"

"Yeah, I was halfway to the meeting—got a late start. Figured I'd hightail it here, then call you guys."

A tall, paunchy sixty-year-old, George's hair was bushy at the sides, as if to compensate for the bald spot on top. Even his clothes appeared bushy, or at least baggy. His serious demeanor and rationed smile were at odds with his inclination to hug anyone he knew more than casually, whether female or male.

"Where are the others?" he asked.

"What's that?"

"Karl, Gail, Jay. Didn't they come with you?"

Henry stared at his colleague. "C'mon, George, when was the last time you saw us hang together once we got to a scene?" He looked around. "There's Jay—with Gail, of course. I guess that's a detective they're talking to. And Karl with his goddamn camera over there—like always, drawn first to peripheral things. What the hell he's doing taking a picture of a cargo net, I haven't a clue."

Ed returned with a pair of latex gloves and moved to take photos of the three women. Henry snapped on the gloves, waited for Ed to complete his work, and leaned his six-foot-one frame over each body, concentrating on each victim's head.

He was proud of his build—far taller than his parents. He theorized that it must be a genetic mutation. He had their black hair and brown eyes, but, in contrast to other family members, he was the only male who appeared top-heavy, with the upper-body contour of a less towering man, perhaps a boxer. Under different circumstances, his smile was rich and beguiling and would pleat the skin around his eyes.

After a cursory inspection, he looked up at Ed and said, "Amazing. Such similarity: young, blonde, pretty, nude, heavy lipstick, polished nails, no jewelry, no distinguishing marks, the eyelid thing. Even the cause of death."

"Shot?"

"Left temple on all."

Henry studied one victim's wound with the larger of the two magnifying glasses he always carried in the right inside pocket of his blue blazer. He once joked that they provided balance, since on his left side was a Smith and Wesson snubby in a shoulder rig. Henry was partial to blazers and had a half dozen or so in his closet—brown, green, blue, off-brown, off-green, off-blue. He maintained it was buttons that made a jacket, and all of his were gold. And there was always a supply of wrapped hard candies in one of the side pockets.

He was particular about shoes, too; his best were loafer-types, easy to slip off wherever and whenever: under a desk, on a plane, at the theater.

Henry put his hand to the side of the victim's jaw and neck; it was cool to touch. The muscles there felt stiff as compared to those below. A slender ribbon of dark crimson lay caked along her left shoulder and upper arm. Midway between the corresponding eye and ear, at a point an inch above a line drawn between their upper margins, was a bullet entrance wound. It was round with blackened and seared margins.

There was no exit wound and no spent shell casings around. "Professional job," he muttered.

He straightened and, while still staring at the body, ran through several mental sequences:

Body cool to touch.
Early rigor mortis in small muscles of jaw and neck.
Early fixed lividity with no blanching.
Dead at least four to six hours.
Edges of wound black and seared.
No soot smudge or powder tattooing.
Hard contact by gun muzzle against temple.
Round, rather than stellate, entrance wound.
No exit wound.
Most likely a .22-caliber handgun.

Henry deduced that since there was no exit wound, the bullet lacked the velocity to penetrate bone a second time, instead ricocheting around within the skull cavity, inflicting fatal damage. He knew that a .22 was a good bet, no doubt a revolver, not a semiautomatic weapon. And, from the way the bodies had been neatly positioned—characteristic of an organized, staged, secondary crime scene—he believed that the women had been murdered elsewhere and transported to the dock. One step remained for confirmation.

"Let's check the overflow lot," he said.

On the way over, Henry was reasonably certain the "hits" were the work of the American Mafia. Their modus operandi seemed clear. But that didn't square with the triangle, for he was just as certain it pointed to the Chinese Triads. He remembered dealing with them when he was a police captain in Taiwan in the early 1960s. They often used a finger or a stick to fashion a triangle from their victim's blood, next to the body.

Was one criminal element trying to implicate the other? Or were they working together? An unlikely scenario.

They walked the length of the paved main lot—stopping to grab a searchlight from Henry's Chrysler 300M—and crossed through a path in the scrub brush. The smaller lot received scant illumination from a single lamppost near the jetty. Ed handled the searchlight like a watering hose as he preceded Henry among empty bottles, newspaper scraps, and tall weeds scattered in the soft dirt.

"Not used much," Henry said. "But there are the tire marks."

They followed the marks forward to the front edge of the lot. Edging closer to Ed and the searchlight, Henry said, "Here's where the car was parked and here's where we see some shoe prints. Looks like a single set on each side of the tracks. Both sets lead to the backseat. What else, Ed?"

"About these sets?"

"Yes."

"No scuff marks. Both sets leading straight to the car. None to the rear. None circling around."

"And therefore?"

"Therefore, if these two people brought the bodies to the dock, they didn't carry them from here."

"But you see something else, correct?"

"Correct."

"And that is?"

"A third set opposite the driver's door—but leading nowhere—like someone just stood there. Not very deep. Looks like the dirt is more compact there."

"Excellent. I agree with you. If I had any of my little gold deputy badges with me, I'd give you one."

Ed laughed and said, "If I had a badge for every time you've said that to me, I could make a living selling them."

Henry pretended not to hear. "So if not from this side, maybe from the other," he said.

They climbed three rotting wooden steps up to the dock and walked toward the water. Tied to the jetty—much like one behind a lakeside cottage—was a flat-bottom racing boat with an outboard engine.

"I'll be . . ." Ed said, his voice lowered.

"Figured," Henry said. "It's a runabout. I'd guess fifteen feet."

"You mean you knew a motor boat would be here? How?"

"Two questions. Answer number one is that I didn't know for sure but, because of answer number two, it was a good bet. If we had a choice of hauling three bodies by either land or sea around here, I'd take sea. It's safer. No traffic jams, for example."

"But why escape in a car and not the boat?"

"Less vulnerable in a car if the bodies are found quickly. Plus, it could have been a matter of fuel. They knew they'd be stealing the boat—from somewhere—and if the only boat they could find had a fuel gauge that registered low, they might not be able to make it back to shore. So someone else was waiting in the car for them. Very carefully planned."

"Why not see if the key is still there and read the gauge?" Ed asked. He hunched over as if to drop into the boat.

"Wait," Henry said, grasping his arm. "Crime scene, remember? Let's let the crime scene people do their job."

Ed stopped short, his grin sheepish.

"But," Henry added, "I'll wager you my whole supply of gold badges that they find some blonde hair in the boat." He motioned with his head that they should return to the others.

On the way, Ed stopped to ask, "Where do you think they came from?"

"Staten Island. Manhattan. Who knows?"

Back near the bodies, the other four GIFT members were talking among themselves and, as Henry approached, Gail broke away from the group, past earshot.

"We've just taken a vote," she said, in her upper-crust British accent, holding out her hand. "Congratulations. You're of course the lead on this case."

"Thanks a lot," Henry said, taking hold of her hand and kissing it. "What if I refuse?"

"You can't. You know more about the Triads than any of us, so it's a no-brainer."

He smacked his lips. "You perfume your hands with Shalamar?"

"How observant."

Ed wandered off.

Gail Merriday was the newest team member and, at forty-two, the youngest. Unmarried, she seemed incongruous in her role as an inspector from Scotland Yard. Too pretty, for one thing. Disposed to wearing tight skirts for another—sometimes the mini variety. Or slacks that were form fitting. She was tall and leggy with short auburn hair, lavender eyes, and high cheekbones. To Henry's eye, she wore little or no makeup; she didn't need any. Known as a swinger in college, she had become a full-blown Romantic, often quoting the English poet William Blake, and his "*see a world in a grain of sand and a heaven in a wildflower*," or flouting social conventions, or speaking against unjust political rule, or in support of Rousseau's "*noble savage*." A Romantic law enforcer! And she had the uncanny knack of keeping such professional and personal sides of her life insulated, one from the other. When questioned, she likened her love of Romanticism, whether in literature or painting or music, to an appreciation of artists plumbing the depths of human emotions and then evoking them, recreating them, stirring them in the listener. Not everyone understood and she would declare, "But you asked, didn't you?"

There was a small mole near the angle of her lips that Henry fixated on, as he frequently did. This time, Gail noticed.

"I have another mole," she said.

"I wouldn't dare touch that one," he countered.

She turned an ear toward him. "Did you say you wouldn't touch or you'd like to touch . . . ?"

"Wait a minute! I didn't mean it that way. I meant I wouldn't touch the subject matter, not the other mole."

"But the mole *is* the subject matter," she said playfully, "isn't it?"

"No, it's not. Touching it is." Henry felt hemmed in. "What are we talking about, anyway? This is a crime scene, a very *unusual* crime scene, and we're talking about moles and other subjects and . . ."

"What subjects?" George said, walking over. Karl and Jay followed close behind. "And what about the Triads? You said you'd explain why you think they're involved."

"You're right, I did."

"Henry, my friend," Karl said, with only the hint of a German accent, "we believe you should assume most of the responsibility for this case."

"I heard."

"And, based on that assumption, what have you deduced thus far?"

Henry resisted the urge to mimic Karl Moser, a longtime colleague. He was the second forensic pathologist in the group and one Henry believed to be as disciplined as George Silvain was uninhibited. More than once Henry thought it revealing that George referred to GIFT as a "gang" while Karl called it a "unit." Henry preferred to stick with the term in the acronym itself: "team."

Jay Palmer, divorced after a brief teenage marriage, sidestepped his way to Gail. The dashing Canadian had never attempted to hide his attraction for her. He was the tallest of the five members of GIFT, having come to them from the Royal Canadian Mounted Police.

"You're asking for a lecture?" Henry asked.

"A *lecturetta*," George responded.

"What's that?"

"A short one."

"There's no such word in English."

"You're right. It's Italian and it translates into a 'diminutive lecture.'"

All but Henry laughed in unison.

He knew he appeared befuddled but pursed his lips for a moment, his method of clearing the air—and his mind—before firing off a retort or launching into a serious topic or answering questions of deep import during criminal trials. Many had commented on it in conjunction with his style of testimony through the years, and lately it was evident even outside the courtroom.

He eyeballed George. "For the umpteenth time, why do you always act like a free spirit?" he asked.

George hesitated and said sternly, "Henry, I bet you don't even know what a free spirit is."

"Does it upset you when I call you one?"

"Yes."

There was no missed beat. "Then you're right, I don't know what it means."

"Clever, doctor, clever," George said.

Like a prizefighter, he made a circular motion with both fists in front of his chest. Henry imitated it.

"Anyway," Henry said, pursing his lips a second time, "I'm afraid to start, but here goes. We all know that different gangs or families have their own colors, their own MO, their own ways to eliminate their targets. Not always, of course, but usually. They're sort of proud of their favorite methods. The Spanish Camorra is a perfect example—they like the garrote approach. The Jamaican Mafia and their bowtie cut is another. In this case we have either two groups working together or only one trying to make it look that way. Let's say there are two. Now, George and Karl have seen plenty of mob hits. But you, Jay, and you, Gail—maybe you haven't yet, so this is for your benefit, and please excuse me if it's old hat to you. Lately, the American Mafia has been resorting to a .22 revolver applied directly to the skull in their executions. Why? First, there are no spent shells to contend with. As far as I know, there aren't any here, but I wouldn't expect any because the murders no doubt took place somewhere else. But even if they occurred here and assuming I'm right about the Mafia, a revolver is the most likely weapon because that's what they use in this type of situation. Second, we see tight contact wounds to the heads of these women—again a dead giveaway for the Mafia signature." He cleared his throat. "Pardon the 'dead' pun," he said before continuing. "I don't know if you took a look at the wounds, but there's no powder tattooing or soot deposits, and they're black and seared. Translation? Hard contact." He went on to speak about low-velocity bullets ricocheting within a skull cavity and never leaving. "We'll see what the autopsies show."

Both George and Karl inspected their shoes as Henry spoke. The younger pair followed along attentively.

"Next, the Triads," Henry said. "The three bodies linked as a triangle obviously refers to them unless, as I've said, the Mafia wants it to look like the Chinese. But I've never seen or heard of that before, and I do know that the Triads sometimes like to leave a calling card. As to the eyes, that might represent something entirely different: a message of some sort, maybe a warning. Incidentally, if there happen to be two groups working together, my hunch is that this is part of a much bigger operation."

"What kind of operation?" Gail asked.

"I don't know yet." As he usually did after a discourse, Henry unwrapped a candy and put it in his mouth. He extended some to the others; they declined.

"But would two rival gangs work in concert like that?" Jay asked.

"If the operation is big enough," Karl said.

"And if there's enough of the green stuff to make it worthwhile for both parties," George chimed in.

They stood in a loose circle for an awkward ten seconds. Karl broke the silence. Hands on hips, he said, "So we had our meeting—I think they're very productive, by the way—then we get called out to this . . . this . . . place by George. And Henry, you will take over. We just spent precious time reviewing forty cold cases and decided on a trip to Sydney for three long-standing ones there—they've been after us for a year—and now we have to postpone the flight. It doesn't affect me that much because, as you all know, I have a lecture commitment back in Germany that I couldn't get out of. But still, is this the best way for us to operate? Who's paying for our time?"

"Meaning?" Jay asked.

"Meaning I often question our value on hot cases. Is it a duplication of effort—a waste—to conjoin five busy people like this? To breeze in and breeze out after anointing someone to take the lead? We do this type of charity work all the time."

"Wait now, wait," Henry interjected, looking pointedly at Karl. "That's why we picked 'GIFT.' Our gift to the world, remember?"

"Yes, I know that," Karl replied, "yet only one of us is put in charge, then typically the others back off—even at our initial go-through at the crime scene. Why should five of us show up?" As usual, he spoke fast—his words in bunches—but there was no mistaking the edge to them this time.

One would have thought such leaders in their field might have clashed more often than they let on. Surprisingly, however, their mutual respect and admiration minimized any professional jealousies, at least outwardly; not to mention the long-standing friendship among the three senior members. This was not to say that Henry wasn't dogged by questions about his skills in keeping GIFT functioning as a cohesive unit. Each member deserved the spotlight based on reputation alone, but now they were a team, which Henry felt obligated to pull together and make work. *He thought about the challenge every day.*

"In my humble opinion," George said, "you have a point, Karl, but what the hell, you never know. The more, the merrier. Remember last year in Stockholm? Eva Erickson? That was no accidental fall down the stairs; we all knew it was premeditated murder. I was in charge there but it took all five of us—every damn one of us—to pool our knowledge before helping to clear the case. What did we get? People appreciated our efforts."

"Plus," Jay said, "as we once agreed, our coming from all over means we get called from all over, so we're filling a global need." He stroked his neatly groomed mustache. "Personally, I'm happy to be part of it."

"But you'll have to admit," Gail said, "this is an exception. How often does a hot case pop up at the exact time we're meeting on cold ones? And we're completely funded. Think of it: a private jet at our disposal." She searched the faces of the others before adding, "Thank goodness for anonymous benefactors."

Henry felt four pairs of eyes on him. It was his turn.

"Why is it we always end up with this discussion, whether it's in Germany or Buenos Aires or Kuala Lumpur, or here in Brooklyn?" he asked, pausing between each word. "Let's just realize, once and for all, that we do exist, that we show up when summoned—remember that was part of the deal with our benefactor, as Gail called him—and that we assign a lead and we confer as necessary. That's our commitment, our profession."

George cut in. "Amen. I'm leaving, guys." He shook each one's hand. "Call me if you need me, Henry." He was most often the last to arrive at a crime scene—it was an anomaly this time—and the first to leave. "In any event, I'll phone you after I finish the autopsies in the morning or early afternoon. Want to join me, Karl? We'll do all three. You can be my *diener*."

"Your assistant? Why not? It won't be the first time. That's a German word, you know. When you're in Hamburg, you can be *my diener*."

"Fair enough," George said. "See you around ten. Same old morgue."

As if on cue, Jay and Gail said their good-byes and caught up to George on the way to the parking lot.

Henry regarded Karl with mild disgust and said, "Same old, same old. You're staying in Connecticut like always?"

"Yes, you still have a bed for me?"

"Of course. Whenever."

"Just for one night though. I didn't elaborate during dinner but BKA has this workshop in Hamburg over the weekend, "Response to Terrorist Incidents," and I'm on the program. I have a two PM flight out of Kennedy Airport."

"What's your topic?"

"Biochemical weapons."

Henry gave him a sidelong glance. "A pathologist?"

Karl stiffened. "Why not? Don't you ever step out of your field?"

"Why should I?" Henry's response was snappier than he'd intended. "But in your case, you *have* to do it."

"Okay, I'll bite. Why do I have to do it?"

"Because they asked you. Unless, of course, you begged them."

Henry feigned protecting his face against a Moser advance. And neither man smiled.

"I'll meet you at my house then," Henry said. "Don't rush because I want to wrap things up with Hal. You can get to Hollings from here?"

"I know my way around these parts pretty well—so the answer is yes." Karl headed for his car and Henry approached Detective Latimore, calling him aside.

"Hal, I'm leaving," he said. "I'll call you in the morning."

"Okay. Meanwhile I'll contact you if anything important develops, like who the hell the girls are. Doesn't seem like much to go on so far. They sure look alike though—maybe they're related. Naturally we'll bring in Missing Persons."

"Good," Henry said. "Now, a couple points of interest. You have more to do than I do. I can be selective at scenes like this and I'm sure when you have a chance to get to it, you'll come to the same decisions and . . ."

"Dr. Liu, please. Whatever advice you have, I'm all ears."

"Well. There's a boat tied up to the small jetty over there. Maybe whoever did this arrived with the bodies by water, put them in the triangle, then fled by car. When you inspect the smaller lot, you'll see some tire tracks and shoe prints. Also, you might want to check if anyone had a boat stolen in Manhattan or Staten Island."

Henry knew that Hal's experienced team would painstakingly comb the boat for evidence and cast the tire marks in plaster of paris, but he wasn't certain it would conclude that the boat might have been stolen. Furthermore, he wanted not only impressions made of the tracks but also an attempt made to determine the type and make of the tires.

"You'll let me know the results of the search in the tire track database?"

"Sure thing."

"Ten to one they're Konaders," Henry said confidently.

"Konader tires? You can tell by what you saw?"

"No, by what I suspect. And I suspect the Triads are in on this."

The detective narrowed his eyes. "But what's the connection between them and Konader?"

"Let's see if that's the make first. Call me when you can. And another thing, Hal—all the shoe prints in the parking lot? Will you be photographing them?"

"Uh-huh."

"With oblique lighting?"

"We can."

"Good. We need all the enhancement we can get. Could you have them enlarged and sent to me?"

"Certainly."

Henry bowed imperceptibly before shaking Latimore's hand. He signaled Ed that they should leave.

They swerved out of the lot, just as a boxy white truck pulled in. The lettering on its side read:

POLICE MAJOR CRIME SQUAD
FORENSIC UNIT

It was 10:45 PM when Henry and Ed arrived at Henry's house at 17 Arrow Place in Hollings, Connecticut, not far from New Haven. Hollings, once a vibrant manufacturing city tucked into a river valley, was on the rebound from the effects of a mass exodus south to warmer climates and better jobs. Many of its one hundred thousand residents worked within four new industrial parks that had changed the nature of Hollings's industry to high-tech and service companies, and, in the process, had rescued its economic base. A few decaying but proud manufacturing plants remained behind along the river bed, a stone's throw from the central district's shops, banks, churches, and a splendid green with towering sycamores, granite war memorials, and a gazebo.

Karl was waiting in a rented blue Lexus that was parked at the curb out front. He got out when the garage door opened and the Chrysler turned into the driveway and into the left bay. Ed emerged from the car and pressed a button on the wall, opening the door for the right bay. The three men greeted each other. Ed jumped into a black police cruiser and started to back out. He stopped, eased forward, and lowered the window.

"Nine in the morning, Henry?"

"Six-thirty."

"Gotcha," Ed said and drove off.

Henry's house was a compact contemporary built in 1973 but purchased by the Lius a decade later. That was the year when Henry decided to divide his time equally between China and the States, teaching at the university-graduate level in both countries: Jiao Tong in Shanghai and Howerton in Connecticut. In addition, he lectured at the State Police Forensic Center. His wife, Margaret, a computer expert, also taught at Howerton for two years, then chose to confine her work to Shanghai. During Henry's six months in Hollings, he would spend a week with her every month.

The gray house was situated on a narrow lot on Hollings's west side and had wide eave overhangs and a low-pitched roof with broad front-facing gables. Similar homes lined the quiet street on either side. The lot was three times deeper out back than in front and extended to another street behind. It was concealed from view by trees and thick underbrush.

The home's interior consisted of a basic kitchen, living/dining room, den, and two bedrooms. Its colors were soft and coordinated, its furniture pieces utilitarian and comfortable. In 1983 when they were house hunting, it was the den that swayed them, the largest room there. Henry would use it as his study. It soon became crammed with books, filing cabinets, two computers, a printer, a copier, a fax machine, a shredder, a short-wave radio, and an elaborate phone console. Three walls were plastered with diplomas, certificates, medals, and awards. The fourth contained shelves of rocks, which Henry had acquired from every country he'd visited and from a few he hadn't. His desk top—a gift from a university that had also granted him an honorary degree—was in the shape of a magnifying glass.

"Nice present, but when I walk around the handle, it gets me right here," he once commented, pointing to a spot well below his beltline.

In the kitchen he said, "Karl, you look tired. Sit down. Take off your hat. Take off your shoes. Would you like some wine?"

"No thanks. I'll take a large glass of ice tea with lemon."

The German physician sat at the table and removed his black beret and pointed shoes—both trademarks. Thin, balding, and loose jowled, he usually moved about as if in a race with the world. He was born in

1939 on the outskirts of Berlin and emigrated to the United States at the age of nineteen. He received his formal medical training at Harvard and Johns Hopkins before returning home shortly thereafter. In 1975 he and Henry met at a forensic science conference in Munich and remained friends, even collaborating on a string of scientific papers. Like George Silvain, he spoke from vast experience in his field.

"Something to eat?" Henry asked.

"No. Thanks again. If it's okay with you, I think I'll turn in. I'm bushed now, but maybe we can chat in the morning."

He rose, paused, and sat again. "One thing though," he said. "Getting back to what I was harping on before, I think we should continue as a brain trust but that you should be in charge of all the cases. After all, you've become a freelance detective of sorts. A super-sleuth."

Their eyes engaged for a few moments. Henry didn't know how to respond to the last sentence, much less the preceding one, so he settled for, "You know where everything is here?"

"Yes, I do."

"Fine. Make yourself at home."

Karl went out to his car, returned with a small overnight bag, and continued on into the guest bedroom.

Henry crossed into the den, expecting to sift through a barrage of e-mails. When he got to the computer, the phone rang—not the usual ring but a low buzzing sound, the one signifying the switchboard at Hollings Police Headquarters. After-hours calls to him at the State Police Forensic Center were normally routed there.

He was informed that Vernon Seal, a veteran crime reporter at the *New York Sentinel*, had called and wished to speak to him. Henry scribbled down the number and punched it in.

"Unfortunately we've never met, Dr. Liu, and I apologize for calling so late, but about the murders at the Brooklyn pier—the three young women? I was there and just missed you. I've already written the story, but I wonder if I might ask you just one question and then offer a theory of mine?" Seal's voice was raspy, each word enunciated with apparent care.

Henry answered, "I know of you. Admire your work. Even caught you on TV a couple times. What's the theory?"

"Well, I don't expect you to know this but just last week I wrote a three-piece story about the problem of white slavery in America. The core of it was that, for some time now, young girls—many from Eastern Europe—are lured here with the promise of legitimate work. Then, guess what? Before they know it, they're turned into prostitutes. So what starts out as a dream of a better life becomes a nightmare they get locked into. The goddamn girl traffickers see to that. And if the girls try to get unlocked, I know for a fact they're beaten and tortured—or worse. I wonder if those three were part of that and resisted too much and paid the price. Anyway, that's my theory. The eye business? My hunch is that that's a signal—pounded into the girls' heads practically from the get-go—either cooperate or else. And what you saw in Brooklyn is happening in other countries, too: Mexico, the Philippines."

Henry covered the mouthpiece and swallowed hard. "I see," he said. "You think the traffickers do the killing?"

"No. I would guess they hire professional executioners."

"Triads?"

"Yes, Triads . . . Tongs . . . the Mafia. Maybe you and I might meet and talk about it."

"Well . . ."

"Look, doctor, call me sometime if you like. You wrote my number down?"

"Yes, I did."

"Good, good."

"And what's the question?"

"The question is, do you have any idea yet about who the victims might be? I mean, anybody missing that you know of, who might fit their description?"

"No. I'm just assisting the police. You might give them a call to get the latest."

"In other words, no identification, right?"

"I don't know."

"Then, may I make a bold statement, Dr. Liu?"

"Certainly."

"You may *never* find out."

"Maybe . . . maybe not. I'll let you know when I run out of clues."

Chapter 2

THURSDAY, OCTOBER 17

The next morning, Karl Moser arose early, gulped down a glass of orange juice, and wasted little time before departing for the morgue. At the door he turned to Henry and groused, "So what good was I on a hot case like this?"

"You didn't hear what Gail said, did you?" Henry countered. "That's not why you made the trip. You made the trip to contribute to our regular meeting." It was a repartee that Henry regretted, but not for long, because he had other things on his mind.

Henry showered, shaved, and bolted down two slices of toast and a cup of tea, then drove toward Hollings's downtown area to buy a copy of the *New York Sentinel*. He selected the route over hilly back roads—the long way. This, together with a beginning rain, gained him more time to think, to assimilate; it was behind the wheel that he sometimes did his best at both.

He squinted through the rain, caught up in a swirl of concerns about what he'd already designated the *harbor case*. He pondered the reporter's cocksure statement about the victims' identification, the real meaning of the open and closed eyes, the international underworld's possible involvement, and whether he wanted to play a key investigative role in the first place. He reminded himself that he was primarily a forensic scientist—that wearing the mantle of super-sleuth was not of his choosing. Over the years, he had stumbled into the world of criminal detection simply as an extension of his work at crime scenes—"the recognition, collection, identification, individualization, evaluation of physical evidence," as he put it to students. Often he found himself in charge of crime scene reconstruction, blood spatter analysis, and the like. His successes, however, nudged him forward into ever-increasing responsibilities, ones fashioned by law enforcement officials, by the public who demanded immediate answers, and by his significant role in high-profile cases including those of O. J. Simpson, JonBenet Ramsey, Elizabeth Smart, Kobe Bryant, and JFK. Even by his appraisal of Monica Lewinsky's stained dress.

Then there was the matter of being overworked, his system overtaxed. Despite a heavy reliance on the belief that frequent doses of tea conferred protective immunities and that basic sleep requirements were irrelevant, he began to realize that forensic casework, teaching, speeches, and endless global traveling were taking their toll. His lower back began to hurt more, ordinary colds lasted longer, and friends complained of his crankiness after extended trips. Even some colleagues' professional jealousies over his involvement in widely publicized cases became a concern.

Moreover, he was bothered by Karl's and George's offhanded comments—less frequent by phone, more when face-to-face—nonetheless, increasingly in recent months. Henry ground his teeth. Too flip? Too pointed? Ignore it all?

The headline on the front page of the *Sentinel* in Aldo's News Rack caught his attention:

Brooklyn Pier Murders
Baffle Police

Back in the car, he read Vernon Seal's four-column article, skimming through most of the early part—the location of the bodies, statements by the police—and dwelled on several of the later sections:

- *Once again, the Global Interactive Forensics Team, a renowned group of forensic scientists and law officials, has been called into a major criminal investigation. Known as GIFT, it is headed by Connecticut's Dr. Henry Liu, one of the world's premier criminalists, who is also considered a master detective by many authorities. Reliable sources indicate that he packs a gun or two.*
- *Other members are Dr. George Silvain and Dr. Karl Moser, forensic pathologists from New York City and Hamburg, Germany, respectively; Dr. Gail Merriday from London's Scotland Yard; and Dr. Jay Palmer from the Royal Canadian Mounted Police.*
- *It is widely known that funding for GIFT is provided by an anonymous source and includes the use of a private jet for so-called hot and cold cases. The group meets on a regular basis in New York City where they select which cases to handle. Rumor has it that its waiting list contains over 900 requests from six continents.*
- *Most police departments worldwide can contact GIFT's central dispatcher in New York City.*
- *All five experts were at the crime scene. Led by Dr. Liu, they reportedly scoured the area but left early. Several law enforcement personnel indicated that Dr. Liu would likely play an active role in the investigation.*

Henry scanned a sidebar:

ABOUT GIFT

- *Mantra: Pooled knowledge, pooled results.*
- *Combined figures for its five members:*
  - *Investigated 35,000 homicide cases.*
  - *Written 200 books and 1,300 articles in professional journals.*
  - *Consultants to 900 agencies.*
  - *Performed 26,000 autopsies and reviewed over 100,000 more.*
- *Their clout circumvents need for certain legal requirements; i.e., they have free rein to examine all physical evidence.*

When he reached home, he still wondered how the reporter knew about the mantra: it was a saying that had originated with Karl and, Henry thought, had not been shared with the media. He was also surprised that reporter Seal, in keeping with the theory he offered over the phone, had not referred to the possibility that the dead women had been prostitutes, particularly in view of his extended story on white slavery.

At 6:30 sharp, he heard the garage door open, gathered up his briefcase and raincoat, and left the house through the inside door to the garage. He gaped out at the rain, which had turned torrential, and felt a draft of cool damp air on his tongue.

"It's like a monsoon," he said to Ed as he slid into the passenger's side of the police cruiser.

Ed smirked in the affirmative. "To the lab?" he asked.

"The lab. The Center. It's really more than a lab, you know."

The ride to the Connecticut State Police Forensic Center took forty minutes, but it seemed like five to Henry, for he played the events of the past half day over and over in his mind. He hadn't come to any new conclusions, at least none he was happy with. His most pressing concern was whether or not he wanted to become embroiled in yet another high-profile case; he was certain that the harbor case had all the earmarks of one. Remarkably, he believed the decision rested on the stock he put in Vernon Seal's theory. Sometimes, Henry's thought processes took on an unusual pattern; he'd choose a theory and then work backward. He ran a hand through his hair. Seal called it a "theory," but it was really a "hypothesis," a concept less established. Seal's no fool though . . . knows the difference. Seasoned reporters deal in nuances among words all the time. He must be *damned sure* then. Surer than "hypothesis" would warrant. And he used the word "theory" twice.

Henry decided that the chances were eighty–twenty he would remain on the case and that he'd better firm up the decision soon, possibly before he'd be checking in with Detective Latimore later in the morning.

Although the prospect of tackling an investigation of such scope intrigued him, he was still unhappy as Ed maneuvered the cruiser into the "Reserved" slot near the main entrance to the Center.

"We're here already?" he asked.

"Yeah, things go fast when you're thinking hard," Ed replied. "I could see it in your face. Did you notice the rain?"

"What about it?"

"It stopped."

The Center was perched atop a hillock in Middletown, overlooking a new community hospital to the west and a cemetery to the east. Henry liked to think its location was symbolic: straddling life and the future on one side and death and history on the other. The building sprawled the length of a hundred-yard parking area and was constructed of one part gray masonry and three parts glass; its green roof could be seen for miles around. The interior was a labyrinth of rooms, some administrative but mostly functional laboratories stacked with state-of-the-art technology and highly specialized equipment to analyze anything that could be analyzed. A separate training wing housed a collection of classrooms whose walls radiated outward like the spokes of a wheel. At its hub was Center Hall, split down the middle by an adjustable partition. Each side sat 150 people. For most of Henry's lectures, the partition had to be rolled back.

They entered his office through a side door. It was 7:10 AM.

Henry draped his jacket over a chair and said, "I'll be here all day, catching up. Look at that desk. You have other things to do?"

"I always have other things I can do: paperwork, tracking computer crime, scam artists—you know, the usual."

"Then go take care of them."

"You're sure?"

"Yes. I'll call if I need you. Your cell phone is on?"

"Uh-huh. If I'm not nearby, buzz me when you need me."

Ed left in the direction of his own office down the hall.

Henry spent the next hour working at his desk, scrutinizing scientific and legal reports, sorting them into piles. At eight, the phone rang several times. Five minutes later, he raised his voice toward the adjoining room.

"You there, Lori? I think I hear you."

Before his administrative assistant had finished her response, he was standing before her desk.

"I'm here in all my glory," she said. Lori Gardner had been associated with Henry for nearly twenty years. With a degree in law enforcement, she also took special courses in homicide investigation offered by the Municipal Training Academy. Later she worked as a part-time constable under the state resident trooper program and assisted Henry both at Howerton and in the field during crime scene searches. Four years later, a conflict arose when the university wanted to transfer her to the Evening Division. She refused and wanted to quit. Henry stepped in and asked her to join him in Middletown. She thus left the university setting and became his administrative assistant at the Forensic Center.

The mother of three and wife of a stockbroker, she was, at forty-eight, a comely, high-spirited brunette who still managed to turn a few male heads at work.

"I know roughly what I've got today," he said. "What do *you* say I've got?"

He folded his right arm across his chest and brought his left hand to his mouth in the form of a fist, as if to keep from speaking while he listened.

"Before that," she said, "I see you went to the Marine facility in Brooklyn last night. There's a big story on it in the *Register*."

"It's no doubt in all the papers by now. They like juicy stuff."

"You're staying with the case?"

"Maybe."

"Is that a yes or no?"

"Why?"

Lori, who had remained seated, swiveled her chair around and clicked Henry's schedule onto a computer screen. "Because it impacts this thing."

"Okay, then, let's say yes—probably yes." He walked around her desk to get a closer look. "Jesus," he said, "how can I do it all?"

"That's what I mean." She turned back to Henry and gave him the half smile he knew meant the decision was his alone.

"We'll take it a day at a time."

"That's fine, boss," she said, glaring. "But today is today. What are we doing? You have so many meetings."

"Cancel them all."

"Next week's, too?"

"Postpone the ones on Monday."

"Then what? You'll solve the case by Tuesday?"

"Lori," he responded, "you didn't listen to what I said. We'll take it day by day."

She saluted him and said, "Aye-aye, sir. So, let's move on. What about your evening events?"

"Cancel them for a week. They'll understand. They read the papers."

"And the student lectures?"

"Those I'll do."

"You have one this afternoon."

"I know. I'll do it."

Lori stared at him for several seconds, fingering her bracelet. "In case you don't know," she said, "it's obvious you're staying with the case."

"What makes you so sure?"

"The gun you're wearing."

He walked back to his office, sank into his chair, and looked around, as if searching for cues of where to start again. The room was not unlike his den/office at home, only twice the size and half as neat. The walls were replete with diplomas, citations, and honorary police hats and badges. Large rocks lined countertops on two sides; smaller ones were stuffed to overflowing in a corner barrel. Behind him was a computer flanked by photographs of Margaret and their two children: Sherry, a vice president at Citibank, and Stanley, a dentist in Hartford.

But it was the stack upon stack of papers that prompted occasional quips around the Center: correspondence, reprints, reports, requisitions, monographs, personal notes. They burdened his desk, the tables, cabinet tops, and several side chairs. Amazingly, while he had trouble naming the wall items without looking, he could tease out a specific paper from the depths of a three-foot pile anywhere in the room.

The only time he spoke to Lori by intercom was when a visitor sat before him or he sensed someone was in her outer office. Otherwise, he raised his voice a notch or two.

"Lori," he shouted, "I forgot to ask you something. Are you busy?" He knew that her silence indicated she was. "Well, drop it please," he continued. "This is important. See if you can round up a three-part series that appeared in the *New York Sentinel* last week. Written by Vernon Seal. Okay?"

"What was it about?" she responded feebly.

"Something like white slavery or prostitutes in America."

Lori suddenly appeared in the doorway, notepad in hand. "Those three girls last night. Do you think . . ."

"Possibly," Henry said.

"Okay," she said. "I'll get right on it." She flipped open the pad. "Now, other than the messages on your desk, here's what you got. A gentleman called from Seattle right at eight. Said his daughter was murdered two years ago, the police have gotten nowhere, and could you please help? I have his name and number."

"Put him on the list, call him back, and tell him the usual." He sifted through the memos of the previous day.

"He got very emotional."

Henry looked up pensively. "Ah . . . tell him I'll call next week."

"Good. Then right after that . . ." She turned to the next page and followed her writing with a finger. "A Basil Vasilakis called. Said he's an officer in the Bureau of Customs and Border Protection. He made a point of stressing that it's part of the US Department of Homeland Security. Hopes you can call him right away—says it's urgent."

The phone rang and Lori excused herself to answer it in her office.

Henry thought about calling Brooklyn first but, after checking his watch, believed it might be too early, especially for the autopsy findings. One of the advantages of his investigating a case in Connecticut was the convenience of dealing with his "own" forensic lab and with the state Medical Examiner's Office. For other jurisdictions, it was more bothersome and time consuming. Not as much, however, in the case of New England or the state of New York, which was part of a coalition that included Connecticut and New Jersey. In terms of availability of information in the least amount of time, the worst was anywhere outside the continental states, although private faxes and encrypted e-mails helped. He would phone Brooklyn closer to noon.

He waited for Lori to get off the phone and asked her to place the call to Vasilakis.

"Dr. Liu," the customs official said, "thanks for getting back so soon. I'll only keep you a minute. As your secretary may have told you, I'm with Customs and Border Protection and I was wondering whether you and I might meet. It's about the deaths at the New York pier last night and I have some information you might be interested in—*we* certainly are. A bit too sensitive though to discuss over the phone. All I can say right now is that it has to do with national security."

"May I ask where you're calling from, Mr. Vasilakis?"

"I'm here on business in Providence, and please call me Basil."

"I see. Well, ah, I'm meeting with a Chinese delegation at the UN tomorrow. Will you be back in Washington by then?"

"No, I doubt it. Could we possibly make it today? I believe it's that vital and I'd be happy to come there."

Henry checked his watch again. "Hold on, ah . . . Basil." He rotated in his chair and checked the schedule on the computer.

"Is 3:30 okay?"

"Yes, indeed."

"You know how to get here?"

"I can easily find out. I heard it's the one with the famous green roof."

Henry waited until 11:30 before he called Detective Latimore, all the while harboring more doubts about continuing on the case. If the caller were correct in his "national security" claim, he wondered about whether he could give the issue its proper time and attention. At the same time, he caught up with his desk work and briefly reviewed several new ideas he considered for his afternoon lecture, "When Science Meets Crime." Widely promoted, it was to be given to law enforcement officials, members of the legal profession, and college students. He was particularly pleased by the advance enrollment of students from high schools. Only recently had they begun offering the subject to their senior classes.

"Good morning, Hal. Henry Liu here. As you know by now, I

prefer to work through you and your department rather than directly with the lab. Anything yet?"

"You bet. I was about to call you in fact. Let's start with the boat. We found it belongs to a Clyde and Yvette Minor from Staten Island. They reported it stolen from a marina over there. We're following up on it. The boat itself? Loaded with hairs—blonde like the girls'. And three separate bloodstains. The typing of one matched one of the girls and the typing of the other two stains was the same and matched both other girls. Am I being clear, doc?"

"Perfectly."

"In fact, we checked with Dr. Silvain, who's already done one of the autopsies. Dr. Moser's doing another. I was there for a while. They say two of the victims look very much alike—like sisters, maybe even twins. The lab's got some DNA going on it. I'll get to the other findings in a minute."

"Good work. Excellent work." Henry scribbled a few words on one of several index cards he kept in his pocket. If he wasn't writing on one, he was shuffling a stack of them. Whenever queried, he described it not as a nervous habit but—pointing to his forehead—"sometimes to help get this engine going."

"Next, identification," Latimore said. "Nothing specific yet. Databank shows all kinds of blonde women missing in the States."

"Getting back to the bodies, was there any evidence of . . . ?"

"Sexual activity? Loads of it. They said in all three cases their vaginas had mixtures of semen, some fairly recent, some old—but they couldn't determine exactly *how* old. Plus Silvain . . . I mean Dr. Silvain . . . said each of them had been sodomized, probably chronically. Their butts were . . . he went on and on about how hard it is to tell with postmortem tissue in that area; he spoke like he thought I knew what he was talking about. Anyway, the thing I remember him saying is that he never saw funnel assholes in three females at the same time." The detective cleared his throat before resuming.

"As long as I'm on the autopsies, cause of death in each case was a single gunshot wound to the head—.22 slug in the brain. Lots of damage in there. One other thing they found. The eyes . . . you know, one open, one closed? They were kept that way with some kind of glue. Why the hell use glue?"

"To guarantee they'd remain in the position the killers wanted. Prior to rigor mortis some muscles relax. For example, the jaw drops down. But the eyes normally remain open. They wanted one closed."

"You mean they'd go to all that friggin' trouble, putting glue around eyelids?"

"The Triads would, if they were just following orders. They were undoubtedly told the message had to be clear—even though they might not understand the significance. Knowing them, since they don't value human life, why should they worry about someone else's motive?"

There was silence at the other end. Henry surmised that the detective was taking his own notes—or consulting ones he had made before.

"Let's see . . . oh, the tire tracks. You're absolutely right, doc, they were Konaders. How or why, I have no idea. By the way, how did you know?"

"This gets sticky, maybe far-fetched. But I took a stab at it. Didn't cost anything at the time. My colleagues in the Detroit area tell me that both the Triads and the Tongs in the United States favor cars with Konader tires and this jibes with what I recently read, that . . . it's right here . . ." Henry withdrew a single page from the middle of a pile of papers on his desk. "Here's an article with the headline, 'World Tire Giant Konader Joins Hands with Chinese Partner.' It says that Konader has entered into an alliance with the Shanghai Tyre and Rubber Company and the joint venture will be called the Shanghai Konader Warrior Tyre Company, with an annual production of eight million radial tires for sedans and 15,000 tons of wire for tires by the year 2010."

"I hate to put it this way, but . . . but . . . so what?"

"Well, Triads who end up here could ship over their cars with them, but they choose to buy American cars as long as they come equipped with Konaders. My thinking is they believe they're indirectly helping the Chinese economy. They're fiercely loyal, or should I say deadly loyal?"

"And with that reasoning you figured the tracks were made by Konaders?"

"I told you it was a stab."

Normally around noon, Henry would wash down a sandwich with a large mug of green tea that materialized from a back room off his office. But he had forgotten to pack the sandwich in his briefcase and was glad about it, for it gave him a chance to get behind the wheel of a car again, this time Lori's.

"Why don't you take Ed?" she asked.

"He's got some things to do. You don't want me to drive your car?"

"It's not that, but you usually have someone with you."

Henry disregarded the comment and took her keys.

Outside it looked like early autumn in New England but smelled like early winter. He felt that kind of earthy chill that bites deep after a hard rain and makes you wonder when the flakes will appear. The trees were still full and radiant in their reds and yellows and variegated browns, especially the maples.

He headed for an old haunt on a side street near the center of town, Fernando's, a Middletown eating establishment that, for sixty-two years, tried to pass as a restaurant but was really a diner, one of those shaped like a trolley, silver and black. Henry spoke of its good food, especially the famous steamed hamburgers—yet favored the place because it was seldom crowded. Besides, it was the slow drive there, two miles, and the change of scenery that often helped him resolve nagging problems.

He nodded. The news from Detective Latimore was not surprising, save the possibility of the twins. But when Henry combined it with his indecision about staying on the case, it fueled a greater urgency to make up his mind at long last. He remembered thinking about twins when he viewed the bodies, even triplets for a split second—that would resonate with the Triads—but the blood typing had ruled it out. He recalled speaking to Latimore at the crime scene and speculating about the stolen motorboat and the Konader tires and the Triads and the Mafia. Now these elements were all but confirmed.

Henry was on familiar ground when confronted with forensic matters. The sleuthing role was something else. He had never assumed the lead in a case with such sweep: international mobsters, a potential white slavery ring, automobile giants, national security. He reminded himself that he was never reluctant to admit to his limitations. Yet, the bond between criminalistics and detection had become tighter.

The sexual findings reported by the detective lingered in his mind. Which brought him back to Vernon Seal's phone call and the articles he had penned about white slavery. Sitting in the car outside the restaurant, Henry pondered. He brooded. He meditated. Finally he opened the door with atypical fervor. All thoughts about near- and far-term intentions had crystallized: he would meet with Vernon Seal immediately and he would remain on the harbor case as its de facto detective.

Alone in a corner booth, he savored the taste of a steamed hamburger, feeling at peace with his decision.

Henry called the *Sentinel* when he got back to the Center. He had put Vernon Seal's number in his wallet after speaking with him the night before.

"Hello, Vernon, this is Dr. Liu. You said last night that I might call you to set up a meeting, and that's what I'm doing."

"That would be, well, ah, I don't . . . fine, let's get together." He sounded distant. "But I don't want to meet here, doctor, or in public, or even at your office because . . ."

"Because why?"

"Because I received a warning to stay away from you."

"A warning? You mean a letter or what?"

"No, a phone call. Not more than an hour ago. It was a man's voice; sounded muffled."

"What did he say?"

"Not much. Something like, 'Look, mister loudmouth reporter, stay away from that Henry Liu. Paddy McClure, too. Got it?' And he hung up."

"But how could anyone know we had talked?"

"I have no idea."

"Who's Paddy McClure?"

"Retired navy man. Now runs a string of bars in New York—the city, Buffalo, Rochester, as I remember. I think a couple in New Jersey and Connecticut, too. Maybe a dozen total. Flotilla One, Flotilla Two—like that."

"Is he a friend of yours?"

"Sort of. We swap stories sometimes."

"In the bars?"

"Sometimes. I don't go in one very often. It wouldn't sit too well at the office. He's got this reputation, you know—well it's really not a reputation. It's a fact."

"What fact?"

"He fixes guys up."

"You mean with girls?"

"Yes."

"Like a pimp."

"No, no, not that. He might direct someone to a pimp, but he doesn't do any of it himself."

Henry couldn't wait to jump to the next question. "Do you think there's any connection between his, shall we say, indirect pimping and yesterday's murders?"

"No way, not with Paddy . . . or even with the pimps he knows."

"Do you know any of them?"

"A couple. At least I'm suspicious. A lot of people are. But you see there's a big difference between pimps and traffickers. Traffickers bring in the girls; practically guarantee their continued use. They hand them over to various pimps, who 'use' them for as long as fifteen years. Then the girls are let go—replenished by young ones. Happens every year. And I gotta tell you, doctor, it's so highly organized in this country—with a chain of command and all—that I'm convinced there's a Mr. Big."

"I see."

"So, if we can meet—on the q.t.—the rest can wait till then. We can sit in a car somewhere."

They decided to make it the following morning at ten. It appeared that Seal, a lifelong New York City resident, knew little of its immediate outskirts; he therefore agreed to travel to Connecticut if Henry knew of a safe, secluded place. He gave the reporter detailed directions to Hollings's abandoned recycling grounds and, before hanging up, they exchanged cell phone numbers. Henry made more notes on an index card.

Lori walked in and reminded Henry of his lecture. At 1:28, he strolled from his office, preoccupied with the meeting with the immigration official later in the day and with that of Vernon Seal the next morning. He had slipped into a long white lab coat and carried a manila folder and a box of slides. The folder contained statistical data only, for he rarely used notes during his lectures, either there or at the university.

The route to Center Hall, though circuitous, took less than a minute. It was Henry's shortcut—through administrative corridors, small classrooms, and a maze of all-too-familiar sections of the lab including those of Fingerprints, Documents, Imprints, Firearms, Photography, Chemistry, Arson, Instrumentation, Trace Evidence, Biochemistry, DNA, Image Analysis, Reconstruction, Toxicology & Controlled Substances, and a Computer Crimes/Electronic Evidence Unit. He navigated around scores of DNA sequencing machines—devices resembling the photo-processing units at retail photo centers—and around fume hoods, benches of stereomicroscopes, and gas chromatographs. An inoffensive chemical smell hung in the air.

He greeted everyone in his path by first name—secretaries, detectives, state troopers, scientific associates, scores of criminalists.

A hush came over the hall as he walked through the door—then loud applause from the three-hundred-plus attendees. Henry mouthed a thank you, proceeded straight to a projection table, and handed the slides to an assistant, Davis Owenfeld, a sergeant with the Connecticut State Police.

The seats were arranged in a semicircular pattern, divided into four sections by aisles running from front to back. Before the podium, six long tables were placed left to right in two rows, one behind the other. All seats were occupied.

The lecture was going well. As was his practice, Henry sprinkled technical talk with his own brand of humor. Eventually his eyes drifted toward the farthest table on his right, and he stumbled on his words when he spotted Gail Merriday, her hands folded demurely on the table before her. She stared at him, a stare rigid and unbroken, and as the lecture wound down, it was more than a scientific curiosity that stirred his wonder about her presence. And about the meaning of the stare.

As the session ended, Henry slipped a candy into his mouth and Gail took her place in a line of attendees waiting to ask him some questions. She was the last to face him.

"Wonderful job, Henry. I hope I didn't unhinge you."

He shook his head. "Not unhinge, shock maybe. What brings you to Middletown?"

"Just passing through."

"How did you know I'd be lecturing?"

"I didn't. I would have stopped by your office anyway." She glanced at the clock on the wall. "Oh my, I really must get going."

Henry wanted to clarify some points but asked about Jay instead. "I thought you were with him," he said.

"Not today, but later. He drove to Boston last night. Said as long as he was in the vicinity, he'd wrap up some business there. We're meeting back in the city tonight."

Henry then brought her up-to-date on the findings from the crime scene. But nothing else.

He walked her to her car, and as she motored off, he waved, sensing something brewing in her. Several possibilities clicked through his mind. He smiled at each of them and dismissed none.

Lori announced that Basil Vasilakis would arrive soon, then deposited three copies of the *New York Sentinel* on Henry's desk.

"Here they are," she said. "Last Monday, Tuesday, and Wednesday."

"Did you read the articles?" he asked.

"Not much. They turned my stomach."

She left the office. He pored over each of the three installments, taking time to underline key points:

- *Unlike drugs, a woman's body can be sold over and over again.*
- *The average price is $1,500 but some "high-quality" girls are sold for $4,000.*
- *Traffickers pose as employment agents.*
- *It takes only a few days to route a teenage girl from country to country; her identity is obliterated by destroying all registration papers and travel documents. There are some payoffs along the way. Ultimately, she is delivered to her final destination, after being transformed into a commodity with net stockings and stiletto heels.*
- *Poor Eastern European towns are a favorite source for these young women.*

Budapest, Bucharest, and Belgrade are especially targeted. The countries of Bulgaria, Greece, Russia, Yugoslavia, Hungary, Romania, Serbia, and Montenegro report hundreds of disappearances.

- *Upon arrival in other countries, they are delivered to buyers who often beat and torture them into compliance.*
- *Every dozen prostitutes can net their owner more than a million dollars yearly.*
- *There is a great difference between small gangs of traffickers and large networks. The gangs vie for the best prices on a small scale. Weekends—when most trafficking occurs—can be expensive for them, so many wait for Mondays to fill orders, even though they get the "leftovers."* Net-*works, however, use the Internet to transact business from a distance, supplying large numbers of bodies to eager buyers all over the world, including the United States.*

At three o'clock, Henry received a call from George, who elaborated on the results of the three autopsies, reiterating what Detective Latimore had earlier conveyed but adding nothing new. Once again, Henry teased him about his habit of prefacing each significant postmortem finding with, "From a forensics standpoint."

At 3:35, Lori ushered Basil Vasilakis into Henry's office. After initial amenities and his refusal of a cup of tea, the immigration officer sat on a chair before Henry's desk, the only one in the room not covered with books and papers.

"I don't have much time," he said, "and I'm sure you don't either, squeezing me in as you have, so I'll get right to the point."

He hesitated as if he were uncertain of his next sentence. Henry studied what he could see of him. He was a bespectacled, rumpled man with the bearing of a Sunday school teacher, hardly what you might expect to find in Homeland Security. Middle-aged, pale, and slightly built, he had an air of delicacy about him, but he reeked of cigar smoke. There was a mild sideways bow to his body, a condition Henry recognized as scoliosis, a curvature of the spine. His shirt was too high and tight, his tie askew. A pen was clipped onto the V neck of a sweater tucked into his trousers; a silver cell phone was fixed to its belt.

"Dr. Liu," he said, "we have reason to suspect that the women found dead last night were couriers for a terrorist group or groups."

"Couriers? Who for?"

"We haven't the faintest idea."

"Okay then, who to?"

"Again, we don't know."

"So why your conclusion?"

"Come again, doctor?"

"Why do you believe they were couriers?"

"Because we received an anonymous phone call from someone making the claim."

"Interesting. Tell me about it."

"Certainly. But first, would it be presumptuous of me to ask if you know who the victims are? Their next of kin . . . that sort of thing?"

"I haven't been told. They're working on it."

"And there have been no inquiries by anyone about details of the tragedy?"

"Not as far as I know. At least none to this office."

"Forgive me, sir. This is all in the line of security concerns. I'm sure you understand."

"Perfectly well. You have a job to do."

"Yes. We follow all leads, large and small, and usually we run into a stone wall."

"You must get a lot of calls these days."

"Yes, but this one was a bit different; it was from a female."

"Oh? Did the call come directly to you or to somebody in your department?"

"It was the strangest thing. A man asked for me, and his call was transferred through several of our personnel before I finally picked up the phone. When I did—as I said, it was a woman on the other end. She spoke about 9/11 and referred over and over again to terrorism and terrorists . . ."

"Did she mention names?"

"No, she used the term, 'international terrorist cartel.'"

"Did she sound Middle Eastern?"

"Not really. Perfect English, maybe a hint of an accent; I couldn't tell. But very, very nervous."

Henry made a notation on a pad, looked off in the distance, then back at Vasilakis. "So," Henry said, "she alleged that the three dead women were couriers for terrorists. Couriers deliver messages. Did she indicate what kind of messages?"

"No, she didn't elaborate, except to say that if the cartel were systematically dismantled, the threat of terrorism would be that much less in this country."

As Henry thought about the statement, the official rose and stated that he had a flight to catch. He again thanked Henry for meeting with him on a moment's notice. At the door, Henry asked a parting question that he knew the answer to and Vasilakis responded: "Yes, you're quite right. Customs and Border Protection used to be part of the Justice Department but, since 9/11, it's been transferred to Homeland Security."

Vasilakis left and Henry summoned Lori into his office. "Please call the Bureau of Customs and Border Protection in Washington," he said. "See if they have a Basil Vasilakis on staff. Did you get a look at him?"

"Sort of."

"Well, describe him as best you can, and if they give you a hard time, put me on the line. And I should have mentioned it before, but I set up a meeting with Vernon Seal for tomorrow morning."

"Here?"

"No, the recycling grounds."

"That creepy place? Why not here?"

"He wants the meeting kept secret and not in New York. It was the only location I could think of."

Ten minutes later, she informed Henry that the description she offered the bureau did indeed fit Vasilakis, that he was midlevel in rank, popular, and highly regarded among his colleagues. In addition, he was in constant demand as a speaker on counterterrorism, both here and abroad.

Henry mulled over the visit. He shook his head from side to side. Why rush in and rush out? They couldn't have spoken by phone?

Chapter 3

LATER THAT NIGHT

At 6:15, Gail was in a tangle of emotions. She felt privileged to be a part of GIFT and recognized full well that in this regard she was the envy of her colleagues at Scotland Yard. Financially she was set, having inherited a tidy sum from her mother, who had perished in a London fire seven years before; her father had died when she was three. Romantically, she tolerated her share of suitors but, on those occasions when it came to the cravings of the flesh, she rationalized away her submissions as rare and discreet, if not reluctantly given.

She expected Jay to arrive at seven, and although she knew her early mood would not mesh with his—he had been persistent but unsuccessful in wooing her—maybe under the right circumstances, she herself might turn out to be the aggressor. Though conflicted, she, in fairness to him, was determined to create the proper atmosphere. She was fond of him and would at least give it a try.

Her apartment was a three-room, second-floor walk-up in Manhattan's West Village. Since joining GIFT, she had stayed there on twenty or so occasions, no more than two days at a time. It was its relative vacancy that helped keep the space neat, far neater than the topsy-turvy rooms in her small London home, one she shared with a female associate at the Yard. But Gail strove to give the apartment a distinct personality, her own blend of elegance, and was solely responsible for the selection of its contents and overall décor—a home away from home where she could experiment with colors, fabrics, and lighting. And no one could object to any selection—not that she would care if they did—because no one visited her there except Jay, and he was always interested in something else. She considered the appearance of the living room, kitchen, and single bedroom as an extension of her sensuous moods, from gauzy curtain material to unique furniture pieces to knotty carpet textures. They were expressed even in the background music she preferred while reading: Baroque harpsichord pieces or the strains of Chopin, Schubert, or Weber. She found elegance in antiques, and the apartment harbored a cache of them, mainly English country style.

The kitchen's workspace was tiny, which didn't matter to her, given the time she spent in it. There was little else than a washer, small stove, and refrigerator. She had installed the 1915 deep sink with a distinctive brass faucet after spotting it at an antiques shop in the city's Soho district.

The bedroom was ablaze in shades of red: the curtains and canopy of a Queen Anne bed, a needlepoint footstool cover, and a quilt fashioned from late-1800s silk scarves. She referred to it not as the bedroom but as the Red Room.

The walls of the living room were covered, perhaps overcovered, with the works of Romantic painters, those that featured deep shadows and faraway exotic subjects. Clearly, her favorite was any of the three Oriental scenes by Eugene Delacroix. This was the only room with a table, a 1780 tavern model wedged into a corner with two matching chairs. Above them a cupboard stored leather-bound books. The sitting area—companion easy chairs upholstered in soft pink velvet and a dark brown sofa—was centered on a chocolate knotty carpet. Pots of fragrant amaryllis plants dotted the room.

Gail stepped out of the shower and thought of Jay as she dried her hair in small rapid strokes and dabbed her skin with a fluffy towel. Her slender but sinewy body reflected years of tennis and gymnastics, yet belied an unmistakable femininity. She tiptoed out toward the bra and panties on her bed; she never liked the feel of damp underwear kept in the bathroom while showering. But still naked and moist, she faced the full-length mirror on the door, regarding her shape. Preening, she ran her fingers slowly over the surface of her breasts and midsection, following her gentle curve.

It was ten before seven when Gail finished dabbing on her best cologne and slipped into a floral blouse, black slacks, and high heels. She had poured herself a glass of Chardonnay and felt fresh and buoyant. Ever the romantic, it was during these times alone when she would fantasize about possible couplings. She refilled her glass to half, turned on soft Mendelssohn, and lit candles. The wine tasted fuller, the scent stronger. The intercom bell rang, startling her. She finished the glass and hurried to the wall speaker in the vestibule.

"That you down there?"

"Nobody but me. Jay." It was a well-rehearsed code.

Gail pushed the button to open the downstairs door and slowly opened her own.

Seconds later, Jay kissed her on the cheek and, with one hand, gave her a package shaped like a wine bottle, holding the other hand behind his back.

"You didn't have to do this," she said. "Do you fancy some, or something else?"

"White wine is fine."

They walked into the living room and sat, she in a chair, he on the sofa. Within a minute, she joined him, an arm's length away.

Jay thrust out his hand, which held a small, rectangular package. "Voilà," he said.

"What's this?"

"Something I've been thinking about giving you for some time now. Want to guess?"

She inspected the package from all sides and answered, "Any clues?"

"Sure, it's something you can't bring to London, but even if you could, you couldn't bring it back here to the States."

Gail gave him a hard look. "Wait a minute; please say that again."

"You can't fly with it."

She opened the package and discovered a small handgun.

"It's a Colt Pocket Nine," he said. "Just right for you in the States. Remember? Airlines?"

"How well I know." She rubbed the barrel of the gun. "It's marvelous, Jay. I can keep it in my purse." She slid closer to kiss him.

Jay gulped down his wine. "Now then," he said, "what can we talk about? Are we going out to dinner?"

"Perhaps a quick bite later on. What do you think?"

"Sounds fine. I have to leave at a decent hour anyway, so no big dinner. And I can't stay the night."

"You never do." She spoke the words with the conviction of one who would rather he *did* sleep over, although she had never made the offer in the past.

Gail refilled their glasses. Seated again, she nudged him with one shoulder and said, "That was so sweet of you to give me such a nice present. That's your reputation, you know."

"What reputation?"

"That you're often hard as nails but are basically a sweet . . . sweet . . . a sweet man."

"Gail, c'mon now. Hard as nails, okay. But don't circulate that sweet stuff."

"Only between us, Jay, only between us. Not a bad quality but, as you like, only between us. You *do* seem sweeter than hard. Yes, I'd say forty-five years of sweetness."

"Not quite yet."

"Not quite yet what?"

"I'm forty-three."

"And about six feet tall?"

"Gail, who cares?"

He was, in fact, six foot two and had dark hair, deep blue eyes, a small mustache, and a broad, slightly uneven jaw.

"Did you know your teeth glisten?" she went on.

"I'm warning you."

"No, really, don't they?"

"Must be the wine."

"Wine makes your teeth glisten?"

Jay was about to answer when she reached over and pinched his lips shut. "All right, I'll quit," she said.

He wore a black turtleneck under a suede tan jacket and there was a swelling near its breast pocket. She patted it and said, "Is it like the one you just gave me?"

"Bigger and longer."

She nodded slowly as if to say, "Of course."

He noticed the hanging cupboard filled with books. "I never asked you," he said. "What do you read? Any of those up there?"

"All of them. The classics. *Madame Bovary*, *Tom Jones*. Authors like Fielding, Flaubert. Did you know that Henry Fielding was a classicist, but deep down, he was a Romantic—even if he predated them? Sure.

He was English, but he fell in love with Portugal. His heart was there. His crypt is in Lisbon. I've seen it. Just like you, you never know: hard on the one hand, sweet on the other."

"Gail, please!"

"Okay, okay. I'm rambling. Sorry." She began to feel flushed but believed her coherence and reason had not deserted her.

They sipped more wine and, after a while, she couldn't believe she had forgotten about the triple murder case. But she wasn't in the mood to discuss it. Instead she said, "Speaking of writers, you know what Emerson wrote, don't you? 'Hospitality is a little food, a little wine and an immense silence.' Well, if you put some thought into that, it doesn't come *near* to applying to us. We've had nothing to eat, we've had loads of wine, and we've been chattering all night."

She drew back again and let her eyes range freely over his upper body. "Look," she whispered, "why don't we stop pretending and go into the next room?"

"I thought you'd never ask."

Under other circumstances, she would have teased him about his salacious grin. But not now.

They got up. She took him by the hand and led him into the Red Room.

In bed, Gail's mind drifted wildly. Still she kept picturing a face through all the movement. It was not the face of Jay, but that of Henry.

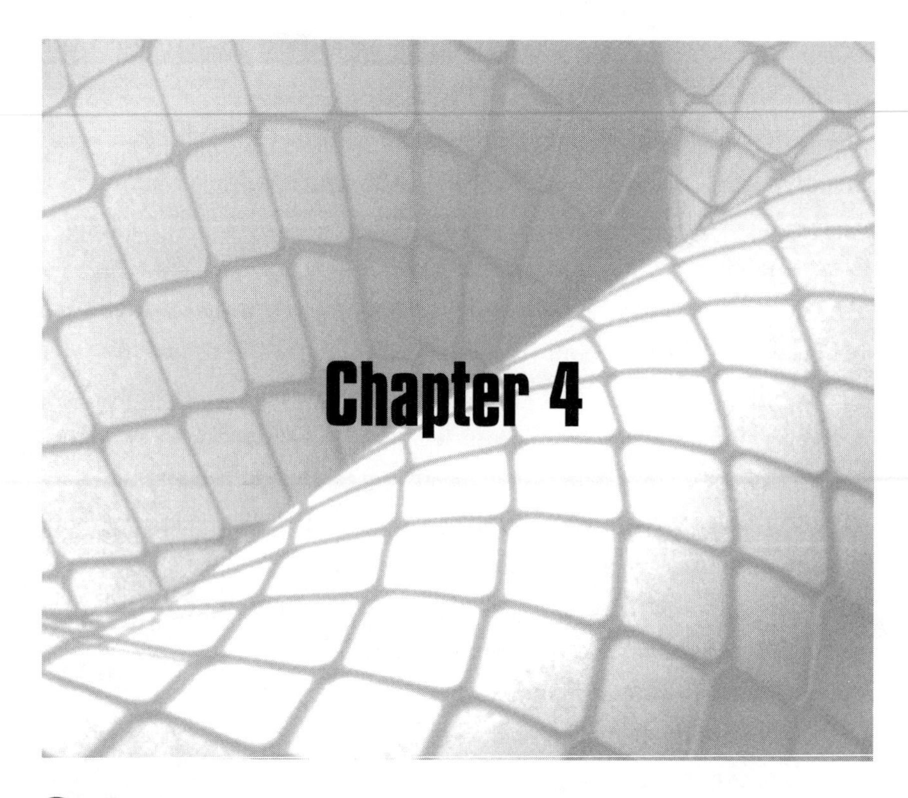

Meanwhile, five hours earlier, Henry had finished with Vasilakis and checked on his assertion that he was an official with Customs and Border Protection. Henry wanted to head home early but sat at his desk trying to unwind. He relished these moments when he could kick off his shoes, close his eyes, and put aside the most recent problems and the leftovers that remained unresolved. But this time, his moment of respite was fleeting, for both the newspaper articles and the quickly arranged meeting with Vasilakis were too fresh in his mind—and they troubled him. The articles? He wasn't shocked at their content, but they reminded him of what he might be in for. And the customs guy? Henry recreated the scene and had lingering questions about its brevity and about the nervous woman who had allegedly called.

It had been a long day. After dinner and a Grand Marnier he retired early.

FRIDAY, OCTOBER 18
9:40 AM

Ed had an early out-of-office meeting so he and Henry drove separately to the Center. From there they departed together in the police cruiser for the rendezvous with Vernon Seal at the former recycling grounds near the border of Hollings with Clemensville. Henry was anxious to find out if the reporter had any notion of the identity of the Mr. Big mentioned in yesterday's remarks. On the way he phoned his office.

"Lori?"

"I was about to call you. You're not coming in?"

"Not this morning." He reminded her of where they were headed. "Anyway, you want to go first, or me?"

"No, go ahead."

"Please see if there are any bars called Flotilla in our area and in metropolitan New York. They're supposed to be all over the place. What I really want is to find out if the owner will be at one of them today at noon. Or will he be at any of them later on?" Henry took a card out of his pocket. "His name's Paddy McClure. If he's at one of them at that hour, get the address. I'd like to drop by to see him if he's available . . . okay? Then call me back as soon as you can, like before ten. Bye . . ."

"Wait! It's my turn. You just got a call from a fellow named Mitroi. Paul Mitroi. Says he lives in Philadelphia now but used to be a member of the Chamber of Deputies—I think that's what he called it—in Bucharest, Romania. They must be something like our members of Congress. He served for over ten years, mostly in a leadership role and eventually . . ."

Henry, a master at stripping the details to the essentials, interrupted. "What's he want? And, by the way, what is this, 'Attention Government officials: it's hurry-and-call-your-local-friendly-criminalist-week?'"

"He wants to meet with you. Said he would still be living in Bucharest, but three years ago his teenage daughter disappeared and a year later was found dead here in the States. Gave some gibberish about the three gals—actually I couldn't make heads or tails out of what he was trying to get across."

"Oh? And he's been living here ever since?"

"That's the way I understand it. Do you want . . . ?"

"When does he want to meet?"

"Tomorrow."

"Where?"

"He'll come here. I told him there's just a skeleton crew here on Saturdays but you're usually in and out. Want to see him?"

Henry paused. "I'd better," he replied. "I'm in this up to my eyeballs now. Make it at eleven."

"So you've made up your mind to stick with the case?"

"Definitely. Didn't I tell you?"

"Please! Since when haven't I had to pry things from you?"

"Don't forget, I pried you away from Howerton."

"That's a matter of opinion. I volunteered to leave."

"*Sure* you did. Anyway, call him and say yes. Where did you say he lives?"

"Philadelphia. Says he wouldn't mind the drive."

Ten minutes later, Lori called back.

"First, it's all set with Paul Mitroi for tomorrow. And I found that all the Flotillas are open for noon trade and right on till midnight. Two are in Connecticut. One's in Westport: Flotilla One Bar & Grille. That's where McClure will be, and he'll be glad to meet with you. I didn't even ask about the others but he went ahead anyway and gave me a song and dance about owning twelve of them—and then he said, in case I was wondering, he was aware that 'Flotilla' refers to a group, that all twelve are his flotilla group . . . that literally he should have named them Flotilla's Number One, Flotilla's Number Two . . ."

"Lori, I get the picture. Did you make it definite?"

"I said you'd be there around noon unless he heard otherwise."

"Good job. I wonder why that's Flotilla Number One?"

"Maybe because he lives there in Westport?"

"Hmm, that makes sense." Henry said he'd probably see her later and reclipped the phone to his belt.

The recycling grounds were five minutes away. The weather that day was the best of the week, nippy but dry and calm.

"Look at that sky up there," Henry said. "Like sapphire."

Ed's expression reflected his certainty that he was about to receive another of the mini dissertations he heard during their drive time. They were mostly about rocks or wind or oceans or the sky or glaciers. Not to mention wild animals. Anything found in nature.

"Did you ever wonder why the sky is blue?" Henry asked.

"Of course. I'd say about twice a day."

"Really—do you want to know?" It was Henry's usual follow-up question.

"Sure, if it makes you . . . I mean, sure . . . why not?"

"Well, it's like this." More predictable words. "It's all about molecules of gases in the air. The intense white light of the sun is actually a mixture of all the colors of the rainbow and each has its own wavelength. The sky looks blue because the gas scatters short wavelengths more than the long ones—and blue is the shortest. So while the long ones reach our eyes in almost a direct line from the sun, the blue waves reach us from *all* parts of the sky, and it appears blue. See?"

"No, but thanks." Ed adjusted the support cushion near his lower back.

Running north to south within a chain-link fence—what was once the Regional Recycling Grounds—was an overgrown strip of land sunk in the middle of a crater, not unlike the bottom of a wicker basket. A roadway of compacted dirt encircled it, while laterally, bushy terrain rose to the level of elm tops based alongside the road below. The high ground formed a rim that sloped on all sides to main streets leading to the city. A year before, the city council had voted to shut down the facility and move to a larger location in nearby Clemensville.

Ed gunned the car up the incline and eased down the other side. Henry spotted a white Chevrolet Malibu parked near the fence ahead. The motor was not running and its door was strangely ajar on the driver's side. The sun's reflection off its windows followed them all the way down, even as they pulled up behind the car.

Henry, surprised that a man had remained so motionless in his car, extended an arm over Ed's chest as a sign to wait. He withdrew his snubby. Ed yanked out his .45. They emerged slowly and, holding their guns with both hands, stuck close to the cruiser, rounding it as they surveyed the slopes on all sides.

At the Malibu, they found Seal erect on the driver's side, his head extended back at a sharp angle. Henry was certain he was Seal, for he had seen him in television interviews. Clearly dead, the reporter was fully clothed. A sports coat rested on the passenger's seat. Neither blood nor a weapon was visible from Henry's vantage point. He leaned in.

Seal's eyes were wide open. His corneas were not opaque and his face appeared waxy and had a blue-gray color. His lips and nails were pale. Embedded in a straight line across the front of his neck was a length of wire. Henry paid particular attention to its ends; there were no handles.

He reached in and put the back of his hand against the side of Seal's face; it was warm. The muscles in his neck and jaw felt soft. He pressed a finger against his cheek; it did not blanch.

Henry drew back sharply as his mind went into a rapid search-and-retrieve mode. He whispered his thoughts to Ed, who was two feet away, combing the area with his eyes.

"Dead less than half an hour," Henry said. "I doubt it was the

Spanish Camorra because their garrotes have handles and they like to leave them behind—you know, their calling card. Poor guy must have left his car and someone nabbed him from behind. Therefore, more than one person was involved. Then they placed him back in—see how neat and symmetrical he is? If this is related to the harbor murders, whoever's doing it is playing musical chairs: trying to make it look like someone else's handiwork. But Ed, if they knew the exact time of the meeting—how, I'm not sure—he must have arrived early. And why did they bother to put him back in the car? If they *did* know the time, weren't they in a hurry? Plus, if he got out of the car, either he must have known them or they ordered him out."

"Do you think they knew he was meeting *you*?"

"I've got to think about that."

Henry inched away to search for tire and shoe impressions and found none in the packed-down roadway. Returning to the car, he leaned in for a final look and nearly missed a scrap of paper tucked beneath Seal's belt. Cocking his head to read a message, he got the answer to Ed's last question:

BUG OFF, LIU.
LET LOCALS HANDLE THIS.

Henry had seen enough of the scene. He called in the crime to Kathy Dupre, a detective friend at the Hollings Police Department, but didn't mention the note.

As they drove up the incline, Ed said, "Wednesday night and today definitely related, right?"

Henry dodged the question. "They must have tailed him here. But what about that message? How did they know Seal and I had talked?" He covered his forehead as if to keep a thought from escaping. "Wait . . . a . . . minute . . . of . . . course!" he said aloud, drawing out the words. "Seal's phone. Bugged!"

Ed nodded slowly. "His phone or yours," he said.

"We'll check them both, and if it's mine, we're in big trouble. Strange though. Usually mobsters themselves don't bother with that stuff. They just carry out the dirty deeds."

"Meaning whoever hired them did the bugging."

"Precisely."

"Frankly, Henry, I'm more concerned about the note than anything else."

"Relax, it's not the first."

"You've gotten them before?"

"Not on this case, but in others."

"This case seems different though."

"Different?"

"Yeah. I wanna call it something, but I'm not sure what."

"I'm anxious to hear," Henry said faintly.

For the past twenty-five years, many of Henry's days had been filled with giving lectures, with case meetings one after another, with phone calls one after another—often interrupted or postponed by emergency responses to crime scenes. And a case would evolve not unlike most others. But this case, a mere forty-eight hours old, had taken on an import, an overtone, which he had never experienced. Was it its magnitude? Multiple characters popping up out of nowhere? All known to each another? Related in some grand design; sharing in a common bounty? Were there more characters on the horizon? Henry was getting deeper into playing devil's advocate with himself when he heard Ed's voice:

"Maybe a 'biggie'?"

On the thirty-minute ride from the recycling grounds to the Center, Henry shuffled a few index cards. He had plenty of time to think some more, and he used it with hardly any interruption from Ed. Four items topped the list: Seal's murder, the note left at the scene, more about

Basil Vasilakis, and the recent remarks of Karl Moser. Henry worked in reverse order.

Karl's remarks had plagued him ever since he'd heard them, not because he considered them overly sarcastic, biting, or even inappropriate, but because they had a degree of merit. Perhaps there *was* duplication involving five busy people, particularly himself. He took a deep breath. Must he not put all other cases on hold? Be more of a sleuth than a hands-on criminalist? But once again he reminded himself of the original arrangement: for hot cases one person takes the lead, either because of geography, expertise, or special interest, while the others remain available for consultation. Yet doubts recurred about his leadership role in GIFT. It was a fine line he was required to walk: knowing when to insist and when to relent; taking the initiative but including the other members whenever possible; assuaging individual egos. Now the reality of another murder, the threatening message, and his decision to notify the other GIFT members—not of the message but of the murder—made Karl's editorializing seem trivial by comparison. Before the day was out, Henry would contact each one of them.

Henry's reflection about Vasilakis centered on what Lori had learned from the Bureau of Customs and Border Protection—that the midlevel official was an apparent expert on counterterrorism. Why? At some point he would check around.

He thought about how convincing he must have sounded to Ed when he downplayed the warning note as simply one of many that he'd received before, when in fact it was his first. But so, in a sense, was this current case—or group of cases—the most complicated he had ever confronted. And Henry had a feeling that this was just the beginning.

His greatest concern, however, was Seal's killing and the numerous questions it generated, particularly when he had never even met the man! He stiffened his back. Was it simply the result of the reporter's three-piece article? After all, it smacked of an exposé. Or was there more to it? Henry dredged up Seal's first phone call. Who were the "sources" he claimed had told him about the eyes: one open, one closed? Or the statement, "The Triads, the Tongs, the Mafia . . . maybe you and I should talk about it." What did Seal know that he wasn't willing to reveal over the phone? Or his bold contention that Henry might never learn the identity of the three murdered women?

At the Center, Ed disappeared into his office almost as if he wanted to be absent when Henry informed Lori of their discovery at the recycling grounds. But Henry was eager to tend to another matter before that. He unlocked the top drawer of his desk and removed an ankle rig and a Kimber compact .45 pistol. Next he repositioned the guns so that the .45 would be at his shoulder and the Smith and Wesson .22 snubby, formerly there, would now be at his left ankle. Like his first warning note, this amount of protection was a first in his career.

Lori appeared and Henry asked her to sit. He gave a brief description of the crime scene—minus the note attached to Seal. He hadn't expected her ho-hum response:

"I figured he was asking for it—after those articles. This is big stuff, Henry; you sure you're really up to it?"

"More than ever."

"Good. I wanted to hear you say it that way."

"Why?"

"So I won't feel so guilty when I clear your calendar for the next solid week."

"But tell them . . . tell them all . . . we might reschedule sooner than they think."

"Good. I like that, too. You still meeting with McClure at noon or does this murder change things?"

"Why should it?"

Lori straightened her necklace. "I just thought maybe you'd have to stick close to home for a while," she said.

"Westport's not that far. We're going."

Two years before, Henry would have done exactly what Lori had thought, even remained at the crime scene longer. There was a time when he focused more on forensics and less on investigations, but since he'd originated GIFT, his priorities were shifting. It was less a matter of interest than of hours in a day, and measuring up to the confidence placed in him by those in law enforcement and—he liked to think—by the other GIFT members. Thus, much as he disliked the supersleuth designation that Karl Moser had bestowed upon him, he felt obligated to act like one.

Lori left and Henry went right to his phone. He took the handset apart. There was no bug. While it was fresh on his mind, he phoned Detective Hal Latimore in New York and requested that he have someone check the phones in Seal's office and at his home. Henry told him about finding Seal's body.

"Well, that's a fine how-do-you-do," Hal said. "All related, no doubt."

"No doubt."

"You're covering it all?"

"Like a blanket. But Hal, one other favor. Get a search warrant for Seal's residence if you can. I want to have a peek—say within the next forty-eight hours. Could you do that for me?"

"You got it, doc."

"Much appreciate it."

"Now—I got a piece of news for you. The DNA results show that two of the babes were identical twins."

"Sad," Henry said. "The same family and as close as twins. But maybe it can help in locating their hometown."

"And doc, I been thinking. You know that glue? Incidentally, the analysis came back as a common variety of Super Glue. Anyway, do you think the eye thing has anything to do with the Mafia's 'evil-eye' talk? I don't know if I'm pronouncing it right, but I think they call it *malocchio*."

"I doubt it. It's probably a signal or a message of some kind like, 'Look, you other girls out there. This is what happens if you stop cooperating.'"

"Then that means whoever killed them—or had them killed—had a stake in the whole operation. They wanted to knock off some merchandise and at the same time warn all the other prostitutes who they control around the country."

"Probably around the world."

"So the operation's a big, big sucker."

"Very big," Henry said. He reminded the detective to call back, gave him his cell phone number, and thanked him before hanging up.

"Lori," he shouted, "round up Ed for the Westport trip, please."

In the hall, Henry stopped by her door and asked that she brief the other four GIFT members about Seal's death. "If you can't reach them by phone, e-mail them," he said. "And see if George could reautopsy Seal after our pathologists have a first run at it."

"You've never taken this kind of tack before," she said.

Henry didn't respond.

Chapter 5

They approached the Flotilla One Bar & Grille shortly after noon. Henry tucked in his left arm to feel the .45 Kimber, just as he had three minutes earlier. Ed had parked the cruiser in an alley two blocks away along Westport's riverfront. Dozens of upscale-model cars were crammed into a parking lot adjacent to the bar.

Crowded and noisy, the interior was larger than Henry had expected; a series of dining alcoves wrapped around a main room at least two thousand square feet. Background music was all but drowned out by chatter. A faint odor of stale beer hung in the air. Fish netting trailed from the ceiling. Shiny walnut wainscoting continued to the floor into an edging of parquet while the floor's central area consisted of narrow strips resembling the deck of a ship. The surfaces of wooden tables were marked with carved initials; occupants sat in plush red and yellow chairs that seemed out of place. To the right, a giant TV screen featured a Fox news show that no one was watching, and next to it, three recessed cabinets contained a rusty anchor, an ancient helm, and a round life preserver. Walls were saturated with pictures of boats and ships, some dating back to bygone sailing.

But it was the bar that stood out, one that spread along the entire far wall, with bar stools shaped like hands. Behind it, liquor bottles filled a score of open cabinets. Above, glassware dangled from a suspended holding device. Bartenders—Henry counted four men and two women—were dressed in tight black pants and shirts with a breast logo: FLOTILLA ONE. The lone exception was a man whose shirt was bright red but also contained the logo. Busy waiters and waitresses were dressed in solid black. The bartenders whipped away clean glasses from overhead without looking. On one side of the bar stood a binnacle holding a mariner's compass; on the other, a ship's mast and crow's nest disappeared into the ceiling. Four cameras rested in the nest, their lenses aimed at different quarters of the room.

Henry and Ed stood near the entrance scanning the room. In a few minutes, a man with a slight limp materialized out of nowhere.

"Ah, Dr. Liu," he said, extending a hand, "and his bodyguard, I presume. Just like a ship's tender. Welcome to the flagship of my flotilla."

Henry shook the hand and introduced Ed. "My tender here is Sergeant Edward Blegan," he said, forcing a smile. "You're Paddy, then?"

"Yeah, that I am. Paddy McClure. At one time Chief Petty Officer Paddy McClure." He and Ed shook hands. "And I wanna warn you: I like to talk. At least that's what they tell me. They say I'm . . . let's see . . . verBOSE."

"That's fine," Henry said. "I like to listen."

McClure, a stocky six-footer with curly russet hair, a droopy mustache, and a black eye patch, looked more like a pirate than a businessman. In his early fifties, he wore a white sweater with sleeves rolled up, baring a forearm with a tattoo of an anchor beneath faded lettering. His face was pocked, his nose bulbous, and his teeth were like ivory pegs. His pants were black and sported a belt with an oversized buckle. A tiny cell phone was clipped to the side of the initials PM.

He blinked his eyes whenever he smiled.

"You ain't had lunch, right?" he asked.

"Right," Ed said. Henry looked at him.

"Well, c'mon," McClure said, "let's go in back. It's mostly storage but there's a table and chairs and . . . ," he held up his hand as if taking an oath, ". . . the service will be the best." He smiled and his eyes blinked as he led the way through a back door into a small room that smelled of cheese and onions.

They sat at a table surrounded by crates and barrels and assorted wine, beer, and spirits containers. Low bebop rhythms, meant for the main room, wafted above them. Henry tried to tune them out.

McClure pushed a button beneath a table and a buxom blonde appeared at his side. She had a pencil behind her ear and carried a pad.

"This is my personal waitress, Tina," he said.

She flashed a nervous smile and curtsied.

"Drinks?" he asked.

"No thanks," Henry and Ed replied in unison.

They ordered sandwiches and iced tea.

"I know you came for a reason, Dr. Liu, but before we get to it, I gotta bring up somethin' and I hope you take this the right way. It don't show up when you're on television but in person? Man! I never seen a Chinese guy your size before. Born here?"

"No, China."

"Bet you played ball there."

"Correct."

"Baseball? Football?"

"No. Basketball."

"You musta been a star over there."

"I suppose so, until I busted my shoulder. Hard to shoot in that condition."

"You did it playing ball?"

"No, kung fu. National championship match."

"During the match?"

"Right in the middle."

"So you lost?"

"No, I won."

"You won with a bum shoulder. How the hell did that happen?"

"Chi-kong."

"Now hold on, doc, you're pulling my leg . . . arm . . . leg. Is it kung fu or . . . what is it . . . chi-kong?"

"Chi-kong is used in kung fu. It's a concentration technique that allows you to withstand the most excruciating pain."

"Now that's one for the books, I'd say. You stay active in that there stuff?"

"Not competitively anymore, but I'm still honorary chairman of the International Kung Fu Federation."

Their meals arrived and, as they ate, they continued to talk.

"So you've built yourself quite a little bar empire," Henry said.

"Empire? Maybe. But it don't make no sense to call 'em bars. Like the sign says, they're bars and grilles. Bars are bars—nothin' to write home about. But a good grille's what brings in the lunch trade. Nights with nice dinners and all—that's a different story. Better watch the lunches though. Get my drift?"

Henry and Ed nodded.

"You gotta try our corned beef sometime. Or the soufflé. Specialty fish. Got a French name but really started by the Germans. Yeah, way back. I read that somewhere. Or, maybe on TV . . . you know . . . those cook shows . . . they show you the inside of pans. Camera's right up there on top of 'em. Fish soufflé. Then some Bavarian cake. So pay attention to the food, I tell my daytime staff; the drinks take care of themselves. Too many businesses, what do they do? They turn around and scrimp on the food. Then they cry like babies when they go belly-up. Think about it. Unless you want some fancy martini bar—they got lots of 'em in Chicago—then drinks are drinks, that's all. Booze. But food's different, my friends. Can make or break you. Make it good and serve as much as they want. Keep 'em happy. That's what I tell my people." He wiped his lips with a napkin. "Now what can I do for you?" he asked.

"As you may or may not know, we got your name from Vernon Seal."

"No, I didn't, but seems like a good guy. Knows his business. Comes into our place in Manhattan a lot."

"Well he won't any more. He was found dead this morning."

Henry was poised for the response.

McClure rose sharply. "Oh, no!" he exclaimed. "He looked healthy as a horse. Worked out and all that."

"Didn't matter. He was murdered," Henry said quietly.

McClure reached into his pocket and jingled change.

"How? Where? Why?" he asked.

"Paddy, forgive me, but I'd rather not go into the details now. Too soon."

McClure sat and folded his hands on the table. "Sorry," he said and lowering his voice added, "gotta be those articles he wrote."

Henry tried to appraise McClure's words and his body language but reached no conclusion. "We can get to that later," Henry said sternly, "but would you mind if I first ask you some questions? Just routine, of course, since Seal brought up your name." He noticed Ed writing on an index card and stifled a laugh.

"No, go ahead, but can I ask why he mentioned me?"

"We were talking about his articles and prostitutes . . ."

"Wait a minute! What's that got to do with me?" McClure's eyelids fluttered and there was no smile.

"Nothing really, but the subject of bars came up and he mentioned you had a bunch of them."

"You're damn right. In five states. Took me ten years to do it."

"What states?"

"New York, New Jersey, Connecticut, Massachusetts, and Rhode Island."

"I imagine in the major cities?"

"Yeah, most of 'em."

"New York, Trenton, Providence . . ."

"Right."

"Boston?"

"Yeah, we're big there. Maybe it was *Cheers*."

"How many do you have in all?"

"Thirteen, but we call the last one Fourteen. Superstitious. Don't look for trouble."

"Do you circulate around?"

"You mean check 'em out? Yeah, I try and spend some time at each one of 'em maybe every couple weeks."

"So you've had these bars . . . ah . . . bars and grilles for ten years. What did you do before that?"

"What else? Tended bar. All over the country; you name the place."

"I see. And the navy before that?" Henry didn't wait for an answer. "Where did you serve?"

"Seal musta told you. Couple places. In 1972 I was a diver assigned to the navy's Coastal Surveillance Force and helped place explosives in North Vietnam's major harbor of Haiphong. The North launched this massive invasion to the South and its troops damn near reached Saigon. Everyone was beat." McClure's eyes narrowed to steely dots and his speech had taken on an unexpected eloquence. "I can still feel the water and hear the strafing." He shook his head as if dislodging a foreign object from his ear. A single bead of sweat appeared at his sideburn.

"Then guess what?" he continued. "Boom, like that—they turned around and shipped some of us to Munich, Germany. That's where they had the Olympics and the Israeli athletes were killed by them terrorists. Can you believe it? Shipping navy guys to where there's no goddamn water except some stupid ponds and streams. You figure it. All we did was hang around."

"Did you get to travel much from there?"

"Sure, plenty. Vienna, Belgrade, Budapest. Like I said, we were useless to them except for some minor patrol duty so we had lotsa leave time."

"Bucharest, too?"

"Yeah, Romania, right?"

"Right."

Henry took out a card of his own and made a quick notation. He glanced at Ed, then at his watch. "Can we switch to something else, Paddy?"

"I'd like to."

"You're aware of the three young women who were found dead at the harbor?"

"Who ain't? It's still playing on the TV. You know, I figured that's what you wanted to talk about. The papers made them sound like hookers and to save you the trouble, doc—no, we don't recommend any in our establishments. I wouldn't touch it. Not worth the bad name. But you know? I gotta be honest. I feel sorry for girls like that, doing that stuff. They need the cash, I guess. So if people want to meet in my place, 'go ahead, be my guest,' I tell 'em." He cupped his hand near his mouth and whispered to Ed, "Long as they buy a meal."

Henry checked his watch again.

"It's not just bars, my friends," McClure went on, "it's fine restaurants, hotels you'll find them. You have one in your own neck of the woods."

Henry's eyebrow shot up. "Where?"

"That famous inn."

"Clemensville?"

"Yeah, Clemensville."

"You mean Cliff Carpenter's place?"

"That's the guy. Some dudes say all kinds of, you know, action went on over there. Maybe still does, who knows?"

"Including drugs?"

"Nah, not that."

Henry scribbled a line and returned the card to his pocket.

"But tell you what, doc," McClure said, "you might want to talk to my manager in Long Island. Hempstead. Flotilla Two. Her name's Felicia Phillips. Smart as a whip. Pays more attention to things like this. She's been around the block, know what I mean? Oh, don't get me wrong—she just knows more people than I do, specially the broads. Looks about fifty but I know for a fact she's at least fifteen more than that."

"Will she be at work, say . . . tomorrow?"

"No, she don't work weekends, but she lives near the place."

"Do you think she'd mind if I paid her a visit?"

"I doubt it."

"Can you call her for me?"

"When?"

"Now."

"No problem." McClure grabbed his cell phone.

"You want tomorrow at . . . when?"

"Say between three and four."

"You got it if she says yes."

McClure made the call, received an affirmative answer, and gave Henry directions to Felicia's home.

"One other thing about that dame," McClure said. "She likes to read the future. Cracks me up when she does."

Ed led the way out of the room, and as they walked near the bar, McClure said, "Come back anytime, doc, and if I'm not here, Roscoe will take good care of you." He pointed toward the shortest of the bartenders, the one in a red shirt.

"Roscoe Fern, this here is Dr. Henry Liu."

Henry reached over and shook his hand. He was surprised at how limp it felt, as limp as the bartender's eyes looked vacant.

After an exchange of pleasantries, Henry and Ed left.

Outside, Henry was glad he'd put on a sweater under his blazer. The air had turned raw. Swollen with moisture about to burst, it felt heavy against his face. The wind wailed against them as they bucked it sideways on their walk back to the car.

They sat in the front seat. Henry played with the heater controls and bemoaned the auto industry's inability to develop a system that gave instantaneous warmth. Ed drove off.

"Well?" Henry said.

"I think he tries hard to sound dumb with all that mumbo-jumbo."

"I agree."

"He's holding back."

"I agree."

"Why mention that Felicia dame?"

"To divert attention from himself."

"Hadn't thought of it that way. That's why I'm just a sergeant."

Henry chuckled. "Listen," he said, "I don't even *have* a rank."

"Nice personal waitress though." Ed timed the comment as if he were dying to make it.

"I'm telling your wife."

"About what?"

"That you notice other women."

"Don't *you*?"

"My answer? I'm married but not dead."

Ed snickered. "You're pretty funny now and then, Henry."

Once on the Merritt Parkway and following a protracted silence, Henry announced: "Another lead though. Are you available tomorrow for Hempstead? It's the weekend, remember."

"I've got a family obligation: niece's wedding. Imagine, just nineteen—and, no, not a shotgun. But Sunday's free. Jake may be able to do tomorrow."

"That's okay. I'll drive down alone. Some thinking time, you know."

"Yeah, I know about that."

Henry's phone vibrated at his hip.

"Doc? Hal Latimore here. Seal's phones? Home and office? They were bugged all right. Microchip transmitters. Also . . . we'll have the search warrant by tomorrow at the latest. You coming down then?"

"Ah . . . let me think a second," Henry replied. He jabbed the air with his finger as he sorted out things to be done. "No," he said. "Make it the next day—Sunday—around midday."

"Good. Let me know the time and I'll have one of my men there to give you a copy and let you in."

Henry took down Seal's address.

They reached the Center forty-five minutes after leaving Flotilla One. It was two forty. Henry strode immediately into Lori's office.

"I'm anxious to hear," Henry said. "Did you make contact with the other four?"

"Well, hello there. Good to have you back."

"Lori, let's skip the crap. And hello. What did they say?"

"You want their exact responses?"

"Yes."

"I got George first. He says you were nuts to go to the grounds."

"Hindsight. What about Karl?"

"He said about the same thing. Asked more questions. Both of them feel the dead women and Vernon Seal have to be linked someway other than through the articles he wrote. And one other thing."

"What's that?"

"Karl said to give his love to the gumshoe."

Henry, not amused, said, "I love him, too."

"I couldn't reach the others, so I sent them e-mails."

"Back to George. Did you mention a reautopsy?"

"Yes. Said he'd be glad to. Well, he didn't say it quite like that . . . more like, 'I thought he'd never ask.'"

Henry pulled up a chair and sat.

"Wow, that's a rarity," Lori said. "This should be good."

"My legs hurt, cramp up at night."

"Plus the bum shoulder. You better get a cot in here."

Henry corrugated his forehead. "What's with you today?"

"I'm sorry. Maybe I'm worried about you."

"Why?"

"All that's going on I guess."

"It's just another investigation. Maybe a little more complicated, but just another investigation. Now—where we came from. This fellow McClure? Quite an actor. We'll probably see more of him. Anyway he set up a meeting for me tomorrow with a woman named . . . Felicia . . . Phillips. Lives in Hempstead, Long Island. From the sound of it, I think she was a big-time hooker."

"Oh? You might appeal to her."

"Me? Too—ah—mature."

"But you look a lot younger than your years. Everyone tells you that. What exactly? Fifty-eight? And don't lie."

"On the button. But there's only one thing: she's seventy."

"Don't be fooled. Seventy with loads of experience, so be careful."

"Yes, Mother, I'll do my best."

"By the way, Ed's got a wedding to go to, so what's the arrangement?"

"I'll drive myself."

Lori sighed. "Speaking of women," she said, "Gail called for you again today."

"What do you mean 'again'?"

"She calls almost every day, says she has no message to leave. But this time she does; wants you to call her."

"In London?"

"No, she's still in the States. You'd better be careful of her, too. How did she ever make the team anyway?"

"Jay insisted."

Lori searched Henry's eyes. "Come to think of it, how did *he* ever make it?"

"George insisted."

"That explains it."

"What's that?"

"Never mind . . . oh, what the . . . maybe I'm stepping out of line, but he also made a comment on the phone that I thought was inappropriate."

"Like?"

"I told him you asked me to inform him about Seal's murder and he said he'd already heard through official channels. That was okay. But then when I asked—maybe it was none of my business—I asked whether he was worried about the way the case was escalating, he said, 'Yeah, that and the Loch Ness monster really keep me up at night.' Sorry, Henry, but that was uncalled for. I'm happy for you about GIFT because it's important and I think you enjoy it, and I've met them all—but George simply . . . well, I'm fond of him but his brand of . . ."

"He's got his quirks just like all of us."

"Sorry, Henry. Maybe I'm just tired." Lori drew her lips back tightly.

"What else?" Henry asked.

"Gail."

"Now back to her."

"I think she has the hots for you."

"What makes you say that?"

"The way she looks at you, all the calls. Besides, a woman can tell."

"That's silly. I told you, I'm too old."

"You said 'mature' before."

Henry cleared his throat. "That's what I meant."

"But let's face it: you're an attractive, young-looking fifty-eight."

"Who says so?"

"I do."

"You perhaps looking for a raise?"

"Okay, *Detective Magazine* said so. Remember? 'One of the five sexiest men in the field, bright, energetic . . .'"

"The article was biased."

"How so?"

"The reporter is Chinese."

"Oh, for heaven's sake! Let's switch the subject."

Henry rose. "Let's," he said.

"So you're going to Hempstead alone tomorrow?"

"I can take care of myself."

"Sure you can."

He turned toward the door.

"Henry," she said.

"Now what?"

"You need a haircut."

He shot her a hard look and left the office.

Seated at his desk, he took out three cards and filled them with notes before placing a call to Detective Kathy Dupre.

"Kathy, this is Henry Liu. Anything yet?"

"I expected you to call. Made a list. Tire tracks? Forget it. Ground too packed. Wait till you hear this though. We looked for shoe prints—saw none. But in the photos we thought there was a funny impression found about a car's length behind Seal's car. We enlarged it, and it looks like a single shoe impression. *One shoe!* I can't explain it unless the ground was softer in one spot just big enough for that one shoe. Weird."

"Sure is. I suppose it's possible."

She continued. "Fingerprints? Just Seal's. The wire? Ordinary picture wire from any hardware store. His Taurus is registered in his name. We did a vacuum of the whole interior. Nothing significant. Did the usual background check. Born in 1955 in Brooklyn. College grad: Ithaca. Four years in the service: Army Intelligence, all stateside. Was with the *Sentinel* for twenty-five years. Then there's . . . divorced twenty years, no children, only family is a younger brother, his wife, and two kids. Lived alone. His wake's on Sunday, two to five. Funeral's Monday morning at nine. That's about it."

"Excellent work. Where's the wake and the cemetery?"

"Wake's in the city. Burial's in Westchester County. You want addresses?"

"Yes, please."

She read them off.

"Much appreciate it, Kathy. Say hi to David. He okay?"

"*Very* okay. He's taking a break from any of his own sleuthing for the foreseeable future. Just practicing medicine. Only house calls. Loves it that way."

"Give him my best and tell him if he ever comes back to this crazy business, maybe we can collaborate on some cases."

"Will do, and I'll buzz you if anything turns up. If there's nothing unusual on the autopsy, I won't bother you."

After hanging up, Henry consulted one of his cards and instead of barking out a question, walked into Lori's office.

"You and your husband doing anything Sunday night?" he asked.

"I beg your pardon," she replied indignantly.

"What I mean is: would you and Martin be free for dinner at the inn? On me."

"What brought *that* up?"

"Haven't been there for a while, the three of us haven't gone out in some time, and I want to touch base with Cliff Carpenter. Three birds with one stone, see?"

Lori thought for a moment and answered yes.

"Good," he said. "Then before the afternoon's out, call them for reservations. Maybe seven, seven thirty. Also, while you're at it, give Hal Latimore a call. Tell him we'll be at Seal's place between eleven thirty and twelve on Sunday.

He moved to Ed's doorway, popped his head in, and firmed up their daytime Sunday schedule. It included searching Seal's residence and attending his wake in midafternoon, a policy Henry always found helpful. Wakes and funerals. In fact, he would have made plans to attend the wakes of the three women if he'd known their identities, and he intended to inquire about formal burials for them by the state of New York. Were these done privately by a designated funeral home or would they be open to the public? If the latter applied, he'd definitely attend them.

He found Gail's phone number in his desk drawer and punched it in. She indicated she'd received an e-mail from Lori about Seal's death. As they progressed into a discussion of the crime scene, Henry sensed a certain detachment in her voice. He gave the gist of what had transpired at Flotilla One and stated he would visit with Felicia the next afternoon, Saturday.

"So you're driving to Long Island tomorrow?"

"Yes, I think I'd better follow up on this."

"Perfect! Why not come visit after you're through. Jay will be here—at least he said he would. We can have dinner. There's a great restaurant down the street."

"I know. GIFT ate there once, remember?"

"Oh yes, of course. So you know where my apartment is?"

"I'd recognize the building. Second floor, right?"

"Right. Do please come."

"Well . . . why not?"

"Alone?"

"Yes."

"Good. Then ring me when you leave Hempstead. Let's hope Jay makes it, but with him, you never know."

Chapter 6

Henry remained at his desk even though he wanted to go home. He'd had plenty for one day. He decided to complete some paperwork that required little concentration: simple calculations, signatures, filing reports in folders, sorting but not digesting three days' worth of mail. These were activities he considered therapeutic from time to time, an opportunity to insulate his mind, a respite from the barrage of stresses and strains.

He hadn't yet replayed the most recent events nor did he expect to until morning, when, after a decent night's sleep, he would have a fresh perspective. He looked at a simple framed card at the corner of his desk; he could recite the words by heart and had applied them to every important phase of an investigation. They had become second nature to him:

REACTION
ANALYSIS
DECISION
ACTION

He considered them his "Four-Step Sequence," and while it had become a ritual to reread the list, he realized that REACTION was virtually automatic, ANALYSIS required contemplation, and the remaining two, DECISION and ACTION, would, more often than not, wait until a crucial moment when he had to, well, decide and act. Sometimes the decision was *not* to act. Use of the sequence was not only the way Henry's scientific mind worked, but also a process he had devised to prevent snap judgments. By 4:15, he was ready to leave.

He felt sleepy on the way home. The metronomic sound of his windshield wipers didn't help as they braved another heavy autumn rain, the second in two days. The highway was slick, the visibility hampered by a fog that had just rolled in. Henry opted to move to the clearer air of higher ground. Approaching Hollings, he drove through a section called Rock Pond Hill, named after its multilevel terrain that surrounded vistas of ponds and streams and craggy rock formations. He turned left down a hill toward the center of town. There were two ways home from that point: into the foggy valley, through the center and on up to the west side, or an immediate right north, circumventing the center and driving two miles west. The latter was longer but better than bucking the congestion of commuter traffic below.

Henry took the right and entered a lightly traveled back route. Within a mile he eased to a stop at an intersection, its crossing roads—familiar to him—lined with trees and stretches of orchard grass. He thought little of the truck he saw in his rearview mirror until it began to bear down from fifty yards behind, sounding like a vehicle with a cracked muffler, giving no indication of swerving to avoid his Chrysler. Instinctively, he floored the brake pedal. The truck slid to a stop, inches short of his bumper. Henry reached for the Kimber .45, but the truck backed up and bolted away. He saw the heads of three men in its cab.

He heaved a breath and replaced the gun in its shoulder rig. At the same time he leaned forward to get a better look at the back of the truck. It was a black 4 × 4 pickup and he was certain it was a Dodge Dakota. He couldn't catch the number on the out-of-state license plate.

For a few seconds Henry sat bewildered. He resumed the drive home and, over a crest several hundred yards away, noticed the same truck parked on a side road ahead. He gunned his car and, as he shot by, heard the muffler noise again. He tracked the truck in his mirror and contorted his face when he realized the same thing might occur at the following stop sign. The next few seconds passed as one. The truck veered to the left, slowed down opposite the Chrysler, then suddenly swerved sharply to the right, forcing Henry off the road. He slammed on the brakes but eased up as he wrestled with the steering wheel to keep from plunging beyond the shoulder and into a ravine below. He lowered the window, expecting to confront his aggressors face-to-face, even through a thick driving rain. He yanked out the Kimber, but as his fingers tightened around the grip of the gun, he winced from a stabbing pain beneath his collarbone, not unlike the sting of a wasp. The gun dropped to the floor. He groped at the spot and felt a pencil-thin object attached at an angle to his left shoulder and, ripping it out, sank in his seat from the searing sensation of unyielding skin. He twisted the object in his hand. It was a dart needle.

His mouth turned dry, his heart began to pound, and his arms and legs felt, at first, weak, then numb. But his mind remained clear enough to reason that his layer of clothes, the dart's angle of entry, and his swift removal of the needle might have lessened the dose of whatever poison . . . toxin . . . tranquilizer was circulating throughout his body. In addition, he deduced, again from the entry angle, that the needle had penetrated just under the skin—subcutaneously—not to the muscle level—intramuscularly. The effect, therefore, might be more prolonged but not as intense. All this in a split second, for the men were at the window.

Henry scrunched into a ball as if totally incapacitated. He let his head sag but, in the process, caught a fleeting glance of the three peering in. Big, smiling, and Asian, they smelled of lime cologne and were dressed in solid black. Medallions dangled from their necks. One man wiped rain from his eye. Above it was a small tattoo of a sword. Three of his fingers were missing.

Though dizzy by now, Henry felt a sudden warmth, strangely reassured that such a response might indicate he'd been injected with a tranquilizer and not a poison. He also theorized that if the men wanted to kill him then and there, they would have shot or garroted him.

They opened the door and dragged him from the car swiftly and silently. His cell phone popped from his belt. He tried to make himself feel limp and let his head swing from side to side.

The men carried him to the back of the truck, hurling him like a rag doll onto his abdomen. He felt his clothing soak up the moisture beneath him. They returned to the cab and drove away. There was no choice but to wait.

Henry lay in a heap, face forward, eyes half closed, his heart skipping beats, his senses blunted, trying to draw upon any slight resolve, any past crisis, anything that might decelerate the throb of the moment. He thought about the .45 on the floor of the Chrysler and remembered the .22 snubby at his ankle. He reached down with his right arm. It was still there!

He was in no shape to use the gun. Perhaps as a last resort; but not right now. Bolstered, however, he opened his eyes wide despite the rain beating down on his head, trickling over his brows and beneath his collar. Believing the cool rain might "resuscitate" him, he tilted his face skyward, running his tongue over his lips to taste the drops. He could do it—a good sign. He ran a feeble hand through his wet hair and could smell the rain's freshness—another good sign.

He conjured up kung fu principles, shook his head, wiggled his toes, clenched his fist—over and over—hoping to retrieve some semblance of equilibrium; even sucked on his candies, thinking that somehow quick energy might help, much as in the case of a diabetic who overdoses with insulin.

Bouncing around in the bed of the truck, he pressed down with both hands and found he had the strength to lift himself briefly and look out through the rain; it had slowed to a drizzle. He did it repeatedly, trying to coincide it with the times when the men weren't looking at him through the cab window. He recognized the surroundings, and when the truck started to grind up High Rock Mountain Road, he had a terrifying suspicion of what his captors had in store. He felt his muscles tighten as he dropped back down and recreated in his mind's eye the bizarre episode nearly three years before: an episode involving Dr. David Brooks, Detective Kathy Dupre's fiancé and an amateur detective of considerable note. He recalled the catchy alliteration of the newspaper's front-page headline—"BROOKS'S BUNGLED BUMP OFF"—and the story of the doctor's escape from the clutches of the Yakuza, Japan's deadly underworld. Brooks's car had been wrapped in barbed wire and towed up the same road to the cliff top for disposal over the edge. But he had extricated himself, and when the truck slowed at a fork halfway up, he had dashed down a footpath to safety.

There was a companion piece to the account, one that told of the Yakuza and their loyalty rituals of tattooing and self-mutilation. When Brooks was interviewed, he described what he had seen through his car window. The paper had speculated on the future of the perpetrators—three men—and whether or not their failure would lead to more mutilation, perhaps another severed finger.

This recollection helped Henry rationalize why he hadn't been killed outright: maybe this was their last chance to redeem themselves. Could it be, even, that they had contacted the Mafia or the Triads and offered their services gratis? And, in some twisted way, that they had chosen to atone for their past failure in Hollings by using the same MO that had previously disgraced them—certain death off a cliff?

Henry knew the story well, as well as the entire High Rock region. Years before, he and Margaret and the kids used to picnic in its forest groves. He was familiar with every bend in the road and could picture its offshoots to rugged terrain and the footpath down to the Sunoco station. He remembered how the family had to come to a complete stop at the fork before circling around a massive rock as high as the tallest evergreen engulfing it. It was there, in fact, that David Brooks had made his getaway.

Could history repeat itself? Would the Yakuza come to a complete stop again? At that very moment, would they look back to check on their cargo?

Henry tried to keep his body moving in small undetectable increments, encouraged by his lucidity, by the disappearance of numbness, and by the anticipation of the rock's appearance. He wished he could rehearse the next few minutes.

The rock loomed through the rain ahead, over the top of the truck. Henry clamped and unclamped his teeth. He felt sweat drip from his shoulder blades even though his clothing was soaked through. He transferred the .22 snubby to a side pocket, rotated slowly to his back, winced from a twinge of pain at his bum shoulder, and braced himself for what he had played out in his mind as "the liftoff." Timing *had* to be precise.

The truck stopped. Henry cast one quick look back and, seeing only the backs of three heads, mustered up every last bit of energy, determination, and trust that his body—once wobbly—would cooperate. In one continuous motion, he doubled forward, scrambled to the tailgate, rose to his haunches, and leaped out like a high jumper in a track meet. He landed awkwardly on his feet but, rather than stumbling to his knees, allowed his body to relax and coil, whereupon his momentum took him in a roll into dense underbrush. He got up, took out the snubby, and hid behind a tree. No one followed after him and he could hear the sound of the truck and its bad muffler fading away.

But he still had to hurry to locate the footpath. It was only a few yards away, and as he approached it, he recalled the many times when little joys or unexpected successes had been taken in stride. They were simply part of an active life's continuum. This, however, was unique. His mettle was being tested just as it had when he blocked out the pain in the kung fu championship. But this was to be a rendezvous with death, and Henry was as much impressed with the manner of his escape as with the escape itself. He trotted down stiffly in the drizzle, thankful, relieved, almost euphoric.

Finally Henry spotted the convenience store at the Sunoco station, about a hundred yards away.

He leaned against the doorjamb briefly before entering. The owner queried him about his appearance; Henry blamed a stalled car and a half-mile walk. He thought about notifying the local police, calling Ed or David Brooks, but, drenched and chilled, he phoned Lori instead and summarized his ordeal. She lived ten minutes away and arrived in seven. It was 5:45 and twilight had set in.

"You smell like gasoline," she said.

"We're in a gasoline station."

"No, it's your clothes."

Henry brought his sleeve to his nose. "You're right," he said. "I must have been lying in some." It dawned on him that since he hadn't detected the odor while being hauled away in the truck, his senses must have been impaired more than he realized at the time. The impairment, he reasoned, must have been progressive, for he had smelled the men's cologne but not the gasoline later on.

"And you're a mess," she said, running a handkerchief over his forehead.

"But a live mess."

"And shivering."

"I'm cold."

She offered him her raincoat, but he refused it.

"I can just see you coming down with pneumonia," she said.

"Never."

"Why never?"

"Kung fu and green tea."

After Henry covered some details, she said, "I'm totally confused. If they wanted to—God help us—kill you . . ."

"Believe me, they wanted to kill me."

"But why not just shoot you?"

"It might have something to do with their botching the job on David Brooks. Remember that case? So, given the opportunity—or begging for it—they reappeared . . . to prove something. Their *own* way. Some people say the psyche of Japanese hit men is the same as latter-day samurai warriors: rigid."

"Lethal's more like it."

In her car, he apologized for getting the seat wet. "So let's see," he said. "At last count we had the Mafia, the Triads, and the Yakuza. Who's next?"

"Don't say that!" she blurted.

"Lori, I'm not talking victims. I'm talking killers."

"Don't mention victims!"

Henry smirked. "It's a good thing you're not out in the field," he said.

She drove off.

"Where's your car?" she asked seriously.

"Just this side of the Spruce and Meadowland intersection."

She continued in the same vein: "You want my opinion? You're going to get it, anyway. From here on in, Ed's got to be with you at all times. Maybe even a second officer." She stared straight ahead.

"Forget it. There's time enough for that."

"Time enough? Time enough?" she shot back, glancing at him after each question. "What happens in the meantime?"

"It all depends."

"On what? On whether they try to kill you again?"

Henry dismissed the last question. "That's it up there."

At the Chrysler, he leaned in, scooped up both his gun and cell phone, and turned to face her. His broad smile felt good. "Thanks," he said. "I'd hug you but you'd only get soaked." He bent down and kissed her on the cheek.

"And Lori? We keep this quiet, right?"

She hesitated, then nodded and said, "You want to eat with us?"

"No. Nice of you but all I want right now is a long hot shower."

As he drove home, he finally conceded to himself that his euphoria—born of enormous relief—was premature. He was shaken by what had transpired and had to admit that Lori's concerns were not ill founded.

He noticed her following him as far as the street before his own.

The rain had become heavy again and before stepping into the shower—a second whiskey in hand—he peeked out a back window. The dense black night matched his mood. He rubbed his shoulder. Where's the thunder and lightning?

Chapter 7

SATURDAY, OCTOBER 19

That night Henry's stay in bed was long and stressful, as sound sleep came hard; his mind fired up, he reenacted each moment of the abduction. And then there was the recurrent dream: wild-eyed creatures chasing after him as he slogged through a swamp that smelled of gasoline.

He was glad when morning came and anxious to run through the past day's activities, applying his personalized four-step sequence to each one. First, however, he wanted to attend to a higher priority.

In the course of forensic work around the world, he had received an assortment of token gifts at hundreds of award dinners: plaques, figurines, badges, arm patches, helmets, night sticks, handcuffs, even a bullet-proof vest. They were displayed around his offices at the Center and the university. But he kept certain others secreted in the attic of his home: the weapons. Among them was a Norinco Type 81 assault rifle presented to him by the Burmese government. It was light, less than a yard long, and was fed from a thirty-round box magazine.

Still in pajamas, Henry removed the rifle from a shelf in the attic, proceeded directly to his car in the garage, and set it under a blanket on the passenger's seat. He pledged to keep it there for the foreseeable future and never again allow himself to be corralled without a fight. All he had to do was avoid a dart needle! But he would be alert for that and next time reach for the rifle before lowering a window.

His march to the attic was as if he were in a hypnotic trance, and it wasn't until he had eaten a light breakfast that he recognized his motivation for additional personal firepower—common sense and an amalgam of fear, anger, and pride. Especially pride, for the ignominious experience of being tranquilized like some wild animal and hauled away in the back of a filthy truck by some thugs. This was something he wouldn't soon forget. Yet he wouldn't be sidetracked, for there was work to be done: a review of yesterday's events; the day's meetings with Mitroi at the Center and with Felicia in Long Island; tomorrow's visit to Vernon Seal's house and attendance at his wake. Henry had always paid attention to wakes and funerals, not necessarily to pay his respects but because they sometimes provided leads. In this case, although Seal had little family, certainly friends would attend. And possibly a few enemies.

He blotted out his roused emotions and within seconds felt mentally and tactically prepared for the day. It was like stopping on a dime, his ability to adapt, to move quickly from one mind-set to another as the situation dictated; mental toughness spawned by early days as a police captain and as a world-class kung fu combatant.

He went out front for the morning newspaper. The Seal murder made the front page, but the story revealed nothing that Henry didn't already know, including the statement that he would undoubtedly play a major role in the investigation.

An hour remained before he expected to leave for the Center, sufficient time to rehash the events of the past day. He jotted them down on one of his cards:

Seal murder
"Intelligent" note on body
Neg. evidence there
Seal—bugged phone
2/3 girls confirmed twins
Gail in NY same time as I'll be in LI
Flotilla One—McClure. Navy. Drops Cliff Carpenter's name. The Inn. Mentions Felicia Phillips. Met Roscoe Fern.
Yakuza

He thought through his four-step sequence; it didn't take long to conclude there were too many gaps to make any final judgments.

Paul Mitroi was a short, skinny man with a pencil mustache and an uncoordinated skeletal gait, each step taken haltingly as if he were waiting for some of his vertebrae to catch up to the others. He looked about sixty and peered over reading glasses when he spoke. A gold crown was visible at the left angle of a smile that seemed to hurt and took forever to disengage. His dark gray hair was straight, parted on the right, and draped over the corner of his left eye. Despite the weather, which had not warmed much, the sleeves of a black collarless jersey were drawn to the elbows. A large ring of keys hung from his belt. But it was his skin that was disquieting—flushed, rough, and weakly attached to his subcutaneous tissue, loose at the eyes and at the angles of his mouth. A booming vibrato voice belied his frail appearance as he stood before Henry at the Center.

"I've waited a long time for this, Dr. Liu."

"Really? I would have been happy to see you sooner."

"But you're not easy to get ahold of."

"My secretary could have scheduled an appointment for you."

"Yes, I know, but you're on the road so much and I hate to commit to anything way in advance. However, I have a moral duty to speak with you." Mitroi looked as if he had just swallowed a mouthful of vinegar.

"I see. But please sit down." Henry waited while the red-faced little man sat heavily on the chair before his desk.

"Now what can I do for you?" Henry asked.

Mitroi leaned forward. "You're a busy man, so I won't take up much of your time. You may or may not be aware of this, but there have been many killings of young women around the world. They're all very, very similar. Carbon copies. The ones in Brooklyn, though, really caught my attention—reminded my wife and me of our own loss." He brushed back his hair. "You must understand: two years ago our daughter was murdered. That changed our lives—we have no other children."

Henry decided to interrupt before hearing a more valid reason for the visit. "I'm very sorry to hear about your daughter's death, Mr. Mitroi. Before you go on—I know it must be painful—but may I ask you a few of the details? My assistant already gave me some background, but how old was your daughter when she died?"

"Sixteen."

"And you came from Bucharest?"

"Yes, Bucharest. I was a member of the Chamber of Deputies. My party was the Romanian National Unity Party. Our Sonia disappeared three years ago, then a year later her . . . her . . . body . . . was found, so we moved here permanently to find out what we could."

"Where did she live here?"

"We have no idea. They found her on a pier in Atlantic City."

"Only her?"

"Yes."

"Shot?"

"Yes."

"For a Romanian, you speak fluent English."

"Thank you. My mother was British and I attended schools near London for over twelve years."

"Then what?"

"We moved back to Bucharest and I became the principal of an elementary school there until 1989—over twenty-five years."

"Communist then, right?"

"Right. The government was communist but not me. Then when that bastard Ceausescu was executed, we began having free elections and the next year my government work started."

"Do you work here in the States?"

"Part time. School custodian."

Henry frowned.

"At least I'm still in education," Mitroi said. He gave his first full smile.

"Can we get back to the change in your life? The grief must have been . . ."

"It was horrible. But my passion has changed now. At this point, I'd do anything to stamp out violence of any sort—anywhere, any time. I hate wars; I hate bullfights; I hate cockfights; I hate wrestling. Even prizefighting now."

"Now?"

"Yes. I was an amateur boxer once—forty years ago, when my weight was up. Hard to believe. Whoever thought then that I'd go through so many illnesses? But I won't bother you with that." Wistful, he stretched his waistband out to the front to dramatize his weight loss. "And I can't give up my allegiance to boxing, but my outlook is entirely different. You see, I view pugilism as an art form. I agree with the Marquess of Queensbury rules, but if I had any say in it, I'd eliminate the bloodshed. Sharp, crisp punches." Mitroi began to shadow box in his chair. "Use your brain more, not brute force. Box . . . weave . . . box . . . weave some more. Jab away. Feint here, feint there. Right hook, left hook, uppercut—but no slashing, no head butts, no grabbing, no rabbit punches. Side to side, in and out. Footwork. Impose your will, not your muscle. Head strikes should count more than body blows, but no brawling, no clinches, no knockdowns."

"No knockdowns?" Henry was absorbed.

"That's correct. In fact, I'd assess a penalty if you knocked someone down. It isn't necessary. It takes talent to know how to pull a punch. They should be stressing finesse and agility, not strength. I watch the matches on TV, hoping these things will prevail—of course they never will—and I don't need to see those animals at ringside, screaming for the worst. It's called 'boxing' not 'attempted murder.' Remember Mike Tyson? Rapes women, bites ears. It's barbaric, I tell you."

Henry felt out of breath. "Interesting," he said. "Can we go back to when you moved here? You came to stay. Why?"

Mitroi picked at his fingernails. "The police were doing nothing. They pieced together what they had, then dropped the ball as far as I was concerned. I wanted justice. I wanted to find things out."

"How?"

"I organized a group to help keep up the pressure—a citizens' action group. And not just because of our own daughter. We have chapters now. Canada, Central America, South America, Europe, the Middle East, all over the United States."

"Sounds like a big undertaking. Has it worked?"

"At least they keep the files open longer. As I said, we want justice, Dr. Liu, that's all. The papers say you're on the case of the Brooklyn girls, but I don't even believe the papers anymore. Are you definitely on the case?"

"Yes."

"Good, good. Then may I offer our services?"

"Which are?"

"We've built up some information about the deaths—mostly a list of the victims, their backgrounds, their countries of origin: Bulgaria, Greece, Russia, Yugoslavia, Hungary, Romania, Serbia, Montenegro, and so on. You know, the demographics."

"The police don't have the same thing?"

"Not in the detail we have. I'm sorry to say it, but they don't seem to coordinate very well, especially if it involves other countries."

"Maybe it's the fault of the other countries."

"Could be, but the result's the same and it's getting worse. This is a monster of an operation, and if we can somehow cut off its head, the monster will die."

"So you have what amounts to a database."

"Yes, perhaps a crude one, but yes, we have one."

"How many files?"

"It's reached over a thousand."

"A thousand murdered young women?"

"Over. Maybe twelve hundred."

"Covering what span of time?"

"We limited it to five years."

"And all killed the same way?"

"The same way: shot in the side of the head."

Henry lowered his voice. "Anything unusual about their eyes?" he asked.

"What they described in the paper this week was the first I heard of eyes so I can't say for sure."

Henry congratulated him on the undertaking and said he would appreciate receiving a copy of the list. "By the way," he said, "did you happen to read Vernon Seal's articles in the *Sentinel*?"

"Yes, I did. They got him for it—whoever 'they' is. Probably the same ones who murdered Sonia. It was difficult but, yes, I read the articles. That whole issue of white slavery is what I'm talking about—why we set up the database. All our chapter heads agree that most—if not all—of the victims were part of it. Or had been. They were sacrificed because they rebelled."

Henry allowed the silence to sink in, his way of expressing further sorrow.

Mitroi got up.

They spoke for a few more minutes as they ambled to the front waiting room. Upon leaving, Mitroi indicated he would send the list and asked if there were any suspects in the Brooklyn killings.

"Too early," Henry replied.

On the way back to his office, he sucked on a candy, not because of a craving but because his mouth was dry.

The windows in his office faced the main parking lot. He looked out and saw Mitroi wander over to a black sedan at the far end. He and a passenger exchanged brief remarks through an open window. Mitroi walked to his own car, a red Toyota, and drove away. The sedan remained behind for another minute and left. Henry wasn't able to determine the make of the car or its license number, but he was reasonably sure two men sat in the front and one in the back.

He wrote some words and phrases on a card, beginning with the group of countries Mitroi had mentioned, pausing between each country; there was something perplexing about them. He shuffled a few blank cards.

His mind wandered to various parallels in the Vasilakis and Mitroi encounters, the most striking of which was his inclination to question their motives: one man spoke of a mysterious phone call and an international terrorist cartel, the other deemed it a moral obligation to share information about murder victims.

Then it hit him! He located the late Vernon Seal's articles in the *Sentinel.* The eight countries cited by the reporter were the same as Mitroi's, those that Henry had written on his card: Bulgaria, Greece, Russia,

Yugoslavia, Hungary, Romania, Serbia, and Montenegro. But, more important, *the order in which the countries were listed was exactly the same.*

He put in a call to George Silvain's home.

"George? This is Henry."

"You're working on Saturday or is this a social call?"

"I work *every* day. You think I'm a pathologist? Listen. Do me another favor . . ."

"Before you get to that," George interrupted, "I just got home. Instead of reautopsying Seal, I drove to Connecticut to join in the original. Nothing unexpected. Straight ligature strangulation. Fractured hyoid bone."

"No physical signs of a struggle?"

"None."

"Okay then. I just met with the strangest guy. Apparently his sixteen-year-old daughter was murdered about two years ago in Atlantic City—at least that's where they found the body. Shot in the head. He's from Bucharest. Name's Paul Mitroi. She disappeared the year before. Makes you wonder about the prostitution ring. Can you find out where they did the autopsy and please get a copy of the findings? That's M-i-t-r-o-i. Please call me. Much appreciate it."

Chapter 8

Henry encountered light traffic on the trip to Felicia Phillips's home in Hempstead, Long Island. He drove alone and at one point reached over to the passenger's seat and patted the assault rifle under the blanket.

He puzzled over the meeting with Mitroi: the circumstances surrounding his daughter's murder, his avowed crusade against violence, his harangue about boxing, the database information, and, above all, the listings of countries that perfectly matched Seal's. Did Mitroi know Seal personally? In that context, Henry harked back to his last phone conversation with Seal and the call that the crime reporter had allegedly received. Why did the caller warn him to "stay away from Paddy McClure and Henry Liu"? Had Seal devised the warning to cast McClure in a suspicious light? If so, why? Did Mitroi fit into the picture in some bizarre way? It would have been clearer if Henry had simply asked if the Romanian knew the crime reporter. He swore at his own oversight.

He passed the Nassau Coliseum and Hofstra University—not far from Felicia's house according to the directions—looking forward to another interview and to any new information it might yield. He disliked the tag "interrogation," yet enjoyed subtly working the process into most of his interviews. There were additional components to traditional detective work: overt and covert surveillance, tailing, photography, archival research, undercover operations. Henry left them for others to perform. Beyond teaching, his professional life had become, instead, a world of crime scene investigations—his stock in trade—along with hours of interviews. After that he would spend even more hours in a solitary effort to decipher, to hypothesize, to negotiate the maze. Until sleuthing had become a greater priority, Henry hadn't appreciated the importance of the interview sessions. Nor their frequency—an endless series strung together as he fished for clues and fresh leads.

He wove his car through residential streets before finding a secondary highway listed in the directions: "Go 1 mile—left on Reservoir Road—third house on right—#9."

A mailbox with "9 Reservoir" on its side was positioned near the road. Set deep into a vast field of yellowing grass and scattered boulders, vines, and apple trees was a large white house with black shutters. It was styled in a blend of farmhouse, Colonial and Victorian, and had a roofed veranda, several round-top windows, two chimneys, and a closed one-car garage. A gravel road circled up to the front door. A towering pole was stationed to the side, its American flag limp in the chilly but still afternoon.

Henry counted the outbuildings: two weathered box houses on adjacent lots and four barn structures in back—six in all. A compound!

After greeting him at the door—"You look like you do on television"—Felicia led him along a foyer lined with pots of dwarfed bamboo stalks and tables of miniature silver cars. They walked through a vaulted great room and broad corridor into a sitting room with cream-colored curtains, lamps with gold accents, and a fireplace. Soft shadows spread through a wide central window sheathed in a fringed coverlet and valance of delicate lace. The room was crammed with books, magazines, and, over its walls, photographs of antique cars. There were several mahogany tables, two Canfield chairs, two wickers, and three more pots of bamboo stalks, similar to the ones Henry passed in the foyer. They sat on the Canfields, facing each other. He detected the scent of either crisp linen or mountain air. A stack of business cards lay on a burl stand next to him. He picked one up. It indicated Felicia's name, address, phone and fax numbers, and e-mail address in black ink. Beneath her name was "Clairvoyant" in red ink. Henry slipped it into his pocket.

From his vantage point, he could see through the archway of a large room off the opposite side of the corridor. Its contents seemed inappropriate to the surroundings: less furniture, more equipment in metallic grays and greens—the pieces one sees in business offices.

Henry motioned in that direction. "You run a business out of your home?" he asked.

"I buy and sell antique cars. Keeps me out of trouble. I'd say 'keeps me off the streets' but that brings back too many bad memories." Only Felicia grinned.

She was a large attractive woman, over-lipsticked, over-mascaraed, and over-jeweled. She wore a green brooch, silver bracelets on both wrists, and a half dozen rings with brilliant settings. Her raven hair was puffed at the sides and light gray showed at the roots near a straight part down the middle of her scalp. A green cardigan hung loose over black slacks that were too tight for her midsection and age. Henry guessed she was on either side of sixty-five.

"Well now, good to meet you," she said, slapping her knees. Her words were deliberate, the sound guttural.

"Likewise. You have a beautiful place here. You live alone?"

"Yes, all by my lonesome."

"A lot of room for one person." Henry waved a hand in the direction of the other houses.

"Well, I like my space. Visitors like to come; some even stay over, you know, even for a week. Old friends, distant relatives, people like that. I love it."

"You must."

"Can I get you some coffee or tea, doctor?"

"No thank you."

"Something stronger? C'mon, it's almost cocktail hour."

"No, really."

"Maybe later then."

Henry stroked his chin. There will be a later?

"So," she continued, "Paddy said you're an interesting fellow. Famous. I don't follow your line of work—although most of the customers at Flotilla do. But I don't listen in much. Like I said though, I've seen you on television a few times. That O. J. thing? Right?"

Henry shrugged.

"Anyhow, doctor, what's on your mind? A little clairvoyance maybe? See if I can help you solve your cases?"

"Certainly you read about the three bodies found at the Brooklyn harbor, Felicia. May I call you Felicia?"

"Of course."

"Of course you heard? Or of course I may call you Felicia?"

"Both." She laughed herself into a cough but managed to add, "You're funny."

"Sometimes even when I don't try to be. Well, our friend Paddy said you might be able to offer a little . . . ah . . . insight into the whole subject of prostitution in this area; or anywhere for that matter."

"He *said* that?"

"Not in those words, but that's what he meant."

Her features fell. "Then I suppose he told you what my profession used to be?"

"I read between the lines."

"Okay, what the hell—it's no great secret; I'll level with you. I'm not proud of what I did, but I was good at it . . . damn good. I paid my dues for twenty lousy years—six days a week—almost all day long. More johns than you can shake a stick at. Young, old, down-and-outs, people in high places. Listening to their fantasies, complaints about their old ladies. Got to travel a lot—South America, Asia, all over Europe. Not bad for the daughter of a strict minister. Then I rose in the ranks . . . up to . . . let's say . . . administration. Served some time for it. Now I'm clean. So there."

Felicia evened out her slacks. "Maybe I'll write a book. I can see the cover now: *History of the Hempstead Hooker*.

"Could be a bestseller. You don't mind then if I ask you a few questions?"

"No, go right ahead. I got nothing to hide anymore."

"You're from this area originally?"

"No, from Mississippi. Natchez."

"Where's your accent?"

"Didn't take those guys at the bar long to change it—if I ever had one. It's you northerners who have the accent, you know."

"And how did you end up in Hempstead?"

"You met Roscoe Fern, I hear. He's originally from Natchez, too. Introduced me to Paddy five and a half years ago—and that was it. I was managing Flotilla Two a few months later."

"So he knew Paddy before you did?"

"Uh-huh. Don't ask me how or how long though."

"I hope this isn't too personal. If it is, don't answer it, but how did you and Roscoe meet?"

"Oh, we go way back. Met at an antique car show. He's got a few of the old jobbies—just like me."

Henry pointed at the walls. "Are any of those yours?"

"All of them, at one time or another."

"How many do you have now?"

"Only four left. They're out back: a 1928 Sport Phaeton, a 1932 Ford, a 1937 Cord Sportsman, and a 1938 Jaguar Roadster. But for a long time I used to own about twenty at a time; got too hard for me to handle."

"*Twenty* antique cars? They must have cost you a fortune."

"Nah. Gifts through the years."

"Gifts? For what?"

"Don't be smart now, doctor." She looked as if she were only half joking. "We went into that already."

"Yes, you're right. I apologize."

"No, no need to," she answered smiling. "You asked if you could ask questions—I said yes—and you are."

"Thank you. It's okay if I keep sliding from one to another?"

"Be my guest; I'm enjoying it."

"Back to Roscoe. Did you ever work for him?"

"You mean was he my pimp?" Felicia's smile disappeared. "Sorry, that one I cannot answer."

Henry strained to withhold his own smile.

"Then can you answer this one?" he continued. "Do you know what he did for a living in Natchez? Tend bar?"

"No. There was a big explosives factory in the south end. He worked there."

"Pardon me a second." Henry took out a card and prior to making a notation said, "I can't remember things for very long."

"That's not what I heard, doctor."

"Okay. Now, did you ever have any association with the Inn at Clemensville?"

"Connecticut, right?"

"Right."

"I've never been in it, but I heard about the place through some friends of mine."

"Male or female?"

"Female. Hookers."

"It was a favorite . . . ah . . . get-together spot for them?"

"Oh, sure. Shacksville, USA at one time."

"You make it sound like a high-class brothel."

"That was its reputation."

"I see. And now?"

"I don't know."

"That wasn't common knowledge, was it?"

"Don't know that either, but they always try to keep those things under wraps, don't they? Good for both sides."

"Did you know Vernon Seal?"

"Didn't everybody? Yes, we had a few . . . shall we say . . . tussles in the old days when he used to bug me about my gals. He called them 'Felicia's Stable.' On top of that he came to me to learn about the future—many, many times. We always ended up fighting."

"About what?"

"He'd argue about what I predicted."

"You read about his murder then?"

"Yes. Too bad but guys like that play with fire."

"Their subject matter?"

"Their subject matter, and I bet every crime snoop prints only half of what they know."

"Why do you say that?"

"Because the creeps tell them to muzzle it or else. Not with everything because it can't look too obvious. Or maybe sometimes their bosses cut the story—for the very same reason. Their editors, right?"

Henry snapped his fingers. "You just gave me a lead, my friend. I should look up his editor."

"Might not be a bad idea."

Henry entered a reminder on his card.

"Do you know of anyone who might have wanted Seal out of the way?"

"Me? No."

"Do you know any pimps?"

"Not anymore."

"Do you keep in touch with any of the hookers?"

"Same thing—not anymore."

"So they don't try to contact you?"

"Why should they?"

Henry took her business card out of his pocket. "How long have you been a clairvoyant?"

"I've dabbled in it for thirty, thirty-five years."

"You use a crystal ball?"

"No, never. I concentrate in a dark room, holding a client's hand. Last time I did, it was for Seal."

"He was here?"

"Yep."

"When?"

"Last week. I forecast some major trouble for him."

"What did he say?"

"Just shrugged it off, said I was crazy."

"You predicted his murder by concentrating in a dark room?"

"I didn't say his murder, I said some major trouble. Sometimes I see things clearly, sometimes not so clearly. Or I dream accidents before they occur."

"Is what you see or dream always bad?"

"I'd say fifty–fifty. I've found my share of lost children." A tear almost formed in her eye.

Felicia's expression froze. She got up and walked over to Henry. "Can I see your hand, doctor?" She reached down and took it.

"You read palms, too?" he asked.

"No—fingers." She knelt down and examined his middle one. Her eyes took on a darkness that startled him.

"Uh-uh," he said.

"Did you say something?" she breathed.

"Ah . . . no. Not that I can remember."

"You're sure?"

Before he could reply, she rose and, grasping his wrist with both of her hands, tugged him into a standing position.

"Would you like to see the rest of the house?" she asked.

"No, I'd better be running along."

"We could start in my bedroom, doctor. It won't take long and you'll be on your way."

"No, I'm late as it is. But thank you for your time and your answers. You've been a great help."

Back in the car, Henry took a deep breath, then another. He edged onto the main road, glanced back at the compound, and, for the moment, came to two conclusions. One, that what appeared to be sexual advances had been off-putting in one sense, flattering in another. But after all was said and done, they were not surprising, given her long life in the sex trade. And two, that in all of his interviews, information he had to extract was more valuable than information offered voluntarily. In Felicia's case, hers fell somewhere in between. Chalk up another one he couldn't quite fathom.

In keeping with Gail's suggestion the previous day, Henry phoned her to say he was on his way. Fifteen minutes later, his phone vibrated.

"Henry? George here. I spoke with the pathologist who did the post on the Mitroi girl. Gunshot to the head, same as the other three. And guess what?"

"What?"

"One eye glued open, one eye glued closed."

At Gail's apartment, Henry had to ring the bell three times before she answered.

"It's Henry," he said over the intercom.

"I recognize the voice. Sorry I took so long but you caught me in the middle of fixing a curtain rod. Come right up. I'll leave the door ajar."

Upstairs, he knocked and pushed back the door.

"Hi, Henry," Gail shouted from the back of the apartment. I'm working on this blasted rod in the john. Maybe you can help me."

He found Gail standing at the foot of a ladder in her ornate, high-ceiling bathroom with an antique sink and single tall window.

"Where's Jay?" he asked.

"Some kind of emergency so he can't be here."

Everything about her was different. Her hair was perfect—no dangling strands, save one across her left eye. Her lips had a rich crimson gloss, and her subtle fragrance was stimulating. She wore a tight wraparound black blouse. Her short skirt was white over black fishnet stockings. Black patent leather high heels rested off to the side.

"This damn rod is hard going in, but I can handle it," she said. "What I can't handle is the rickety old ladder. Could you support it for me?"

"Yes. Sure."

Gail climbed to the second from the top rung and widened her stance its full width. Henry looked up. She was wearing a garter belt but no panties!

"There," she said, snapping the rod in place. Turning, she descended frontward, posing at each rung, feeding him the same laser stare he remembered from Center Hall.

"Gail," he said, his voice unsteady. "As you might expect I'm having trouble with this. It's kinda hard in more ways than one. I mean, what's going on here?"

She braced herself and released the tie to her blouse. She spread it open in slow motion, exposing her breasts to the level of his eyes.

"No, Gail, don't!"

"Can't we go into the next room, just one time?"

"We'd better not. I'm tempted, believe me, but I'm sorry."

Gail slowly descended the steps while Henry stood transfixed. She kissed his mouth and drew herself tightly to him. Her kisses moist on his face, he stepped back. Gail tried drawing him close to her again. But he shook his head no. Gail took a deep breath and collected herself.

"Sorry for the passion," she said, while tying her blouse closed. "I feel so foolish now, but it *is* a fragile earth, isn't it? Thank you for understanding. I don't know what came over me." Her eyes turned misty. "Still friends?" she asked.

Henry kissed her lightly on the forehead. "Still friends," he said, then walked toward the door.

"Henry?" she whimpered.

He glanced over his shoulder.

"Still colleagues?"

He nodded.

"And this is only between you and me?" Her chin quivered.

He nodded again and headed for the front entrance.

Driving away, he felt no guilt over what had taken place. First Felicia and then Gail! But Gail was really something! Yet, he had not really succumbed to her temptation. While visions of her anatomy danced in his head, he wondered if there would be a next time.

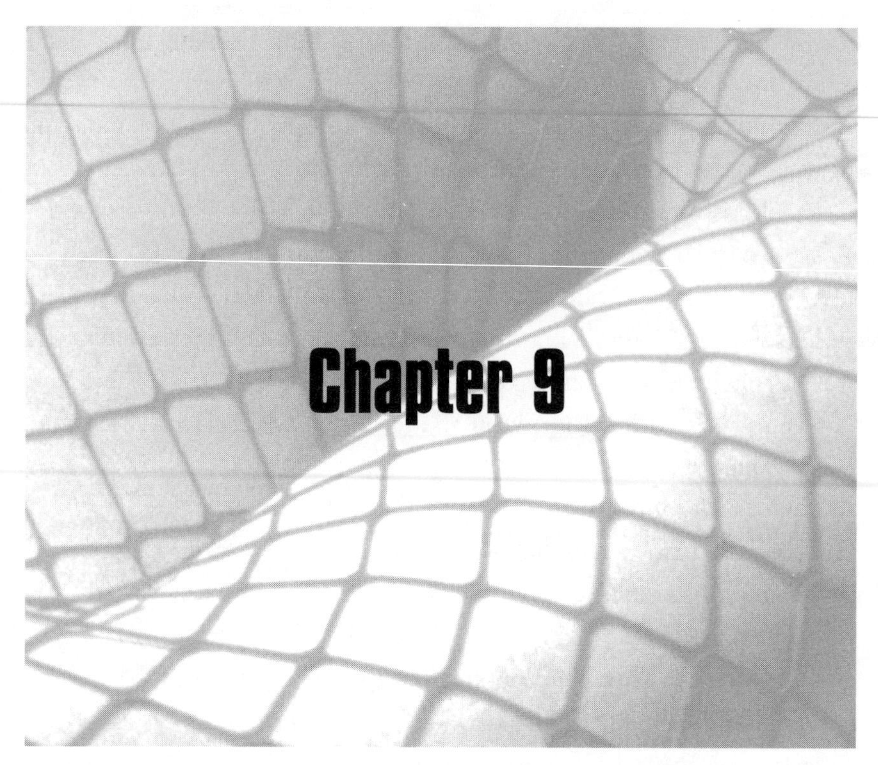

SUNDAY, OCTOBER 20

The following morning, Henry awoke with the two women on his mind. Under ordinary circumstances he might have enjoyed meeting with them, though not to the point of consummation. But under ordinary circumstances he might not have met them in the first place. Each presented a problem of a different kind; one was too enticing and the other was the reverse. They both posed an investigative problem as well: one, more and more, appeared to be a Scotland Yard misfit, and the other had a past that deserved further scrutiny.

He decided, however, that both women would keep for the time being. Recognizing that while each was titillating in a unique sense, he had a deeper concern plaguing him. Somebody was after him: the Mafia, the Triads, the Yakuza. Or all three wanted him dead.

He once had a coworker who, rather than admit he was worried about something, would say it gave him "pause." Pause or not, Henry was worried stiff. His personal arsenal spoke volumes: the .45 at his shoulder, the .22 at his ankle, and the assault rifle on the seat of his Chrysler. Before turning in for the night, he would position the handguns on his nightstand; when in the car, he kept tabs on all three guns with the regularity of a Brinks driver checking his flanks through the mirrors.

Henry tried to humor himself: three mobs were after his scalp, but two women were after his body. So why worry? Plus it was more than likely that underworld elements were not acting on their own; once a kingpin was nabbed, it would be like calling off the dogs. So just nab the kingpin.

In that connection, he never thought he'd reach the stage where he resented a relative lack of participation by the other GIFT members. Why complain? After all, the crimes had occurred almost in his backyard and the four had bowed to his investigative prowess. Initially he felt honored, but as the case became more complicated and his life put in jeopardy, so, too, did their absence become more irritating. Furthermore, he was as much upset by his own reaction as by their lack of participation.

GIFT's charge was for the five to work in concert wherever possible. To share expertise. To share the load. This wasn't happening and he blamed himself, even questioned his leadership skills.

He defined excuses for each person by the first thing that came to mind. Karl: too far away. Jay: too preoccupied. George: too absorbed in autopsies. Gail: too absorbed in, well . . .

But that exercise didn't ease his mind. There had to be a better way, a closer collaboration. Beginning Monday, he would call each one, not to voice his distress, but to assign tasks. Henry ran his fingers over his lower lip as he considered possible obstacles. Karl and George would not present a problem. In the case of Jay and Gail, however, there might be time constraints imposed by their agency superiors. If so, he would contact the superintendent of the Royal Canadian Mounted Police and the chief inspector at Scotland Yard. Once the other members had returned to the loop, he was confident a better team effort would emerge.

Ed picked Henry up in the cruiser and they started for Vernon Seal's apartment on Manhattan's lower east side. It was 10:15 on an overcast, dank Sunday morning. They both wore tan raincoats. Henry referred to the addresses that Kathy Dupre had given him: Seal's and Freed's Funeral Home.

"These should be easy to find," he said.

He summarized most of the conversation he had had with Felicia but never referred to Gail. Little more was said until well into the ride when they stopped at a traffic light. To the side, a monastery sat on a hill overlooking manicured grounds of pin oaks, honey locusts, and sycamores.

"Beautiful," Ed said, "and I hear your mind clicking."

He often took liberties with Henry and Henry never discouraged it, absorbing both ribbings and compliments in stride.

"I suppose you're up to one of your . . ."

"No, I'm not," Henry said evenly. "But come to think of it, pick a subject, Ed, any subject. You're the only one who listens to me lately." It wasn't true, but it reflected the mood he was in.

"What subject? I don't have a subject."

"Anything that crosses your mind. See what happens."

The light turned green and Ed started up again, checking the cloudless sky, a pond, a few more trees—nearly crossing the center line in the process.

"Well?" Henry said. "It doesn't have to be about nature, you know."

"I . . . uh . . . make it . . . make it about . . . time!"

"Time?"

"Time."

"You want a statement about time?"

"Sure. Anything. A lecture, a sermon—but a statement will do. Ready—set—go."

"Okay," Henry said, scratching his head. "Try this on. A moment in distant time is odd. When viewed from the front, it's right there. From behind, it's so far away."

Ed registered a look worth capturing on film.

They both laughed.

"I don't get it," Ed said, "but who cares? You sound loose, my friend."

"Easy for you to say," Henry stared straight ahead, sighed, and added, "I'm not at all. Not for a minute." Figuring it was as good a time as ever, he gave a detailed account of his abduction up High Rock Road.

Ed listened intently without interruption. When Henry finished, Ed pulled over to a soft shoulder and stopped the car.

"That's it," he said. "We get you another cruiser."

"I like this one."

"I mean an additional one. Following us. Or you, if you're alone."

"You've been talking to Lori."

"No I haven't. And I don't have to talk to her about this." Ed stuck out his chin defiantly, his voice raised a notch.

"Thanks for your concern. I can manage the way it is. Really."

"Sorry, but you're too close to all this. You've *got* to have more protection. I insist."

"Really, I . . ."

"I insist. I never have before. Now I insist. Listen to me. Does this sound like me? But I said it before and I'll say it again. This case is different—blows my mind—and that means from the MOs, to the motives, to the perps, and to what-the-hell-else this case is all about. I tell you, Henry, they'll stop at nothing. It's like a war—and wars require manpower. So why don't we simply arrange for another squad car to tag along wherever you go? Or wherever we both go? Jake would be perfect for the day shift. He's on today in fact."

Whether it was related to Henry's slouch since the truck episode or its revisit in conversation, his shoulder began to hurt. "I suppose you're thinking about a car at the house, too?" he asked.

"Absolutely. Twenty-four hours, wherever you are. For nights we can get Collander. I'm not talking forever, just while the case is hot."

Henry folded his arms over his chest, glanced at Ed, out the window, then again at Ed. "Okay," he said. "You win. Let's try it."

Ed got back on the highway. "It's the only way," he said.

"So maybe I'll put the Norinco away . . . no, I'll put it in the trunk."

"What Norinco?"

"The one on the front seat."

"You mean you've got an assault rifle on your front seat, but you gave me a hard time about another bodyguard?"

"I didn't give you a hard time. It's the only way."

Seal's apartment building was not unlike Gail's on the west side, but its interior was a different story. His, three rooms, was smaller—with little furniture and even less in the way of decoration.

A uniformed police officer greeted them at the door. He smiled broadly and handed Henry an envelope.

"Search warrant, Dr. Liu, compliments of Detective Latimore. I'm Officer John McConnell. I can let you in—then I'm on my way. The door will lock behind you when you're through."

Henry put the envelope in his pocket, shook the officer's hand, and thanked him. The officer saluted and walked away.

Since Ed's convincing argument for added security, there was a new bounce to Henry's step as he led the way in a walk-through of a bedroom and two combination "everything" rooms: kitchen, dining area, study, sitting room. Study? Desk, computer, printer, phone, locked filing cabinet, and a few books. Sitting room? Easy chair, side table, floor lamp, and TV set. The apartment smelled of old garbage and the floorboards creaked under colorless, threadbare carpeting.

A large framed photograph hung on the wall above his desk; it was flanked by four smaller ones. They depicted paddocks at Belmont Racetrack with the same gray horse and the same inscription: *Belmont: Filly-Fa-Fa.* Scrawled in longhand on the border of the center photo were three lines that Henry assumed Seal had penned:

Decent writer
Terrible gambler
Can't stop either!

Henry sought to reconcile the condition of the place with Seal's career in journalism. He put the blame on gambling, but neither dwelled on it nor asked Ed's opinion. Henry was more intent on locating bank statements and old e-mail messages.

Ed had slipped on latex gloves; he handed Henry a pair.

"I think it would be wise to hurry this up," Henry said, snapping on the gloves.

He opened the middle desk drawer and found a folder labeled "To do." In it was a single sheet of typed notations:

International proportions—elab. $$ billions—repeat E.

Europe prin. supply—delivered everywhere, say you name it—top boss in U.S. of A.—say unnamed sources—elab. line of work, meets people, ideal cover.

And then a full paragraph:

Take the case of Paul Mitroi, a once proud member of the Chamber of Deputies in Bucharest, Romania, and a survivor of the notorious dictatorship of Nicolae Ceausescu. Mitroi's sixteen-year-old daughter mysteriously disappeared three years ago and was found shot to death a year later. Where? In Atlantic City. On a pier. Strike a cord?

Henry wrote some words on a card and returned to the desk. He rummaged through a drawer and under an assortment of papers found an appointment book and a savings passbook. The appointment book contained a few entries—deadlines, doctor and dentist visits, a Broadway musical. But one stood out: SHOWDOWN. The word was printed under the date he was murdered, October 18.

The bankbook covered a period of a year and a half and showed a current balance of $2,878.65. Henry checked the deposits and withdrawals and noticed two distinct patterns: withdrawals averaging $750 were made about every two weeks and deposits of $5,000 each were made approximately every two months. He withdrew a calendar card from his wallet and matched the dates with the days of the week. His hunch was correct: the withdrawals occurred on either Thursdays or Fridays and there was no order to the $5,000 deposit days. His last observation was that additional deposits had been made in a willy-nilly fashion, all in the $2,500 range.

Henry's snap appraisal took the form of a two-part question: One, was Seal heavily into gambling or saddled with regular debt payments? And, two, was he receiving cash payoffs? He searched the desk for bank check statements and found none.

Ed had been looking over his shoulder. He took out a miniature camera and asked if he should photograph the material.

"No, let's finish with e-mails and get out of here," Henry replied. "Others will take care of that."

Henry booted up the computer, hoping that while Seal's messages had been password protected, there would not be a demand for verification. There was not; Seal had instructed the computer to bypass that step for easier access. But in scrolling through incoming and outgoing messages, the screen remained blank.

"Damn!" Henry said. "Deleted."

He rose and looked at Ed, who in turn was inspecting the surface top behind the printer.

"Look," he said, raising a wire basket containing several sheets of paper, "e-mail copies."

Henry flipped through and set five of them aside. They read the short unsigned messages together. Henry glanced back and forth at his calendar card and calculated the timings as he read:

Incoming, September 28, three weeks before Seal's murder:
Tell your man it can be arranged. It's a big pie.

Outgoing, October 4, one week later:
Did you receive the three articles?

Incoming, same day:
He says don't like them but go ahead.

Incoming, October 16, two days before murder:
NO. DO NOT PRINT THIS. UNDERSTAND?

Outgoing, same day:
TELL HIM TO STUFF HIS FINGER YOU KNOW WHERE.

Once in the cruiser, Ed radioed Jake with instructions to drop everything and meet them at the funeral parlor. He read the directions on Henry's card, then gave a brief rationale for his request of additional security; he asked Jake to remain outside as backup protection. Henry recorded their findings on several other cards. They munched on nutrition bars, which Henry kept in his briefcase.

Freed's was located across town, pinched into a row of town houses, shops, and retail stores. A red brick structure with two massive white columns, it looked more like an administration building or a library than a funeral parlor. It was set on a sliver of land with barely enough space—on either side—for a thin person to squeeze through. Henry surmised there was a back door that opened into a parking area for hearses or directly to a parallel street behind. Two stern shaved-head men in funereal attire stood curbside, opening car doors, greeting mourners.

"Drop me off," Henry said. "I'll meet you inside."

"Uh-uh," Ed snapped. "We go in together."

They circled side streets until Ed, exasperated, backed into a No Parking space a few blocks away. He placed an *Official Police Business* card on the dashboard. Henry emerged from the cruiser and pulled up his collar against a stiff wind.

He preceded Ed into the parlor. The anteroom was twice as wide as deep. Against the left wall, an oak stand contained a guest book and a stack of memorial cards. Beyond twin archways that led to a large receiving room, double lines of mourners stood waiting their turn to kneel before a simple closed casket immersed in rainbow floral sprays. String music oozed from an overhead speaker. The air reeked of fresh flowers superimposed on old ones. A small empty alcove on the right contained a fireplace, landscape paintings in thick frames, and several settees in taupe and burnt orange. On the other side, an archway spanned the entire length of a larger alcove. Attached to one of the lateral piers was a brass plate with the words *Meditation Section*. Henry, initially more concerned with blending in with the mourners and the collective demeanor, stared straight ahead but could tell that the section held about fifty or sixty people and was filling fast.

At the head of a reception line on the right, a tall middle-aged man shook hands with men and embraced some women as they filed by. He could be heard introducing some of them to his wife and two teenage sons. Behind them, several people sat on folding chairs.

Henry was conscious of supporting his weight principally on one leg, the one on the opposite side of his sore shoulder. Five minutes passed before he and Ed knelt briefly before the casket; they rose and turned to face the tall man.

Henry extended his hand and said, "Unfortunately, I never had the pleasure of meeting your brother, but we've spoken on the phone. I'm Henry Liu and this is my assistant, Ed Blegan. So sorry for your loss."

The man shook their hands. "Yes, I knew it was you. Thank you for coming. I understand you're involved in the investigation."

"Yes—and this is hardly the time or place but if you'd like to speak to me later about anything you feel is important, please give me a call." Henry found and surrendered the last business card in his wallet.

"I appreciate that, doctor. Thank you very much. All I can say right now is that my brother was a good guy who I guess tackled something far bigger than he counted on."

Henry expressed condolences to Seal's sister-in-law and nephews and signaled Ed to follow him into the smaller alcove. They sat on the orange settee with a clear view of the reception line. Henry noticed that about a quarter of the people who came through ended up in the meditation section. Eventually they would saunter in themselves, but first Henry wanted to observe the reception lines.

A trim distinguished-looking man with white hair entered the alcove and approached them. "Dr. Liu," he said, "how do you do? I heard you introduce yourself to Richard Seal. I was sitting in the row behind the family. But of course I recognized you anyway. My name is Maxwell Pierce and I'm the managing editor of the *New York Sentinel*."

"Pleased to meet you," Henry said before introducing Ed. "You were Vernon Seal's boss, I take it?"

"Yes. I'm happy to say that nearly the whole staff is here to pay their respects . . . although, forgive me, that was a poor choice of words . . . there's not much to be happy about, really."

"Mr. Pierce . . ." Henry said.

"No . . . please . . . Max."

"Max, then. I'm glad you came over. I was going to call for an appointment. Could we get together soon?"

"Absolutely. Maybe tomorrow? Monday is usually a zoo at the paper, but late morning would be fine. Or the afternoon. We have our editorial powwow earlier."

"So you won't be going to the funeral?"

"No. As I said, Mondays are tough. We all came here instead."

"I see. Well, we're going to the cemetery. It's over in Westchester County. How's, say, eleven or so?"

"Perfect. I look forward to it."

Pierce left and entered the meditation section. A few minutes later, George Silvain and Detective Latimore appeared in line, one behind the other. They exchanged glances with Henry and Ed and, later, joined them in the smaller alcove.

The detective sat on a settee opposite the others.

"I *thought* you'd both show up," Henry said.

"Duty calls," Latimore said. "I promised your Detective Dupre I'd cover for her here."

George gave Henry a bear hug before sitting next to Latimore.

"Anything new?" George asked.

"Nope," Henry replied. "Duty for you, too?"

"Just thought I'd mosey over. I knew Vern for a long time actually. He was a good friend to my office and to medical causes across the board." George played with a spot on the carpet with the toe of his shoe and then said, "Pretty clear he was killed because of the articles, don't you agree?"

"Yes," Henry said. He thought briefly about sharing the discoveries at the Seal apartment but, since they were in a public place, decided against it. Instead, he addressed Latimore: "Anything turn up on the harbor IDs?"

"Negative. They'll be held at the morgue for a while longer. Then private burials and I suppose some kind of . . ."

"Wait," Henry said, spreading his fingers in a stop sign. He watched as Paul Mitroi came into view, walked through the line, knelt at the casket, and spoke briefly with Richard Seal. But he bypassed the meditation section and headed for the front door.

Henry bolted over. "Mr. Mitroi," he said, "have you got a minute?"

"Oh, Dr. Liu. Hello there."

Henry motioned him aside. In the haste of the moment, Henry

couldn't decide whether to be subtle or bold. He opted for bold. "Yesterday, you didn't mention you'd be coming to the wake."

"Frankly, it never crossed my mind."

"You obviously knew Seal, then."

"Obviously. He was always very kind to me . . . understood our loss. That man had so many connections and helped in putting together our list. You know, the one I mentioned at your office?"

Henry nodded. "Speaking of the list," he said, "could you clarify something? Do the names on it represent women reported missing or just those confirmed dead?"

"Dead only."

"And all identified or not?"

"Some yes, some no. Mostly yes."

"What percent? Can you say?"

"I'd say roughly eighty percent."

"Eighty percent identified?"

"Yes."

"So for an identified one, her hometown is listed, right?"

"Not necessarily. Sometimes the best we can do is narrow it down to the country but not the precise address. Something to do with bureaucratic privacy laws in certain countries."

"I see. Their ages are sometimes listed, I take it?"

"Sometimes. Plus whatever other data we have on them. You'll see when you receive the list. Incidentally, doctor, when I got home Saturday, I sent it out to you as promised. UPS Ground. You should get it, maybe tomorrow."

"Many thanks. Now . . . the individual names . . . how current are the ones with positive IDs even if only by country?"

"Very. If the cops act fast and get together with missing persons bureaus—or vice versa—then the information is merged fast. I receive merged files every single day."

"Where?"

"In the computer room of my home."

"Do you look them over every day?"

"Usually, but I haven't for the last couple."

"But would you say, as they all come in, that they appear to be prostitutes?" Henry suddenly realized the implication of the question as it related to Mitroi's own daughter. Without changing expression, he added, "What I mean is, the majority of them."

"Yes, the majority. Perhaps—in going by what the police and medical people supplied us—perhaps all of them. Even our daughter. We like to think that most of them were tricked . . . forced . . . brainwashed."

"I'm sorry I brought up a delicate subject, my friend."

"That's all right. It is as I said."

"May I ask about two other things that bother me?"

"Certainly."

"When you cited some of the countries these women came from, you gave them in the same order that Vernon Seal quoted in some articles he wrote. Have you read the articles?"

"Yes. Vernon sent copies."

"And?"

"Excuse me?"

"The list of countries was a perfect match. Coincidence?"

"I believe it's the way we listed them in our database and, as I said, Vernon was familiar with it."

"He saw it?"

"I'm not sure about the final form, but some working sheets—I'm sure he saw those."

"Okay—and I thank you for your cooperation, Mr. Mitroi—just one last question. When you left my office yesterday, I happened to glance out the window and saw you go over to a car there. Would you be willing to say whether you knew the people in it?"

"No problem. They were strangers. Asked me for directions."

"To where?" Bold again.

"The shortest way to Providence."

"And you told them?"

"Yes. I said I wasn't from the area but that probably Interstate 95 was the best."

"Do you recall whether the car was there when you arrived?"

"I don't remember seeing it. I didn't even notice it when I came out. They called me over."

Henry thanked him again and Mitroi went out the door.

By the time Henry had returned to his seat, he was caught by surprise. The immigration officer, Basil Vasilakis, had arrived, apparently paying his respects, and was headed for the meditation section. George and Detective Latimore had also moved to the same alcove. Henry signaled to Ed that they should follow.

The section was a plain room with inadequate lighting, poor ventilation, and a musty smell. Straight-back chairs were arranged in a half dozen rows—ten to a row. All but the back row were occupied. A single aisle ran the depth of the room on the left.

They walked toward the back, nearly passing by Felicia Phillips and Paddy McClure, who were seated next to each other in the third row on the aisle. Henry reached out to shake their hands, leaned over, and whispered, "You both came"—not a question but said in a way that demanded an answer.

"We were among the first to arrive," Felicia said. "An old acquaintance, as you know."

"Ditto," Paddy said. "Vern was good to all the Flotillas."

Henry thought he detected the man next to Paddy move his head closer to listen. All he processed, with others waiting behind them in the aisle, was that the man wore dark clothes and might have had a scar near his left eye.

Henry and Ed proceeded to the last row and sat next to Vasilakis, whose chair was the last, against the wall on the right. Within minutes, others filled in the remaining seats.

"Well, Dr. Liu. You made it," Vasilakis said.

"Yes," Henry said, his voice muted. "I'm afraid there's a possible link between Seal's death and the harbor murders."

"Certainly looks that way. You must have to attend many wakes in the course of your work."

"They can be helpful sometimes. Sometimes not. Not as helpful as for politicians." Neither man smiled.

"What brings *you* here?" Henry asked.

"National security."

"National security regarding Seal?"

"Sorry, I'm not at liberty to say."

Henry paused as if to convey he was digesting the reply. "May I ask then, did you know Seal?"

"Not directly. I knew *of* him, of course. He had quite a good reputation as a journalist. From his recent articles, I knew he was interested in so-called white slavery. There's that courier business I informed you of already."

"You get the *New York Sentinel* in Washington? That's where you're from, right?"

"Just outside. My department gave me the clippings."

"And this subject is tied in with national security?"

"Sorry, Dr. Liu. I wish I could be more helpful."

Henry felt an elbow at his right rib cage. He looked at Ed, who gave an eye signal toward the aisle. Two bulky men in light blue pinstripes sat slouched back in the end chairs, heads facing down and to the right.

Ed cupped his hand over Henry's ear. "Those guys at the end? They leaned over. Kept staring at you. Caught me staring back—then they turned away."

"Probably nothing," Henry said, but he tucked in his shoulder to check on the .45.

A gaunt man in a navy blue business suit came into the room, flashed a puny smile, and said, "Good afternoon, dear friends. My name is James Freed. Reverend Sterling wanted so to be here this afternoon but at the last moment he took sick. He's asked that I lead you in a special prayer he composed in memory of Vernon. It's on the inside of these folded memorial cards, which I'll hand out. We can recite the prayer together. The reverend will be very pleased."

The funeral director advanced down the aisle, stopping at every row to count out a stack of ten cards; he gave a stack to each outside person for distribution across the row.

Henry received the last two cards. He passed one to Vasilakis and looked at his own. On the first page he noted Seal's dates of birth and death along with a short passage from scripture. He turned to the inside page. A small Post-it note was affixed along the top. The note read:

YOU'RE NOT STUPID.
ONCE AND FOR ALL, DROP THE CASE.
WE MEAN IT.

Henry's immediate conclusion was that whoever wrote the note wasn't stupid either. He turned sharply to his right. The two men near the aisle were gone. He rubbed his chin. One guy received the stack, the other one slapped the note on the next to last card? A good bet.

He sighed and handed the card to Ed.

"You're being stalked," Ed said in a manner that suggested he didn't know what else to say. He looked toward the aisle. "Should we go after them?"

"Forget it. They're on a highway by now. But I want to check with Freed."

They sat through the brief prayer. Henry wished Vasilakis good luck, got up, and, along with Ed, worked his way toward the front of the room. There was no trace of Detective Latimore, Paddy, or Felicia, but George had remained behind, leaning against a wall.

"You need me for anything, Henry?" he asked.

Henry showed him the note. George shook his head.

"Not the first, not the last," Henry said.

"You're not worried?" George asked.

"Not particularly."

"Then why show it to me?"

"Because I love you," Henry replied, putting on a mischievous grin.

"That's *my* line," George retorted. "Now I suppose you'll hug me?" He pushed himself off the wall. "Well," he continued, "I'm glad you can make light of it. Call me anytime if I can help. Incidentally, do the other three know what's going on?"

"We notified them about Seal, but I'd better call them in a day or two—bring them up-to-date. Thanks, George. I'll be in touch."

George walked out as Henry noticed the funeral director leaving the Seal family. Henry approached him.

"Mr. Freed, I'm Dr. Liu," he said. "Sergeant Blegan here and I are part of the investigation team assigned to Vernon's case. I have a question for you. May I?"

"Yes, of course, doctor. Pleased to meet you." They shook hands.

"About the memorial cards. Why were they handed out when there's a supply of them on the stand over there?"

"Oh, those? They're different. The ones on the stand are one-page cards. The ones I handed out are two-pagers with the personal prayer inside. To be honest, we only had sixty of them made up. Just enough as it turned out. We never expected our meditation section to be so filled."

"Much appreciate it," Henry said, backing away.

He checked his watch. It was 3:45. "Let's go," he said to Ed. "We've got some thinking to do."

The man who had been sitting next to Felicia and Paddy materialized out of nowhere.

"Dr. Liu," he said, "my name is Augustine Minotti, but you can call me Augie. Can we talk for a few minutes?" He glanced at Ed. "In private? Like in the small room over there?"

Augie was a square man in a black wool overcoat that brushed the floor. Henry thought its weight brought him down a few inches. He twirled a fedora in his hands. Clean shaven, his ponderous head was set deep into his shoulders and had little or no swivel. He appeared around forty and had straight black hair, a big nose, and elongated ears. His bushy eyebrows appeared pasted on, and he looked like a raccoon around the eyes. With a semicircular scar on his left cheek and a droopy mouth on the same side, he expelled his words through the opposite corner. A scratchy voice seemed forced from somewhere lower than his vocal cords, like an amplified whisper with the volume turned up.

"You may not know me, doc, but I heard plenty about you . . . you know . . . here and there . . . and I have great respect for people like you. That's what counts. Respect. I always say that and I believe that. It's important in my kind of business."

"And I have great . . . I mean . . . thank you. What business are you in?"

"It's like a calling. Yeah, that's it, a calling. People call and, like *that*, I get paid. Nice arrangement. And when I'm not getting called, I deal in wine."

"Wine?"

"Yeah . . . you know . . . you drink it. Taste's what makes it and we make the best." He bunched his fingers at his lips, gave them a loud kiss, and flung his hand up in the air like releasing a bird. "Besides age, wine's got to have the right taste and the right color—them two they call the body of the wine, but I don't go for the word 'body'—taste and color's better, know what I mean?"

"Let me understand. You sell wine?"

"Yeah, wholesale. We make it. We have the best winery in the country, bar none. Maybe the whole world." He gestured as if embracing a giant globe.

"Where?"

"Upstate New York, the Cayuga Vineyards and Winery. Finger Lakes area. Near Ithaca. You been to Ithaca?"

"I lectured at Cornell a few times."

"I got an office in Chicago, too."

"Where do you live?"

"Both places. Now can we go talk alone?"

Ed inched closer to Henry. "It's okay, Ed."

"Let's go talk . . . uh . . . Augie," Henry said.

"I'll be at the archway," Ed said.

On the way in Henry asked, "So you own the winery?"

The two sat opposite each other at a settee grouping. Augie placed his hat beside himself and rotated it so that the crease in the crown faced forward.

"Worked my way up—in everything. As a kid, I delivered messages to a baker in St. Louis. Got paid in crullers. Now I'm in management."

"But the winery. You own it?"

"Let's say we acquired it."

"We?"

"Yeah, I have a partner."

Henry assumed a quizzical expression.

"Sorry, doc, it's what they call a silent partner."

"*It* meaning a man or a woman?"

"You got it. A man or a woman. What's wrong with a woman partner? They're good with wines. Good tasters."

"I didn't say anything was wrong."

"And I didn't say it was a woman, neither." Augie crossed one leg over the other. "You got any more questions before we get down to real business?"

"Yes, three. Unless I think of more as we go along."

"Shoot. I got a little time."

"If you're from Chicago and Upstate New York, why come all the way to a wake here?"

"Because him and I are . . . were . . . buddies. He liked the ponies, you know."

"You went to races together?"

"Sometimes."

"So you knew Seal pretty well?"

"I already told you that. Buddies . . . you know . . . buddies. Next question?"

Henry took out an index card. "Okay if I make a note?" he asked.

"That's another question?"

Henry ignored him and printed a single word, deliberately taking his time.

"There," he said, "now question number two. The people you sat next to in the meditation room. You know them?"

"Paddy and Felicia? Sure. I have a beer at their places when I'm in the area."

"Care to elaborate?"

"What?"

"Final answer?"

Augie scowled. "What's with this 'final answer'? You think you're Regis? I answered the question, didn't I? You got one more."

"Are you computer literate?"

"Come again?"

"Can you use a computer?"

"Certainly. Ain't good, but good enough. I have a secretary, you know."

"I don't suppose you'd give me your e-mail address?"

"You suppose right. I can't remember it anyway. Wrote it down at home."

"Chicago or Upstate New York, right?"

"Right." Augie uncrossed his leg and leaned forward, forearms on his knees. "Okay, doc," he said, "time to cut the bullshit. My client wants you off the case, or else. No more foolin' around."

"What?"

"*Sta zitto*. Be quiet. You want me to say pretty please? Okay, pretty please. Now it's my turn. It would be easier to turn around and have you zapped, but our Chinese pals don't want that."

Henry held off running a finger along his sticky collar. "The Triads?" he asked.

"Yeah, them and the Tongs. We get along most of the time and we want to keep it that way. I got to level with you though, doc, it's a heavy choice to make—if you don't get your ass off the case. We want to stay pals with them guys, but there'd be this here big payoff to bump you off. Really big. Like I said, a heavy choice. Best thing is you just let the local cops handle it and bug off."

"Like the notes said?"

"Yeah."

"You wrote them?"

"Who, me? Naw, my client. My biggest caller."

"You were responsible for the note I received five minutes ago?"

"Yeah, that one, too."

"But why—when you planned on talking to me?"

"Just to be sure you got the message. So be smart. Go back to the fingerprints and blood and stuff. What's the other thing? DNA? Maybe play a little detective on the side—you know—bank robbers, the second-story sharpies. This one's too big for you—know what I'm sayin'? I heard of you . . . I like you . . . respect you . . . I really do." He leaned back smugly. "Think about it," he added, "you're not a cop—technically."

Henry was stunned he knew the word. "I'll give it some thought," he said.

Augie stiffened. He jumped to his feet. "*Adesso basta!*" he fumed. "Enough is enough!

You got forty-eight hours, doc. Wrap it up or else!" He spun around to leave and had to yank his overcoat to keep from losing his balance.

"Wait," Henry said. "You have the phone number at the winery? I might want to contact you."

Augie took a few steps and turned around slowly. He gave Henry a full inspection before walking up to him. The capo's face had flushed, highlighting his scar against the dark red background. He inserted his hand under his coat.

Henry reached in and took hold of his .45.

"Here!" Augie said, whipping out a business card. "They know where to find me, day or night."

"I didn't think guys like you carried business cards," Henry said.

"What do you mean 'guys like me'?" Augie stepped closer. "Look, pal," he said, "I run a legitimate wine business—just as legitimate as what you do for a living."

Henry finally ran his finger beneath his collar as he watched the square man storm out the front door.

Ed burst in. "What happened?" he asked.

"What else? He threatened me. He's behind the notes. No surprise there. Gave me forty-eight hours."

"Mafioso?"

"Uh-huh."

"Why didn't you pull out your gun and call me in for the arrest?"

"Because he's not Mr. Big and we need this bozo still out there." Henry tried to sound calmer than his stomach. "The case won't be solved one piece at a time. Trust me."

"But the forty-eight hours?"

"He's bluffing. It's probably the only number he knows over ten."

Henry put the mostly blank index card back in his pocket. He'd become disinclined to add to it.

"We're out of here," he said. "Let's see who shows at the funeral in the morning."

"At what church?"

"No, we skip that—go straight for the cemetery. You know my views."

Henry held that in homicide investigations gravesites were more productive than churches. That people intent on collecting leads often skipped the religious service itself and focused on the gravesite. For it was there that interested parties such as law enforcers, attorneys, and perps themselves tended to congregate. Especially the perps. Not all but many. Not in the confines of churches or synagogues but outdoors, in the open, where—for whatever reason—they could appear or disappear at will.

To a degree, Henry was shaken by the complexity of the past couple of hours. The location. The attendees. The confluence of grief, sympathy, volatility. Obvious danger. Once again, the question of his key role in the investigation tumbled through his mind. It could be so easy handling the customary cases; they were generally routine, less stressful. Not this time. He was faced with the specter of pushing an ever-enlarging snowball up a hill, hoping it wouldn't reverse course.

But since early childhood, he had often called upon a tiny secret habit—a gesture performed without notice, a fetish of sorts. It was a fleeting flick of his head, quick as a spark, as if to rid himself of a thorny issue or a bad thought. The bad thought now was the advice of the new warning note and the follow-up threat by the mafiosi capo.

Henry flicked his head twice, and muttered his own version of the note:

ONCE AND FOR ALL
DROP DEAD

Outside, Ed said, "How's that for service?" He waved in the direction of a car double-parked across the street. It was a facsimile of their Taurus police cruiser only unmarked and gray, not black. Its occupant slipped out and beckoned them over.

Jake Miller was a uniformed Connecticut State Trooper, straight out of central casting: tall, trim, closely cropped brown hair, square jaw and shoulders. His pants were charcoal gray with vertical blue and yellow stripes, his shirt a gray wool blend; it bore a multicolored patch of the state emblem. There was a gold badge on the left side of his chest and the right was plastered with several medals. His shoulders sported blue and yellow epaulets. The leatherware was patent with brass buckles and snaps, and a holstered gun hung from his belt.

"I just arrived," he said.

"Thanks for coming," Henry said. "Your cohort here talked me into it, so blame him."

"Jake," Ed said, "let's work it so we're both with Dr. Liu at all times during the day. I'll be nearby, you as outside backup. Say seven to seven. I'll arrange for some other officers to share night watch at his residence."

"Fine," Jake said. "I figure you can wrap up this one early, Dr. Liu."

"Want to trade places?" Henry quipped. Ed led the smiles.

"Did you see anyone in a long coat leave the parlor in a hurry?" Henry asked.

"Matter of fact, yes. A guy in one of those pinstripe suits ran over to him—you know, the kind with the wide lapels? Anyway, he came around the corner, said something to him. Then a sedan pulled up, they jumped in, and took off like a bat out of hell. I almost went after them but remembered my duty here—plus we're not in Connecticut."

"You get the make of the car?" Henry asked.

"Yes, sir. Cadillac. Black. But I couldn't see the plates in time."

"You want to walk or ride, Henry?" Ed said.

"How far away is your car?" Jake asked.

"Five, six blocks."

"Hop in."

The two cruisers reached Henry's house in less than two hours. He spent most of the time mulling over what he termed "action items," a phrase he'd borrowed from an industrialist friend. He thought of the discoveries at Seal's apartment and the people at his wake. But he kept returning to the behavior of the capo, menacing in his words, brazen in his long black coat. The guy must have known that Ed was a police officer, and only thirty feet away. All the while, Henry fingered his index cards, writing nothing down.

Ed dropped him off at six. "The cemetery in the morning," he said, "leave at eight?"

"Make it 8:30. I checked the map. People probably won't arrive till ten."

Ed drove off and Jake remained parked out front. Henry went inside and within minutes headed for the shower. He looked forward to dinner with Lori and Martin at seven, despite a cluttered mind and a feeling that he had just assumed ownership of the misery of the world. For the moment, his only solace was the piece of candy in his mouth.

Chapter 10

LATER THAT NIGHT

At 7:15, Henry and Jake reached the Inn at Clemensville in separate cars. Built in the early 1900s and perched on a steep hill, it resembled a Gothic stone mansion from a distance, but up close one could see more wood than stone. Its arched entrance featured THE INN deeply etched into a keystone, beneath which voussoirs were wedged between twin curves of dark hardwood, matching the floors inside. Within, everything else was light and airy. Outer walls of casement windows, each set straddled by stained-glass lancet sections, lent a bright ambiance to complement the building's exterior. Rows of marble support columns separated groupings of old wooden tables and chairs.

They found empty spaces in the dimly lit middle parking lot—out front, but a hundred yards from the main entrance. Jake maneuvered his cruiser so it faced the building.

The wind had not died down, and Henry could feel light moisture in the air. He got out of his car and paused a moment. It was his favorite view of the inn, its black contour outlined against a veil of shifting mist. The moon was camouflaged somewhere above a massive side chimney.

He recognized Lori's car as he walked by. The two, along with their spouses, had dined there several times over the years, when Henry's wife had visited from Shanghai; this was the first time without Margaret.

Inside, he took in the cinnamon fragrance and the familiar waltzes that had always greeted them. He strolled through the foyer, past the lodging desk and sweeping staircase leading to the inn's upper two floors. They contained thirty-six rooms. Word had it that the inn's longtime owner, Cliff Carpenter, relied heavily on a bed-and-breakfast trade. But as Henry neared the small reception room, he recalled the accusations of both Paddy McClure and Felicia Phillips. He stopped and cast a sidelong glance up the stairs. Lucrative, he was sure.

Lori and her husband, Martin, were seated in the reception room and rose when Henry came in. He complimented her on her attire, tasteful jewelry, and broad smile, calling it "sunny."

"Does dressing up do that for you?" he asked.

She wore a black dress, silk shawl, a choker, and pearl earrings. Her high heels were burgundy, and she carried a matching beaded evening bag.

"Same smile as at the Center," she answered.

"No comment," he shot back.

"And I don't think I've ever seen you in a turtleneck or in that kind of jacket," she said.

"Tired of ties. Same old blazer—just a weird olive color. But see, a nice shiny tan inside." He unbuttoned the jacket, spread it wide, and quickly rebuttoned it. "Sorry," he said, "I didn't mean to show off the gun."

"It's no secret, Henry. Knowing you, you probably have another one on you."

"Maybe two."

Henry shook Martin's hand, then stared at his own. "Whoa," Henry said, "you got stronger. We have to get you involved in kung fu."

Martin, grinning, replied, "Good idea. I could use it sometimes at the office."

A stock broker for twenty-four years, he was a solidly built six-footer with thinning gray hair, a broad jaw, and a wide face. Its outer edge formed a straight line down from his eyes, giving him an expression of strength. His voice was similarly strong and commanding. He wore a dark blue business suit and a gold tie over a pale blue shirt.

A maitre d' greeted them warmly in the crowded main room. He ushered them to a table against the far wall.

Over drinks—Chardonnays for the Gardners, a Manhattan for Henry—they spoke small talk until Lori asked what had transpired since his escapade with the Yakuza. He started a skeletonized version of the weekend's occurrences when he interrupted himself.

"Wait," he said, sniffing to each side. "I smell something."

"Bad?" Martin asked.

The unmistakable, high-pitched racket of smoke detectors pierced the air.

"Smoke!" Henry exclaimed. "I can hear something going on down there." He pointed to the floor beneath their table and, trying to keep his voice down, said, "I hope I'm wrong but . . ."

His last word was muffled by the crash of broken glass below, followed by a wrenching blast that evoked a variety of raw cries from patrons who had leaped up from their tables, poised to scatter. Most of them did, crushing against one another, knocking over chairs, shouting and shoving, losing their balance in a burst of pandemonium. They squeezed out of every exit. A few elderly people remained near their tables, clinging to one another, their faces twisted in horror and uncertainty. They were whisked outside by streaking passersby and cool-headed waiters.

Smoke grew dense: white, gray, black, yellow, green. Flames surged up between the walls and floor, spewing their whooshing sounds and igniting curtains as they licked along the walls and floorboards toward the center. An intrepid employee aimed an extinguisher at the gathering blaze but soon gave up and ran to assist with evacuation.

Henry wasted no time. Favoring his shoulder and back, he grabbed Lori's arm. Martin grabbed the other. They pulled her past the tables and immobilized diners to the front and out the door. En route, they each shouted incoherently, engulfed by the screams of others and the crackling sound of fire on the loose.

Outside, Henry ran into Jake and motioned for him to escort Lori and Martin to safer ground. At the same time, he caught the smell of rubber grating on blacktop and heard the roar of a speeding car. From the right, the car—a white compact—zoomed from behind the inn and continued down the narrow bend. He heard its shifting gears, saw the weaving, the panic. All four looked at one another. The car disappeared into a stretch below and, within seconds, their faces drew taut at the sounds of screeching brakes and a thunderous crash, louder than the noises of the human and fiery tumult behind them. Lori sank her head in Martin's chest.

"You three go check," Henry said, breathing fast. He wiped sweat off his brow. "I'm going back in."

"Don't do it, sir," Jake said. "It's too hot. Too late."

"We'll see. There's a motor vehicle accident down there. Call for backup. Go check."

"Wait here for us, promise?" Lori screamed as she removed her high heels and scampered with the two men down the road.

Henry stood at a safe distance before the inferno, his senses piqued but his sensibilities sickened by the harsh odor of the burning, the sounds of collapsing beams, the taste of smoke, rolling and surging. He heard a dog's whimper and saw him crawl out, his fur singed. Henry knew he had to screen out the chaos: the swirling fire; the coughing, moaning, and screaming; youngsters fleeing helter-skelter; the huddled elderly, stooped and straining to look back; the wail of distant sirens getting louder.

He summoned *chi* from deep within, a concentration technique—an energy—one that is an integral part of kung fu. He crossed his arms in front of his face, prepared to dive into the building. But he was driven back by a solid wall of heat and shooting sparks. He retreated and, peering back through the darkened debris, thought he heard the spray of feeble sprinklers. He saw no one yet shouted, "Crawl! Stay down! Crawl!"

He ran around the side of the inn. Trees were scorched and scores of people filed down an iron fire escape. They joined clutches of patrons, silent and crestfallen, their faces reflecting the flaming colors of red and gold. He wanted to speak to each one of them. But he decided there was nothing more he could do there. He dashed back to the front and down the one-way road to the junction. He found Lori and Martin shaking their heads and Jake making notes in a pad. The car lay before them, bathed in rising, wispy vapors, accordioned against a tree.

"He's crushed," Jake said. "The engine's in his seat."

Henry eased up to the car, bent over to look in, and felt strangely affected by what he saw, more affected by a red shirt than the blood that drenched it darker. A chord had been touched but he didn't know why. He looked closer. On the shirt was a logo that read: FLOTILLA ONE. The bartender in the red shirt! Felicia's friend!

He straightened and winced at a familiar stabbing pain in his lower back.

"Let's alert the firemen up there," Henry said as he, followed by the others, hobbled up the steep incline toward the burning building. It was becoming a mere shell. The fire drafts were louder, the smoke denser, and the smells more acrid.

An aerial ladder, elevating platform truck, and three pumpers had just arrived, as had four police cruisers and several ambulances. All the vehicles, save one, came from neighboring Hollings. Other emergency cars and trucks poured in. Henry couldn't decipher the static of radio receivers filtering through open doors and windows.

He pulled a policeman aside and, motioning in the direction of the lower road, whispered in his ear. "Car crashed down there. Guy's deader than a doornail."

"We'll take care of it," the policeman answered. "Hey, you're Dr. Liu! How you doin'? Good to see you." Red and yellow hues flickered over his face.

"Likewise. Wish it weren't here though."

Scores of firemen streamed from the vehicles and crisscrossed about. Most wore helmets, knee-length coats, gloves, and boots. Some wore masks attached to air cylinders strapped to their backs. Several connected a hose from the largest pumper to a nearby hydrant and shot a stream into the core of the fire. A half dozen men, unwinding booster lines from reels, siphoned water from tanks in the smaller pumpers and sprayed the outside walls and surrounding shrubs and trees.

"Get the snorkel going!" the obvious battalion chief barked into a bullhorn. "Get those fumes out!"

The platform truck moved into position at a safe distance from the least active side of the fire. Its cagelike platform held three men who were hoisted aloft. They used pike poles and axes to cut a hole in the roof.

Paramedics stood ready with stretchers. Jake and Martin volunteered to man one.

Lori appeared stunned and Henry embraced her. She broke her

silence. "I can't bear it anymore. Can we leave? And have you noticed the way you're walking? Grabbing that back of yours? You should be in a hot tub. The firemen can handle it. You can get a follow-up tomorrow."

"Maybe you're right, but in a minute. I have to check back there." He led her to a grassy knoll and sat her down, noticing for the first time that dried blood was caked on her lower leg. They agreed the underlying wound was superficial. She said, "Let's get Martin."

"I'll be right back," he said over her protest.

Henry searched all sides of the inn, sniffing, blowing his nose, sniffing again. He bumped into firefighters and their apparatus, tripped over hoses, and caught a glimpse of the few who were either being escorted or carried to rescue vehicles. In the darkest recess he could find, he leaned against the back of a tree and ran through several mental sequences:

Point of origin? Probably basement. Clear inverted cone with apex at bottom.

Professional or amateur? Professional.

Accelerant? Absolutely. Fast fire. Initial black smoke: organic material, probably gasoline. Yellow, brownish red: nitrocellulose base to help spread. Trace of ammonia used to offset gasoline odor.

Explosive device? No doubt. Initial blast maybe from pipe bomb.

Henry had additional thoughts but stopped short, wondering why he should bother, for everything pointed to Roscoe Fern as the arsonist. The man from Natchez. The man who once worked with explosives.

He stepped out but remained in the shadows. He recognized some men passing by: the fire marshal, detectives, members of the media. Exhausted, he had no desire to stay at the scene any longer, much less confront them. But the battalion chief spotted him and bobbed his head, trying to get a better look.

"Who are *you?*" he asked.

Henry was not used to being unrecognized in the Hollings-Clemensville area.

"I'm Henry Liu."

"Sure you are. And I'm Elvis Presley."

Henry drew closer, away from the shadows.

"Well, I'll be! Dr. Liu. Sorry about that. You're everywhere, I hear."

"Not quite, but I try to get around. Think it was set?"

"Set? Can't say for sure, but I wouldn't bet against it. The cellar had that flammable stench coming up from it."

"What do you make of the car? Didn't it nearly hit you guys as you came up?"

"Damn right. We swerved and cussed. Thought he was going to plow into us. Made the tree instead. Dead I assume?"

"Very. I saw him."

Henry encouraged the chief to resume his duties, shook his hand, and walked away.

He returned to Lori. Martin was there and suggested they leave to tend to her leg at home. Jake walked up.

"We can eat at our place," Lori said. "I can always scrape something up."

"No thanks," Henry said. "Appetite's gone. Let's fend for ourselves. We'll try this again some other time." He looked back at the burning structure and added, "Some other place."

Henry had difficulty weaving through lines of cars on the winding road below. He passed a TV van. He looked up at the inn. It was flooded by the sweeps of blue strobe lights and was still receiving a fusillade of water.

Jake followed behind.

At 17 Arrow Place, a question Henry had put to Lori was still on his mind: "Did you make the reservations in your name or mine?"

So was her answer: "Yours."

Chapter 11

MONDAY, OCTOBER 21

Henry once read that the pace of news transmission was so fast, it was like riding on a hockey puck. The next morning he felt that way. And a little stiff.

He read the newspaper and wondered whether the reporter had received the story secondhand. She indicated that the blaze was of suspicious origin but made no mention of a man in a red shirt who sped from the scene and died in a car crash. Nor did the article cite any deaths or injuries in the blaze.

Ed came by for Henry at 8:30 sharp, and they left for Seal's place of burial in Westchester County's White Plains. Another unmarked cruiser tagged along.

It was calm and warm for late October. Leaves in shades of brown, yellow, and orange drifted about. Henry wore a solid black suit and a gray tie; Ed appeared uncomfortable in a state police uniform.

"Looks too tight," Henry said.

"I haven't had it on in six months."

"You mean it shrank?"

"Very funny." Ed tugged at his collar. "You read about the fire last night no doubt?"

"I was there. About to have dinner."

"You were there?"

Henry related all he could remember about the inferno—detail after detail—considering it as an initial run-through of what he wanted to evaluate during the ride.

"So you think it was set?" Ed asked.

"Undoubtedly."

"By the guy in the crash?"

"Yep."

"Red shirt. The bartender we met? Didn't that Felicia babe say he was from Natchez? Explosives background?"

"That's the one."

"You think he—or whoever hired him—was after *you*, or what?"

"I'm not sure yet. Seems like an awful lot to go through just to get to me."

Ed accelerated past a string of cars on the Merritt and Henry said, "We're early so maybe we can take it easy. It's not too far from Greenwich."

Clemensville was a small town—actually designated a borough—with a local constable as its only law enforcer. It had a voluntary fire department and relied heavily on neighboring Hollings for major police and fire protection. Henry planned on phoning Hollings's Detective Kathy Dupre at 9:00 to see what had turned up about the fire.

In the meantime, there was plenty to think about. Uppermost in his mind was whether or not the fire was meant to coincide with his arrival at the inn, a possibility he had minimized with Ed just moments before. Was there any connection to Felicia's and Paddy's claim that the inn was a favorite haunt for prostitutes? If they were correct, was Cliff Carpenter aware of it? He *had* to be. Or did he have it torched for insurance purposes? Henry dismissed this possibility out of hand, for although he was never close to Cliff, he knew him well enough to reason he wouldn't jeopardize so many lives during a dinner hour. Besides, such a scenario was unlikely, for the alarm had sounded and the sprinklers had worked; in a deliberately set fire, they would have somehow been disengaged. Plus, it would have more likely occurred in the middle of the night.

Henry was tapping his foot on the floorboard. How much did Felicia and Paddy know, anyway? Who dispatched Roscoe Fern to the scene? Had someone told him about the reservations? If so, who? If not Cliff, could it have been a prostitute who informed Felicia who informed . . . ?

Henry would adopt a working hypothesis that the sole purpose of the fire was something other than his own death. If, however, his elimination were part of a dual purpose, so much the better for the perp. There appeared to be no relationship at all between the ongoing investigation and the fire, except for two items: one, the revelations of Felicia and Paddy, and, two, the recently deceased Roscoe Fern.

But his thoughts and hypothesis aside, Henry was convinced that the investigation had taken him to a point where he needed to be armed with thorough background checks on everyone he came across, alive or dead. And that included two people he hadn't interviewed yet: Maxwell Pierce at the *Sentinel* and what he hoped would be a downcast Cliff Carpenter.

The phone buzzed at Henry's hip. It was 8:40.

"Good morning," Lori said. "You okay?"

"Yes. And you? How's your leg?"

"Sore, but it could have been worse. I wanted you to know that Gail called."

"Gail Merriday?"

"Of course."

"Now what?"

"Says she's not going back to London until next week. She'll be at her apartment if you need her. Whatever that means."

"Good, I will. Strange, I was just thinking about her and . . ."

"What?"

". . . and the others. I can use her to dig up all she can about Felicia. I don't trust that woman."

"Felicia or Gail?"

"Felicia." Henry paused. "For your information, Lori, Gail came to us as a highly skilled and motivated senior inspector at Scotland Yard and she . . ."

"Of course," Lori said.

Henry informed her of his trip to the cemetery and asked her to set up interviews with Maxwell Pierce and Cliff Carpenter, if possible. She should expect him at the Center by three. He ended the conversation by briefing her of his intended conference call with the other GIFT members shortly after his arrival.

The time had come to engage them more. For starters, the background checks would be ideal. He took out a card, thought about geography for a minute, and printed the following:

TASK—FIND OUT ALL YOU CAN
KARL—MITROI
GEORGE—VASILAKIS, MAXWELL PIERCE
GAIL—FELICIA, ROSCOE FERN, CLIFF CARPENTER
JAY—PADDY McCLURE, AUGIE AND WINERY

He studied the card and felt playful attaching the word "tasker" to the GIFT members and "taskee" to those they would investigate. He ran each taskee through his mind and determined that such a group, with the exception of Roscoe Fern, comprised his suspect list for Mr. Big. Or is it Ms. Big? He reflected on whether or not it was too great a leap to assume that a single mastermind was at the center of his burgeoning case. Why not a syndicate—like the Mafia itself? He narrowed his reasons to three or four. First, the nature of the warning notes: the wording and the proper punctuation. Of course, a consigliere might be a college graduate; he could have chosen the words. Second, European suppliers would most likely deal with an authority other than a mobster. Third, the "To do" folder Henry had found in Seal's apartment stated that the top boss lived in the United States. How did he know? And fourth, Henry was convinced that any single individual on his "taskee" list had the wherewithal to develop and manage an international ring of prostitution.

Henry settled back and placed a call to the Hollings Police Department.

"I just missed you at the inn last night," Kathy Dupre said. "Heard you were there having dinner. Isn't that ironic?"

"Very."

"The fire was contained by nine. We hung around a little longer."

"What have you got so far?"

"The fire marshal says there's no doubt it was set. You know about the car crash?"

"Yes."

"He's got to be the one. We're still checking him out."

"Any fatalities? The newspaper did a terrible job."

"One. A dishwasher. Some injuries though, and smoke inhalation. About seven or eight wound up at the E.R."

"Was Cliff Carpenter in the building at the time?"

"No. He came by later. Said he was out of town. He was a mess, poor guy. He put his heart and soul into that place."

Henry didn't want to pursue the issue, but he did offer that the man in the crash was one Roscoe Fern and that he was employed at

Flotilla One in Westport. He avoided, however, the question that Kathy raised about irony.

"Would you do something for me, Kath? See if you can find out where Cliff will be early this afternoon. I want to see him."

"We've already asked him to be here at eleven. You want to come down?"

"I can't. We're on our way to a cemetery in New York—the Seal case. See where he'll be around 1:30. Do you mind?"

"Not at all. I'll set it up and call you back."

"Much appreciate it."

Ten minutes later, she returned the call.

"It's all set. You can use my office. We won't keep him long this morning and he's willing to come back at 1:30. I won't be here—have an appointment in New Haven—but make yourself at home."

"Excellent. I owe you another one."

"After all you've done for us? Forget it."

Riverside Cemetery in White Plains was set in a hollow among sugar maples, butternuts, and cottonwood trees. Henry and Ed put on sunglasses and left the cruiser in a rutted dirt parking area. They followed several people along a path that circled among tombstones, flowers, and flags toward a white and gold canopy visible several hundred feet ahead. Behind them, the backup officer veered off to the right. Seconds later, Henry spotted him in a cluster of trees on higher ground but with a clear view of the canopy. And also of Henry and Ed. They took a position against a stony ridge short of the canopy. Ed gave a finger wave and the officer, who held a rifle vertically at his right flank, waved back with his left hand.

Henry was certain none of the seated few could see them; the bright sun was at their backs and reflected off the front end of a nearby hearse and the brass handles of a casket resting on a rig.

The twenty-minute ceremony proved to be unremarkable except

for some observations that startled Henry. One concerned Felicia and Paddy, who sat separately among four rows of folding chairs, she in the middle, he on an end chair. A minister was ending a brief eulogy when Augie, still in his overcoat despite the balmy weather, sauntered over and whispered in Paddy's ear. They exchanged picture smiles and the capo departed along a path at the far edge of the gathering. Before long, he was joined by the two companions from the wake. This time, they were dressed in dark pinstripes.

Another was the presence of Maxwell Pierce, who had previously declared he wouldn't attend. The ceremony over, Henry hailed him aside.

"I thought you couldn't make it," he said.

"Early on at our meeting," the editor responded, "we decided that one of us *had* to be here. Vernon was with us a long, long time. See you soon?"

"Yes. We could talk here, I suppose, but I think your office would be better."

"I agree. You know our address?"

"I have it written down. See you there."

Henry was keeping one eye on Paddy and Felicia and noted they did not leave together.

On the drive to the *Sentinel*, he persuaded himself the trip to Riverside was worth the time and effort if only to see Felicia and Paddy ignore each other and the capo make contact with the Flotilla guru. He would ponder over the significance of both matters at a later time, perhaps on the way home.

He inserted a candy into his mouth. Certainly the last half hour was a far cry from the last gravesite visit when he learned virtually nothing. It was during the case of a hood who had been gunned down in a car wash. Henry had little to go on. Discouraged and grabbing for straws, he attended both the church and burial services. He expected blood out of a stone and what he got was another stone: only three people showed up at both services, all close family members!

Around eleven Henry and Ed walked into the *New York Sentinel.* Henry had visited television studios, radio stations, and movie sets before, but never the newsroom of a daily newspaper. It was there on the second floor that they located Maxwell Pierce. A busy switchboard operator had pointed them upstairs. Pierce was moving about in a sprawling open space without partitions or windows. The lighting was recessed and abundant; the smell of paper and ink permeated the floor. Scores of men and women sat at computer terminals, thinking and typing—mostly thinking. Some stood before more fax machines than Henry had seen at office equipment dealerships. Other workstations were crammed with desks and stacks of newspapers and reference materials. He was impressed with the quiet hum of the room, relative to the number of people preoccupied with their work, not noticing him or Ed or even their fellow workers alongside. But Pierce did.

"Dr. Liu," he said, "and is it 'Ed'?" They shook hands. "Come, let's go to my office."

The office was on the other side of a counter that ran the length of the newsroom and faced it head-on. From the outside it looked like a storefront with pane glass windows on either side of a central door that itself was half glass. Henry thought it curious that the upper part of the door was covered by a blind, but the large side panes were not.

The room had scuffed-up wooden floors, a single window, and a metal desk, a table, and filing cabinets. Computer hardware, printer, scanner, copy machine, and overloaded bookcases occupied the corners. The computer featured the word "MAX" floating across as a screen saver.

Pierce slid another chair beside the one already positioned before his desk. The three of them sat.

The managing editor's shirt was rumpled, his pants creaseless. He wore dark blue suspenders and matching sleeve garters. A plastic protector lined a breast pocket, which was stuffed with pencils and pens.

He dusted off his desk top with an ink-stained hand and put aside a pair of industrial-size scissors before addressing Henry.

"May I offer you some coffee or tea?"

"Not for me," Henry replied. Ed shook his head no.

"Well," Pierce said, "what did you think of the fire at that Connecticut hotel?"

Mere mention of it produced an unwelcome spasm. Henry tried to be inconspicuous when he gave his lower back a brief rub and straightened his posture in the chair.

"One word? Set."

"It sure reads that way, especially when a guy hightails it out of there and smacks into a tree."

"Did your paper print the story?"

"Yes, indeed. We took it off the wire services. Did he survive the crash?"

"No. The story didn't indicate that?"

"No. Just that he crashed and his condition was unknown."

Henry looked down at the floor. "Strange," he said.

"But don't forget, the account of it no doubt was written right after the crash," Pierce said like a newsperson defending his own.

"Still strange. He was killed instantly. Upon impact."

Pierce appeared wounded. "Anyway," he said, "you wanted to see me. How can I help?"

"I mostly wanted to hear about Vernon Seal, but first—on another topic—you're no doubt familiar with the case of the women found dead at the Brooklyn pier?"

"Yes. Sad. Very sad."

"Were you aware of anything unusual about their eyes?" Henry deliberately avoided mention of eye closure or glue.

"Sure. They were all blue."

"But if it were more than that and, for whatever reason, someone wanted to keep it out of your paper, could he or she?"

"It depends on who wanted to keep it out."

"Vernon Seal?"

"Easy. He wrote the story."

"You?"

"Yes. I approve the stories."

"And their contents?"

"As far as it's humanly possible for me. I try to read every word."

Henry wrote a couple of words on a card. "Fine," he said, "now about Seal. Did he ever submit stories you rejected?"

"Years ago but not in the last decade or so."

"Do you recall any of your reasons for rejecting them?"

"Oh, yes. Vernon was great with words but some of his ideas were too way-out. He tended to glorify criminals, gave them weird names like 'Georgio, the anti-God.' Or fancy ones. I remember he called one the 'shark spinner' in a story about a mobster who liked to dispose of loan shark competitors. Then there was—what was it?—the 'snitch crusher.' My favorite though was the 'machete meister.' I almost let that one go through."

"So he coddled criminals, at least in his writing. What else about him?"

"He was an inveterate gambler. The horses."

Henry didn't dare mention the pictures he'd seen at Seal's apartment.

"He owned one once. Lost his shirt on her. Filly something-or-other. He was a great reporter though. Loved his work. Dug into stories with everything he had. I'll say this about him: he would tackle *anything*."

"You have a theory on why he was murdered?"

"I've been thinking about it ever since Friday. Probably because of what he was covering for the paper. Serious stuff. Apparently big business. Got him killed—that's my guess."

"Did you give him the assignment?"

"No. He came to me about it and together we decided on how much coverage."

"So there was a three-part series—and was there more planned?"

"Yes. Another three-parter."

"Had you seen what it was about?"

"Not specifically. He gave me a memo stating it would be more of the same only with more details."

"I don't suppose you keep memos?"

"No, I don't."

"How about his interpersonal skills? Was he well liked by your staff?"

"Very."

"Any enemies?"

"Not that I know of except those he recently wrote about. No, to the ordinary person, he was a terrific guy."

Henry added more notes and noticed that Ed had taken out a card and written something down.

"Getting back to horse racing," Henry continued. "Did Seal ever miss work because of it?"

"No, I think he went only on Saturdays. There must have been some off-track betting during the week. There were always racing forms around."

"Did he go alone?"

"As far as I know. No one else from here ever went with him, although he did try to get me to go once or twice."

"Can you give me a ballpark of what his salary was?"

"I'm not certain. Maybe in the sixty, seventy thousand range."

Henry entered the figures on his card and searched the air for a moment. "That's about it," he said and rose from the chair, concaving his back. "May I take a peek in his office?" he asked.

"You're welcome to, but it's all been cleaned out. There wasn't much to begin with."

"That was fast. What happened to his belongings?"

"Belongings?"

"Yes. Notes, copies of past stories he wrote, that kind of thing."

"The police confiscated it all, but, I tell you, there wasn't anything of consequence. Over the years, he never let much accumulate here. Curious."

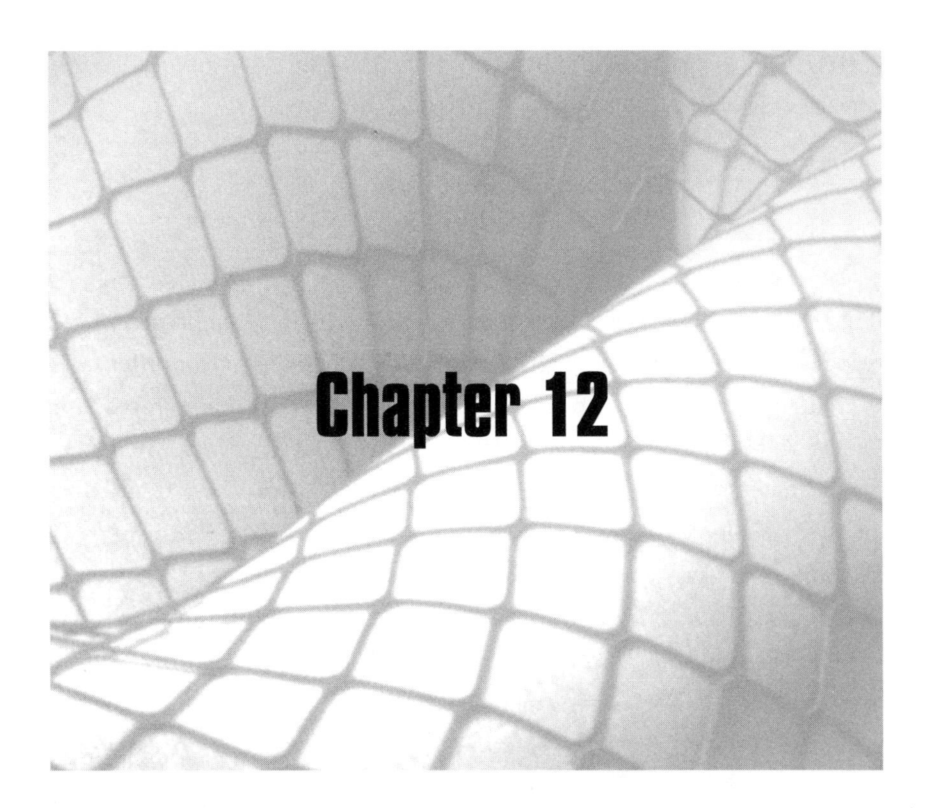

Chapter 12

Henry spent the greater part of the drive back on the Merritt shuffling cards and trying to untangle an ever-widening web of inconsistencies. And getting nowhere. The latest strands comprised the behavior of Felicia Phillips and Paddy McClure at the cemetery, Maxwell Pierce's showing up, and the apparent familiarity of Paddy with a gangland boss. Henry scratched an imaginary itch above his ear. Maybe Felicia and Paddy simply had an argument over the bar and grille business. Maybe Pierce felt guilty about his initial decision to skip the burial ceremony. Maybe Augie wanted Paddy to know he'd be eating soon at one of the Flotillas. Each explanation was feasible, but taken together, a hundred-to-one shot.

Henry asked Ed's opinion.

"I wouldn't trust any one of them," he answered.

"What stuck out the most?"

"McClure and the hood. Buddy-buddy. You?"

"Same thing."

Henry didn't add another peculiarity. At the newspaper, why didn't Pierce query him about the hypothetical issue to be kept out of the paper—the issue related to the victims' eyes in the harbor murders?

Henry incorporated the latest revelations into the broader picture. In many of his other investigations, at an estimated midway point, he would take stock of what he had, what he still needed to do, and what he had no control over. Plus he always stirred in a little bit of luck. In this investigation, however, he couldn't tell whether or not he'd reached the midway point or even if luck would enter the picture at all.

They stopped at a McDonald's for a take-out lunch and turned into the Hollings Police Department's parking lot at 1:20. They climbed the steps of a new prefabricated entranceway, harsh against walls of blanched brick and pitted mortar. Greeting friends at the dispatch window, they were buzzed into a maze of hallways and interconnecting rooms. The floor creaked beneath half partitions and shiny modular furniture as employees traipsed about their filing cabinets and worked their computers.

"As long as we're here," Henry said, "let's pop in on Sparky."

They proceeded directly to the Lilliputian crime lab—past benches of microscopes, chemical bottles, and the brothy smell of petri dishes. Henry knocked once before they entered the criminalist's office.

Walter Sparks, fortyish, looked anemic and had an anemic handshake. His black hair was slicked down and parted in the middle. He wore wire-framed glasses, which he peered over when he spoke. Trained under Henry, he headed up the lab shortly thereafter.

"Hi, Henry . . . Ed. No doubt about it: open-and-shut case of arson. I was about to call you about it." He sat at a large table and pulled over a pile of Polaroids and two trays of ash fragments. "Looks like multiple points of origin; traces of gasoline and ammonia; the usual charring and alligator patterns from the pictures. And look here." He slipped on a pair of plastic gloves, slid over another tray, and picked up a small metal cylinder. Holding the distorted object as if he were guarding a piece of kryptonite, he declared proudly: "Pipe bomb."

The three men talked about the tragedy of the fire, the cost of rebuilding the inn, and, for the next five minutes, the burgeoning interest in forensic science around the world.

Finally, Henry glanced at a wall clock and said, "Well, Spark, you must have lots to do and we have another commitment. Thanks for the input. Much appreciate it."

Henry had been in Detective Dupre's office many times but never without her present. Cliff Carpenter was not there when they arrived. Ed sat on a worn easy chair and Henry felt like an interloper as he took Kathy's seat behind her desk.

Her office was a spacious rectangle that was part of the original wing not included in the department's renovation program. The walls were empty, save for a calendar and a picture of Kathy and her fiancé, Dr. David Brooks. Basement-style hinged windows circled the room. A small counter held a smattering of papers and books. Fluorescent lighting fixtures were suspended from a high ceiling; one flickered. There was no door, only an opening the size of two doors. The smell was old but scrubbed.

Designated "Kathy's Chamber," it was far removed from rooms packed with sophisticated detection, communication, and database equipment; far from the Firearm Storage Room and the Evidence Storage Room; far from the Interview Room and the holding cells. Kathy's large barren space held but a file cabinet, a swivel chair, a makeshift serving table on casters, and a gray metal desk containing a king-size telephone assembly. The few words Henry and Ed exchanged while they waited for Carpenter sounded like echoes.

Henry heard distant footsteps approaching. "Here we go again," he said, "another round of questions." Once again, he harked back wistfully to the more hands-on discipline of forensic science. But he also reminded himself that his interviews were with a variety of people, in a variety of venues. It was a defense mechanism he'd recently adopted—one that seemed to dull the perceived monotony of interrogations.

Cliff Carpenter had the reputation of a man whose smile lit up any room he entered. Not this time. He paused at the entrance as if uncertain about what to do next. Henry and Ed quickly converged on him, taking turns shaking hands and offering condolences over his loss. Carpenter thanked them and indicated it was a long time since he'd seen Henry but wished their meeting was under less trying circumstances.

The proprietor of the Inn at Clemensville for thirty years seemed to look *through* Henry. His face bore the haggard lines of a refugee, or of one who had just lost his life's savings. Reddened eyes shone through horn-rimmed glasses. He possessed a stubble of facial hair that Henry guessed was three days old.

Carpenter wore his usual crew cut and double-pocketed shirt—this one ivory in color. Henry remembered the others as white, cream, and pale gray.

He pointed to a chair for Carpenter to use while he and Ed returned to their seats.

"Cliff, thank you for coming over," Henry said. "I'm sure you have many other things to do."

"Mostly sleep," Carpenter replied.

"Well, this shouldn't take more than five minutes, and if you feel you can't answer some of my questions, that's perfectly all right." Henry knew that sometimes a dodged or unanswered question had more significance than a straightforward one. "I'm sure you realize the fire was deliberately set?"

"The fire marshal and police informed me earlier today."

Carpenter's features thinned. He clenched and unclenched his teeth.

"Any idea why or by whom?" Henry continued.

"Not at all."

"No warning, no threats?"

"None."

"You knew I was about to eat there, I take it?"

"Yes, I saw your name on the reservations sheet."

"Did you discuss my reservation with anyone before the fire?"

"No, but it's on a clipboard on a stand as you go in."

"When is it put there?"

"Each day around noon. Before that, it's kept at the counter . . . you know, the one in the lobby. Right by the phone."

"Did you know a fellow by the name of Roscoe Fern?"

"The police asked me the same question. No, I didn't. They think he set the fire. What do you think?"

"I would say so."

Carpenter got up, walked in a circle, and slouched back in his chair.

"Sorry," he said. "Nerves, I guess."

"Just a couple more things, Cliff. How was business?"

"Excellent. The economy's picking up and that usually helps . . . uh . . . helped us."

"You had insurance on the place, of course?"

"Yes, but it wouldn't come close to replacement costs."

"Will you?"

"Will I what?"

"Replace it."

Carpenter took a deep breath before answering. "Dr. Liu, I can't even think about that. Maybe it's time to call it quits. Maybe that's what they had in mind."

"They?"

"They . . . he . . . she . . . them. Who knows? They're all bastards." Carpenter's shoulder twitched.

"I can understand your feeling. Now the last question and it's a sensitive one. Were you aware of a large number of trysts at your place? Trysts for money?"

Carpenter responded without hesitation. "I suppose that goes on in all motels—hotels—inns—lodges—boarding houses—you name it. I have no control over it."

Henry reassured Carpenter that his responses would be kept in strict confidence, wished him well, and thanked him for his cooperation. The proprietor left, his shoulders more slanted than when he arrived.

Henry explored Ed's face. "So?" he asked.

"Holding back, but not very hard."

"I got the same impression."

"By the way," Ed said, "how come you didn't take notes?"

"I didn't want the guy to think he was being interrogated."

Ed raised an eyebrow.

Henry felt as though it had been weeks since he sat behind his desk at the Center. He sorted out a busy weekend's worth of index cards, put all but one into a folder, and replaced the others with a fresh supply. The one he held back dealt with the tasks he'd assigned to the GIFT members. He studied it, called Lori in, and gave her the card with instructions to set up a conference call as soon as possible.

By three o'clock Eastern time, 9 PM the time in Germany, she returned and announced they were all on the line.

"I can't believe it," he said after activating the conference call apparatus. "I really expected two or three of you to be available on such short notice. "There *are* four of you there, right?"

Karl answered, "Right" and George, Jay, and Gail followed suit.

As the responses came through, Lori handed the task card back to Henry and scribbled a note on a pad, placing it before him. It asked whether she should leave the room. He shook his head no.

"Good, everybody's accounted for," he said. "So let's begin by my assuming you're in the following places as we speak. Then I'll go into why I've set up this call. George, you're in New York City. Karl, you're in Hamburg. Jay, you're probably at your RCMP headquarters. And Gail, I understand you'll be in Manhattan for a while."

Each answered yes.

"First and foremost then, you've got to know that this is getting to me. I can still coordinate, but I need help. Did everybody hear about the fire last night?"

All but Karl answered in the affirmative.

"What happened?" he asked.

Henry summarized the event as well as the essentials of his meeting with Cliff Carpenter and noted that he'd met Roscoe Fern at Flotilla One three days before.

"This is how I look at the big picture," Henry continued. He glanced at the task card. "If I'm considered de facto in charge, I've got to be allowed to act that way. Okay?"

No one replied.

"Okay?" he repeated.

The yesses trickled in.

"Fine. Here's what I propose and it's understood that I preface these requests with a please. Are you with me so far?"

He waited for a unanimous yes, got it, and then George said, "What's the proposition?"

Henry related the essence of his encounters with Mitroi, Vasilakis, Pierce, Felicia, Fern, Carpenter, McClure, and Augie, and included whatever he knew about their backgrounds. He then assigned the research tasks.

He could taste the silence, hear the ticking.

Finally Karl cleared his throat and said, "Henry, my friend, your voice is a dead giveaway. I've never heard you so frustrated. So I'll go you one better, and I hope everyone else is in a position to agree with me—given your workload. I not only vote for the new approach, but I would make an additional recommendation. Because of the obvious complexities of the case, we should—each one of us—devote as much as a whole week to living in the United States. Then we can function as a unit and bring this case to a close. Remember, we call ourselves GIFT. We're global. We deal in forensic issues. We should work as a team!"

Henry gaped at Lori. "Thanks, Karl, and believe it or not, folks, this was not prearranged."

The phone rang on what Henry recognized as a private line in Lori's office. She left.

"Now, George," Karl went on, "you're already there. So are you, Gail. Jay, you're close by, but should get closer if you can. That leaves me. I've got to think on that one."

Henry was about to ask him to move in with him, but George beat him to the punch.

"It so happens Harriet's going to a three-day convention in Atlanta tomorrow," he said, "AAUW stuff. So it would work out fine."

Karl accepted the invitation and said, "Then once we're a manageable distance from each other, we can meet every day for, say, breakfast—give our reports, divvy up some more, depending on what transpires, and so on. Henry would still take the lead, of course."

No one spoke for a moment.

Karl continued: "Henry, you're not saying much."

"I know. Call it shock. I couldn't have asked for more."

Jay chimed in: "I agree with everything that's been said, and I'm absolutely sure our superintendent wouldn't have a problem with my absence for a mission like this. He's told me more than once how proud he is to have the Mounted Police represented on our team."

"It's Monday," Henry said. "Can we start by meeting Wednesday morning here at the Forensic Center at eight? That give you enough time, Karl?"

"Plenty. While I'm over here though, I'll get the ball rolling on the Romanian. Mitroi's his name?"

"Paul Mitroi," Henry replied. "Chamber of Deputies in Bucharest."

"We haven't heard from you, Gail." George said. "You with us on this?"

"Count me in. I'm here anyway but yes, yes indeed. Good thinking, Karl. I would gently suggest, however, that we aim for a week and then take it from there."

"Good idea," Karl said. The other three men concurred.

Henry believed she sounded too enthusiastic, even eager. "Now then," he said, why not . . ."

Lori burst in. "There's a call on the private line I think you'd better take," she said. "It's Natalie from the dispatch office."

Henry apologized to the team and took the call.

"Dr. Liu," Natalie said, "there's just been a suspicious death in Budapest and the Hungarian government doesn't want it to become an international incident. They asked for GIFT."

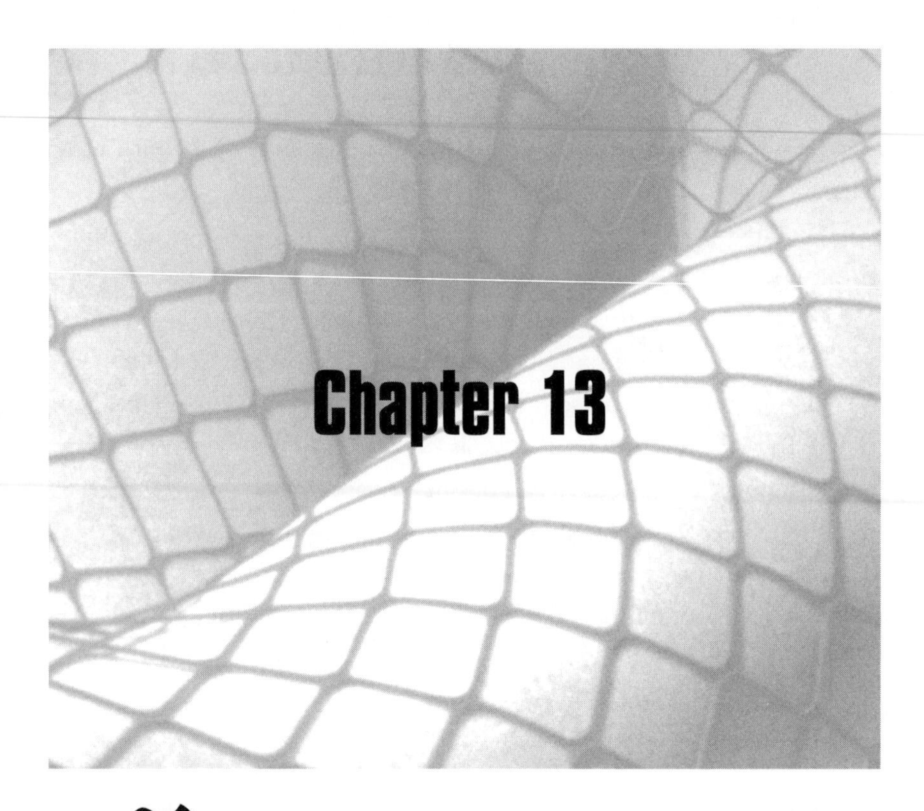

"Give me the particulars," Henry said.

"I took it all down," Natalie said. "First of all, it's nighttime there, a little after ten. Budapest is hosting a three-day conference called, 'Democratization. The Goals of a Free Society and How to Reach Them.' It's their sixth annual . . . on the same subject . . . by invitation only. Many of the surrounding countries are having problems adjusting to a democratic way of life and diplomats and other dignitaries are arriving at the conference in droves. The person on the phone identified himself as Fedor Kocyk. Says he's the commanding officer of the Central Police Commissariat and he was calling at the request of the Hungarian government. A little accent—speaks decent English."

"I know Fedor. Good man. Met him at a law enforcement symposium in Paris around ten years ago and we've worked many cases together ever since. Other countries ask for his advice. He's very accommodating and very professional."

Natalie continued: "They're now winding down from a dinner and opening ceremony. The sessions start tomorrow; I think he called them plenary sessions. Let's see . . . the dinner and conference are being held at the Marriott hotel. About two hours ago they found the body of a woman who fell or was pushed from the seventh story. Her husband claims it was an accident. The police think otherwise."

"Hmm. Back up a minute," Henry said. "What countries are represented? Did he tell you?"

"Yes. He just said Eastern European and I said like which ones? He spieled off Hungary, Bulgaria, Romania, the Czech Republic, Slovakia, Croatia, Bosnia, Serbia, and Montenegro like they were on the back of his hand. I had him repeat them so I could write them down in case you asked."

"Probably had them listed before him. Did he give the name of the woman?"

"No."

Henry heard her snap her fingers. "Damn," she said, "I should have inquired."

"Hold on, Nat," he said. He covered the mouthpiece and signaled Lori over. "The team's still on the line," he whispered. "Speak to them from your office. Indicate the rough nature of this call and to stay put."

"Real rough," she said. "I mean, what's it all about?"

"Suspicious death in Budapest. The government is requesting our assistance. I'll give them the details when I learn more. Maybe in a minute or so."

Lori left as Henry resumed his conversation with Natalie.

"So he didn't say anything about her identity?"

"Only that she was the wife of an American dignitary."

Henry covered his forehead with the palm of his hand as if to smother the charged circuitry of his mind: Government request. Long-time alliance with Fedor Kocyk. GIFT had to fly to Budapest.

He thought it over for another few seconds and said, "That's all we need, Nat. He left his number, I hope."

"Yes, I have it."

"Please call him back. Tell him we'll be there ASAP."

"Will do. He said he'd reserve five rooms at the Marriott in your name plus make other necessary arrangements."

Henry told her to make it six rooms, that Ed was going. He thanked her and returned to the conference call, giving the others the details as he understood them.

"So I suggest we pack our bags and leave as soon as we can," he said emphatically.

The response was unanimous and positive.

Around 4:45, Henry opened a package that arrived by UPS. It contained a computer printout of data opposite women's names. A cover message from Paul Mitroi read:

I hope this proves helpful, doctor. In your work, please keep an eye out for anything that might shed light on our daughter's death. Thank you.

Henry combed the list and found the following on page four:

Surname: unknown. Age: 18, ***twins****.*
Location: NY. Born: Budapest, Hungary.

GIFT's sleek white jet liner was scheduled to fly from its secret New York location by way of Montreal and Hamburg—to pick up Jay and Karl—and land at Budapest's Ferihegy Airport at 2:40 PM Tuesday. From past trips abroad, Henry knew that the amenities of the plane would allow sleep to come easily and keep jet lag to a minimum. He also knew he wasn't allowed to carry a firearm.

His custom was to read up on a country he was visiting for the first time, obtaining all he needed from the Internet. Though he felt tired shortly after boarding the plane, he browsed through most of the sheets he had about Budapest:

> In December 1992, Budapest celebrated its 120th birthday—the anniversary of the unification of Buda and Pest. But the metropolis on the Danube River can actually look back on two thousand years of history. And it is fast regaining its splendor. Once the center of culture in the Austro-Hungarian Empire, the city and its buildings and treasures were neglected or damaged by a succession of invaders and occupiers. But with a democratic government in place since 1990 and a lengthy series of renovations, it is rebuilding many of its historic landmarks.
>
> The capital of Hungary, Budapest, is the heartbeat of the country. In hilly Buda—on the Danube's west bank—there is evidence of its political and imperial past, with the Royal Palace and the National Gallery—the embodiment of the history of the Hungarian people. Though Buda is marked by defeats and victories, its national pride has never diminished. On the east bank, there is Pest, the city's contemporary face, a thriving center of commerce and art, filled with cafes, restaurants, boutiques, and theaters.
>
> The city-splitting Danube is an integral part of the life of the city, not only in terms of its beauty, but also its vital use as a waterway for commerce and tourism. Three impressive bridges link the two sides: the Chain Bridge, Margaret Bridge, and, at its narrowest point, the Elizabeth Bridge.
>
> Worthy of note in its communist past was the year 1956 when the people of Budapest rebelled, demanding freedom of speech and social reform. Soviet troops quickly responded and crushed the rebellion in a matter of days.

Henry was especially drawn to a paragraph taken from the 1903 writing of Arthur Synons in *Cities*:

> In Budapest there is nothing but what the people and a natural brightness in the air make of it. Here things are what they seem; atmosphere is everything, and the atmosphere is almost one of illusion. Budapest lives with a speed that thrusts itself, not unattractively, upon one at every moment. . . . The people with their somber, fiery, and regular faces have the look of sleepy animals about to spring.

Henry then put the sheets in his pocket and dozed off.

The plane landed on time. GIFT was greeted by a police contingent and escorted toward the center of the city. When the group reached the area of Castle Hill, Henry asked the driver to circle to a higher elevation so they might have a panoramic view of the city. The air looked and felt and smelled pure, more like that of a Connecticut village in spring than on the rim of a European metropolis in mid-autumn.

The car pulled alongside one of several bastions and the driver said, "See. Look. Beautiful."

They all agreed, and when they continued on, Henry took out the sheets and glanced through the last page, which contained a snippet explaining why Budapest is considered the "Pearl of the Danube." It also referred to the city's recent attempt to decrease the number of illegal aliens and to dampen its robust sex industry. The latter, it claimed, had given rise to the sobriquet, "The Bangkok of Europe."

Henry folded up the sheets and returned them to his pocket. They crossed the Elizabeth Bridge in the direction of the nine-story Marriott on the left. He looked up and down the river and sensed that every street and building had a tale to tell. Certainly the hotel did.

At 3:50, they spun through the revolving doors. Henry, usually more impressed with guest rooms than lobbies, stepped aside and put down his suitcase. His eyes darted about, quick to suggest that the "Marriott" sounded too contemporary; the "Marriotti" would be more appropriate. Plus he expected to see more people, some bustle.

It was less of a lobby than a grand hall anchored by a Victorian circular ottoman. A potted palm in its center had stalks that stretched to a massive chandelier hanging from a ceiling of coffered glass octagons, no doubt Murano. The ottoman was not tufted or velvet as one might expect in an English hotel, but was covered in ivory cotton and embroidered with a Veronese shield. All around there were columns in multicolored marble, sisal carpeting, and slipcovered club chairs; a quadruple-width staircase led up to a cluster of stained-glass windows. Soft music and a decidedly jasmine aroma filled the air.

A man in a gray suit and vest, gray tie, and brown shoes appeared from behind a column, a thin gold chain looped across his chest. He was surrounded by six uniformed policemen.

The man walked straight to Henry. Silently each extended his hand and each attempted to arm wrestle the other to submission. After several grunts, they chuckled and called it a tie.

"You remember, do you not, Henry," the man said, "when we drink too much of our famous whiskey and we had little contest?"

"That was no whiskey; that was turpentine."

"What is turpentine?"

"It doesn't matter. How are you, Fedor?"

"Very good. I am glad you came here. It means much and I will soon tell you why."

Fedor embraced Henry tightly.

"You hug stronger than George here," Henry said and introduced Fedor to the two youngest members of GIFT and to Ed. "You know George and Karl, of course."

Fedor pumped their hands as he spoke. "Certainly. The best forensic pathologists . . . how you Americans say . . . in the business?"

An impressively proportioned man, he was almost as tall as Henry and broader at the shoulders. In his fifties but younger looking, he had thinning gray hair, bushy eyebrows, a large bushy mustache, and fleshy hands. His eyes were crinkled at the corners, his smile animated but slightly drooped as if paralyzed at one end. Henry recalled their first meeting when he noticed Fedor's nose deviated to the opposite side of the droop. He figured that Fedor had once taken a nerve-damaging punch to the face but never asked him about it.

"It's quiet here," Henry said. "The conference is still going on?"

"Yes. They will finish at four. Then you will see the rush."

"Where's it held?"

Fedor pointed to his left. "Down that hall. In grand ballroom."

"How many attend?"

"Usually about six hundred."

"And it's all by invitation?"

"Yes, they are very strict. You are all welcome to attend, but I am sure you have other things to do. And of course you are invited to big reception and dinner tonight. Now, you are registered on same floor—number six. We have signed for each of you. Your . . ." He glanced at a clipboard, ". . . your Natalie gave me names. I am sure you want to go to your room but first . . . please . . . may we visit the side room for us to talk? A minute or two only. I will tell you what kind of evidence we have to this date. There is still much light outside. After you see your rooms, we can visit crime scene together. We believe it was murder and not accident. We tell media that death is suspicious until investigation complete. There is no paperwork yet from forensic consultant, but I spoke with him on phone. He thinks murder—pushed off balcony."

"Any evidence of rape?" Karl asked.

"None."

Fedor dismissed the policemen to a corner of the lobby and led the GIFT members and Ed toward a closed room beyond the registration desk. He alerted the concierge who ran ahead of them and opened the door. Its brass plate read "Stellar Room."

They filed in. It was not unlike a small conference room—plain, well lit, mirrors on three sides, no windows. A long table with chairs occupied most of the space; before each chair were paper and pencils. While the others took seats, Henry noticed that Gail had disappeared, though she had said nothing to the rest. Nor did he call attention to it.

Henry sat next to Ed on one side, George, Karl, and Jay in a row on the other. They appeared to huddle about something and Fedor, at the end of the table near Henry, whispered in his ear, "After you check in, could we meet here privately fifteen minutes before others join us to visit crime scene?"

A coinvestigator with Fedor in many past murder cases, Henry well remembered how often they both had gravitated toward each other at critical moments.

Henry answered yes.

"I like one-on-one for some things. You do not mind, do you?"

"No," Henry whispered. "Like before. I understand."

"You explain to your colleagues?"

"Yes, I will."

"Now, my friends," Fedor said, turning to the group, "may I call for drinks?"

They all declined.

"Anyway, I have arranged for you to attend the reception and dinner tonight. Then, you can make up for no drinks now."

Gail walked in. "Sorry everyone," she said, "had to powder my nose. You know how it is."

Fedor consulted his clipboard again. "First, all the newspapers and other media carried story of GIFT coming to Budapest and reason why. And Henry, you received . . . how do they say . . . top billing? Know you well in this area."

"They heard of him because of the work in Bosnia," Jay said. "Right next door."

"Correct," Fedor said. "The story mentioned ICMP and mass grave identification work."

Fedor continued. "You maybe think, if we conclude murder, why do we call you? Answer is this is high-level conference and government wants to prevent political problem. Wants independent opinion. GIFT is well known now—like Interpol. If you agree is not accident, that is all we ask. If you do not, then we have consulted with the best."

"Thank you for that, Fedor," Henry said, "and we're glad to help. Now, I was told the victim was an American. Are other Americans here?"

"Some from your State Department were invited."

"I see. What's the name of the deceased?"

"Helen Vasilakis."

"Vasilakis?" Henry said stiffening. "Was she married?"

"Yes. Husband was Basil Vasilakis."

Henry shuddered. *How many men named Basil Vasilakis could enter his life?*

The others sat back.

In a stark period of silence, Henry watched as Fedor slowly checked the expression of everyone in the room. Finally he said, "You know of him?"

"I think so," Henry responded. "What's his position back in the States?"

"We questioned him. Said he is with your customs agency."

"That's got to be him," Henry said.

"Walks a little bent to the side?"

"Yes, he must have spine trouble," Fedor said.

"But what's he doing here?" George asked. "Customs is with Homeland Security now. These are ambassadors with the State Department. Am I not right—sorry—isn't that right?"

Only Henry caught the slip and wondered if he would make one before long.

"Yes, that is my understanding."

"Do you have access to the invitation list?" Karl asked.

"We have," Fedor answered timidly. "We should have checked. I am sure he must be on it, however, or why would he *be* here?"

"Who knows?" Jay commented.

"They were staying at the hotel?" Gail asked.

"Yes."

"We'll talk to him later," Henry said, "but I've got to say, I can't believe it."

"What?"

"That he popped up here. That it was *his* wife."

"Can I add my two cents?" Ed asked.

"Of course," Henry said.

"Truth is stranger than you know what."

"Amen," Gail added.

"I have autopsy report," Fedor said, pulling out a collection of pages from the clipboard. "Translated into English for you."

"It's already typed out?" George said incredulously.

"You are not that fast in your country?" Fedor replied.

"The autopsy, yes. The report, no."

"Government wants it that way in this case."

"What's it show?" Karl asked. "Not the nitty-gritty, just the essentials."

Fedor spread out the pages on the table. They got up and, leaning over, perused them like a group of builders inspecting architectural drawings. Seated again, Henry plucked out a single page and said, "Excuse me a minute; this is what I want. You can mull over the others if you want."

He read the Anatomical Summary, word for word:

1. Forty-eight-year-old white female seminude body fell 100 feet from balcony onto concrete courtyard. Weight is 115 pounds. Height 5 feet 2 inches. Body habitus is nonobese and the abdomen is slightly rounded.

2. Multiple skull, rib, vertebral, and long-bone fractures are present.

3. There are multilinear brush-burn-type skin abrasions over the upper back, right arm and shoulder, right breast, right abdomen, left elbow and forearm, and the right lateral hip-thigh-leg area.

4. There is a patchy bright red skin abrasion on the right frontal-temporal scalp.

5. The skull has multiple massive open comminuted fractures including a 9 × 6 completely open defect of the right calvarium through which the entire brain has been traumatically avulsed, and a widely gaping comminuted transverse transpetrous hinge-type basal skull fracture, depressed fractures of the right orbit and cheekbones, and comminution of the entire calvarium, with receipt of multiple small calvarial (right frontal

and parietal) fragments, which were found scattered in the courtyard along with pieces of brain.

6. There are two fractures of the mandible, one depressed at the anterior right side, the other nondisplaced to the symphysis.

7. There is an oval ¾ inch red contusion to the inner mucosa of the right lower lip. There is a red abrasion to the vermilion border of the lower lip. There is a ¼ inch red contusion to the inner mucosa of the upper lip.

8. The back of the right hand has a 1 inch red contusion, which upon dissection is found to be prominently hemorrhagic in the distal inter-metacarpal area of the 2nd and 3rd metacarpals.

9. There is anatomic evidence of high-velocity translational impact to the right side of the head and body associated with clotted bilateral hemothorax, hemorrhagic lung contusions and lung lacerations, and heart lacerations.

10. The body organs have an odor of alcohol congeners.

11. The toxicology results are as follows: femoral venous blood ethanol .22 gms pct. Aortic clot ethanol .15 gms pct. Vitreous ethanol .11 gms pct. Urinary ethanol .26 gms pct. Stomach contents ethanol 4.50 grams. All other drugs tested are negative, including rohypnol and GHB.

"One other thing," Henry said, "and I'll be right with you." He put the pages into a pile, thumbed through them, and pulled out another page that described the face:

A careful search is made for petechiae of the face and eyes; none is found. The right optic globe is traumatically collapsed. The left optic globe is intact with a white sclera and cloudy cornea. The bulbar and palpebral conjunctiva are very pale. I aspirated clear vitreous from the left optic globe for purposes of toxicology after examination.

Henry stopped reading when the report went on to other facial features, but he reread the eye findings.

"Sorry for the delay," he said. He looked at George and Karl. "Of course you two pathologists wouldn't think of reading what I just did."

"Why should we?" Karl asked. "We're going over the body and organs ourselves tomorrow."

"Good," Henry said. "Double check the eyes."

"Nothing about it in the report?"

"Nothing suggestive of what we're thinking."

"Where's the body now, Fedor?" George asked.

"City morgue."

"No trouble in our examining it?"

"Not at all. I have already told them that members of GIFT would inquire there."

"Not just inquire," Karl said, "reautopsy."

"Inquire, examine, reautopsy. Whatever is your pleasure. And on this whole visit . . . I forgot to mention, gentlemen . . . ah . . . and lady, of course . . . whatever you need, if we have it, we will provide it."

"As long as you put it that way," Henry said, "I'm curious about something. Perhaps you can share some information. In Budapest—all of Hungary for that matter—has there been a change in the missing persons rate?"

"Big change. Big increase every year."

"Who are they? Is it a pattern?"

"Young women. Some finally found dead."

"Found dead where?" Henry asked.

"All over, but most in your country."

The meeting ended after they had agreed to reconvene in forty-five minutes. Fedor indicated he would bring along photographs of the body (even though they would visit the sites), the courtyard where the body was found, the balcony, and the room registered in Basil Vasilakis's name.

The group emerged into a kinetic blur and scattered in the direction of the registration desk. Henry noticed Gail peel off toward the rest rooms. He tagged along a short way and said, "Powder your nose again?"

"You know how it is," she replied.

Henry's hunch was too acute to let it go. He made his way to a clerk at the far end of the desk, away from the others who were getting their keys. He identified himself and the other five in his group.

"Can you tell me if any of our rooms are adjoining?" he asked.

The clerk checked her computer. "Only two. Rooms 604 and 606."

"Am I in one of them?"

"Yes, 604."

"Who's in the other?"

"It was Dr. Moser, but then I see a request was made by Dr. Merriday to make a change. To put *her* there."

"And you did?"

"Not me. One of our other employees."

"And now Dr. Merriday and I are in adjoining rooms?"

"That is correct unless you require another change."

"No," Henry said. "It's okay . . . I guess."

Chapter 14

On the elevator back down to the Stellar Room, Henry postponed what he had already postponed while showering and shaving—arranging his thoughts in some reasonable order. They were a jumble in his mind, simply tossed there while people asked questions and fired suggestions—and while he himself collected observations, made preliminary judgments, and generated his own questions. A reorganization of his thoughts would have to wait. Besides, many of his questions could not be answered until the following day, Wednesday, when George and Karl would substantiate, correct, or add to what he had already learned. Not that he denigrated the report of a Budapest pathologist, but, in Henry's view, Drs. Silvain and Moser were the best in the world.

Fedor was waiting for him twenty minutes before the others were expected. They sat on opposite sides of the table.

Fedor spoke first. "Thank you, Henry, for understanding. I do not mean to be secret and I know your friends and colleagues are specialists, but I trust you the most. Not only that . . . like I say . . . one-on-one easier for me. Even in Commissariat, when we have group discussions . . . everybody talk at once . . . not good for me to concentrate."

"It doesn't surprise me, Fedor. It's okay."

"Good, good. So I know you are here for the death, but may I bring up other subject which I believe links our two countries?"

"By all means."

"You in America call it 'white slavery.'"

Henry felt a twinge in his shoulder.

Fedor went on. "We in Commissariat were notified of murder of your distinguished reporter because of reference to our country in articles he wrote. Then we follow his writing, read of murders of three girls in New York. Maybe work of Triads?"

"Maybe."

"We learn this morning that two may be twins and at same time we learn that twins missing from Budapest."

"You know their names?"

"Yes."

"I'm sure our government will expedite the proper identification and transferal here if necessary. If there are problems, let me know."

"Thank you. But this is part of much bigger problem we have. Prostitution. Here and as export. From here and from our neighbors. Regional problem and we try to handle it as regional—set up responsible person in each country to lead inquiry. I want to share something with you, my friend. Many of my comrades call me stupid, but it is what I think."

Henry took out a card, dated it, and added a note.

"We have this conference many years now," Fedor continued, "because people in region have trouble with democracy. Most of them want it because of bad history with other political forms, but they have trouble to adapt . . . adopt?"

"Adapt."

"I say it is like man in prison for forty years and then he is let out. Have trouble to adapt. He is on own. Does not know how to open bank account, register for things, use credit card, change phone service. You know?"

"I can only imagine."

"Even worse East of us. Romania good example. They are slowest to develop. Now here is important point and it is my belief. The slower a country in . . . what you say . . . catching up, the more young girls want to escape to better life. They read magazines, watch TV, hear about better clothes, more money. They see much . . . ," Fedor elevated his arms in supplication, ". . . much opportunity. But they do not see what they escape to."

"I would guess Bucharest suffers the most along those lines."

"No, Transylvania."

"North of Bucharest, but still in Romania, I believe."

"Yes. It is not too far from Bucharest. You have been there?"

"Never, but I've heard of the myth of Dracula. Saw some of the movies."

Fedor shook his head. "Unusual you bring that up. There is man in Bucharest who owns Count Dracula Club. His name is Mugur Popa. He likes single name, just like Dracula. Everybody knows Mugur in Eastern Europe. He helped lead opposition against Communist Party leader Ceausescu. He is direct descendent of bad, bad man, Vlad the Impaler. Vlad kill many people on wooden stakes in fifteenth century. They say Mugur now sign up young Transylvania girls to be employees on cruise ships."

"And?"

"And many never come back home."

"So you think there might be a connection with the prostitution rings?"

"I am not sure."

"Why hasn't anything been done about it? Check it out?"

Fedor rubbed his thumb over the other fingers.

"Payoffs?" Henry asked.

"That is correct. But the parents cannot be bought off. They make trouble and three were killed. Made to look like accident."

"You think it would be worth it for me to make a visit to . . . Mugur?"

"Yes, of course. I can arrange private plane for tomorrow. Maybe one-hour flight. I know police officials in Bucharest. We do this right way, get permission. Mugur always questioned, even by me—used to it. Always have proper answers. He will think he is big shot—questioned by famous person from America."

"Good, let's set it up for around noon. I'll bring Ed along. You want to accompany us?

"No, he is too used to me. Someone fresh is better. I bring you map of area before you go. And I arrange for travel from airport. A policeman will drive you to Mugur."

"And can you arrange two other things before I go there tomorrow? First, I'd like to question Basil Vasilakis in the morning. This room will do." Henry paused to rub his shoulder.

"Nine is good?"

"Yes."

"And second?" Fedor asked.

"I hope I'm not imposing on you but, because of the flight over, I'm not armed. Would it be possible to borrow, say, a .45 and a shoulder holster? Also some extra rounds?"

"Consider done. I will secure them before evening over. You want one for Ed, too?"

"Perfect. Much appreciate it."

Ed and the other GIFT members entered the room as if they had assembled outside beforehand. From there Fedor took the group through an outside courtyard that was defined by cobblestone walkways lined with small sassafras and Chinese catsura trees. They angled among grassy triangles before reaching the opposite side of the hotel. Fedor saluted a police officer, who lifted a length of yellow crime scene tape allowing access to a cement patio. The figure of a body was outlined in chalk about four feet from the building's edge. Seven stories of balconies spanned the south face; their railings and balusters looked like giant combs as viewed from below.

Karl and Gail wandered about individually, taking close looks around several bushes and boxes of plants and flowers. Jay and Ed did the same thing, but as a unit. George was busy taking pictures. Henry counted the balconies, drew lines in the air with his finger, and paced off distances from the chalk outline to various spots near the building. He took out a magnifying glass and studied the leaves of the plant closest to the outline.

Fedor motioned to the group to form a circle; he stood in the center.

"Which one was hers?" George asked.

"Say again, please," Fedor replied.

"Which balcony up there was hers?"

"Count seven stories. In the middle."

George counted up seven and pointed to the most central balcony.

"Yes," Fedor said.

George snapped another picture.

"But her body landed way off line," Karl said. "I'd say a full fifteen feet."

Fedor said, "Let me tell you what we know and what we piece together." He removed several sheets of paper from a manila envelope and, both glancing at the others and reading verbatim, he said. "According to paperwork and discussion with investigator this morning and with Detective Boc of Homicide Department and after my view of decedent at death scene and my investigation here, we determine that decedent was forty-eight-years-old lady. Name of

Helen Vasilakis, wife of Basil Vasilakis. They live in Virginia, USA. He attend conference as member of United States Bureau of Customs and Border Protection. They both check into hotel yesterday afternoon at two twenty-two. Room number 746, which we will go visit. Body found at eight last night. Last seen alive by husband at 4:45 PM before he leave for speech."

"Excuse me for interrupting, Fedor," Henry said. "What speech?"

"He give speech and answer questions from 5:00 to 6:45.

"Oh? On what topic?"

"Counterterrorism. He give expert speeches all over Eastern Europe. Good reputation."

"So he had an alibi," Jay stated.

"Good one. Maybe two hundred people listen to him. He say that go to room at about seven and wife not there. He report her missing at front desk at 7:30."

"I'm curious," Karl said. "He never looked over the balcony?"

Fedor's features and upturned palms expressed uncertainty.

"And why didn't she attend the lecture?"

"He say she hear him too many times already."

"Where's the husband now, by the way?" Henry asked.

"With cousin in Albertirsa."

"Where's that?"

"One hour away. His parents Hungarian, you know."

"Do you consider him a suspect?" Gail asked.

"Husband usually . . . how you say . . . good bet. But in this case, he giving speech when she go over rail. So we remove him from suspicion list."

Both Henry and Ed made notations on their index cards.

"Now," Fedor proceeded, "guest in hotel saw body lie face down as you see there. I read you: 'Ambient temperature 68. Body temperature 95.4. Skin purple liver color. Lips and nails pale. Early nonfixed lividity. Blanch with touch. Body warm to touch. Detect no rigor mortis. No insect activity. Estimation time of death under three hours. Body in light brown waist-length garment with straps. Body nude under garment. No tattoos, scars, jewelry. I estimate only moderate amount of blood around body, maybe 150 cc but much on garment—some dry, some wet. Largest part of brain three feet from body, farther out from building. Like you see there, body has head closest to building and feet point away from building with legs apart. Much brain material splattered on window of ground-level office you see there. Next I give you photographs." He handed a package to Henry, who in turn handed it to Karl.

"The rest of you might look them over first," Henry said, making a deliberate effort toward unity.

Up in room 746, Ed and Fedor, near a police officer, remained by the open entrance door. Henry hung back for the broadest view, and George and Karl milled around separately. George took several more pictures. Gail and Jay scoured the room in tandem, checking the furniture inch by inch, as if looking for trace evidence. One could have made arguments that each of the two wanted first rights to a discovery or they simply enjoyed the closeness. Either way, and all sexual suspicions aside, Henry liked what he saw. Professionally, they brought talents honed from distinguished service at Scotland Yard and the RCMP, both within the aegis of the same Commonwealth. But now in Budapest, the aegis was GIFT, and any sign that indicated a cohesion, a mutual trust—even a grand style among its members—pleased him. Making GIFT work was becoming a near obsession for him.

The hotel room was not unlike Henry's or those found in many world-class hotels. It included two beds with swooping headboards carved with scrolls and shells, an elegant sitting area, a deep sofa, and upholstered walls dotted with pictures of Hungarian landscapes.

Luggage lay closed on one of the beds. The bed nearest the balcony was unmade. A black purse, a pair of black women's shoes, and a red blouse were on the carpeted floor between the unmade bed and the balcony. A pair of brown men's shoes was on the floor of an immense closet. Two dress shirts, a blue suit, and two ties hung on hangers to the left. To the right, a printed skirt and a pants suit.

Other than Henry's initial assessment of the room, he spent no time doing what the rest of the team was doing. Instead, he moved forward onto the balcony and concentrated his examination there a full ten minutes. Despite his trademark of painstaking thoroughness, he realized the determination of murder over suicide had already been made by Fedor and other law enforcement officials. Earlier, the commander made it clear that GIFT was summoned because of political considerations. In short, the Hungarian government, in its democratic infancy, didn't want to be poisoned by an international incident, so GIFT was the perfect antidote.

Henry summoned the team members for a quick consultation, then called Fedor out. "In the States," Henry said, "we sometimes use a stunt coordinator in cases like this." After explaining the meaning of "stunt," he persuaded Fedor to have a human-shaped dummy dropped from the balcony at different angles. He also recommended the construction of a mock railing that was expandable in height. The expansion, Henry pointed out, would allow persons of varying height to test their own stability at the railing and to simulate what it might have been like for Helen.

He reentered the room and, eyeing the sofa, walked over. "Your forensic people are done in here, I assume?" he asked Fedor.

"Yes."

"Were there any bottles of liquor found in the suitcase or any in the room for that matter?"

"No."

"Any taken from the room's liquor cabinet?"

"No."

"Did they lift any prints from the railing?"

"No."

"Not even hers?"

"Correct."

Henry sat, took out a stack of cards, and filled out six of them, front and back. He rose and, facing Fedor, said: "Okay, here are our impressions thus far. Of course we'll have Gail's and Jay's reconstruction of the scene later and George's and Karl's autopsy input tomorrow." He scanned the room and saw that the others were paying attention. The police officer stepped out and Ed closed the entrance door. "I'll read off what I have, the others can add or subtract, and then Jay or I will either e-mail the preliminary version or dictate it to whatever terminal you wish."

"Dictate to central office. Anytime before you leave country. Tomorrow, is that not right?"

"The red-eye flight. I hope you understand, Fedor, that we're smack in the middle of an investigation at home and cannot stay long to enjoy your hospitality."

"Yes, of course. To verify murder and not suicide is satisfactory—and thank you very much. Will satisfy press, will satisfy my boss, and will satisfy international community. But with your permission, may we have GIFT commitment that, after we find murderer, we may use your team at trial if necessary?"

"By all means. A phone call away as they say."

Fedor looked pleased.

Henry read from a card: "Prior to her demise, the decedent had consumed a significant amount of alcohol. It is not clear where she had obtained it. There apparently is no history of depression or alcohol abuse." He looked at Fedor. "Is that correct?"

"Correct."

Henry alternately consulted his notes and cast about for the right word or phrase. "By toxicology testing at autopsy, her alcohol level was .22 percent. With her body weight, she must have consumed at least eight drinks. Autopsy findings are consistent with her being alive when she hit the ground. The manner of death appears to be homicide, as the decedent seems to have been pushed or dropped over the railing, and the following is presented as the basis for such an opinion:

(a) The height of the balcony railing is forty-five inches, which is over midchest level on the decedent, nearly two-thirds her height. This is consistent with her needing assistance to go over the railing, given her intoxicated state.
(b) She was found in a seminude state. No underwear or stockings were found in the room.
(c) She appears to have landed on her head and right torso area. Since there were no injuries to the palms of her hands, she did not appear to have restrained her fall. This is consistent with a semiconscious or unconscious state during the drop. Also, in those who jump, there are typical ankle/feet fractures, and they were not present in this case.
(d) She landed close to the face of the building. However, while falling, she moved an estimated fourteen or fifteen feet laterally along the side of the building. This supports a theory of being pushed over the balcony railing. If she had jumped or fallen, one would have been expected her to have landed at a point farther away from the face of the building and in a straighter line with the balcony.
(e) Abrasions on the back of the hands, some bruising on face, and hemorrhage in the neck are suggestive of an additional injury just prior to the drop.
(f) Maybe there were two people involved in her death.

He rearranged the cards and returned them to his pocket. "Anything to add, anyone?" he asked.

All but Karl shook their heads no. "Probably not," he said, "but we still have the body to go over ourselves. And I suspect that Gail and Jay will examine the clothing, hair, and body for trace evidence."

"Very impressed," Fedor said. "And now I must go. You may want to confer as group." He removed a sheaf of papers from the clipboard and handed them to Henry. "Here is most of file," he said. "Copies in English. You may keep for record." Before leaving, he checked a pocket watch and said, "Remember reception and dinner in less than one hour."

Henry scanned the headings on the papers:

Autopsy Report
Radiology Report
Forensic Report
Microscopic Report
Coroner's Notes
Toxicology Report
Sexual Assault Evidence and DNA Data Sheet
Investigator's Report

"You guys want to see these?" he asked.

Jay probed the others' faces and replied, "Not really. We know our role here and it's just about completed except for checking on the autopsy tomorrow—and having a drink or two tonight."

"That's not part of the role," Karl said.

"It is for me," Jay snapped.

"Speaking of checking," Karl said, handing a package to Henry. "Here are the photos. We've all seen them."

Henry gave them a hasty once-over and said, "Before we disband, let's get our signals straight for tomorrow. George, you and Karl check with the coroner, right?"

"Right."

"And reautopsy the body?"

"Right."

"Gail, I have two things for you to do if you're comfortable with them. The first I didn't want to bother Fedor about today—he's got this murder on his mind. But earlier he talked to me privately for a minute. They have a huge prostitution problem here. Wonder of wonders. Incidentally, he knows all about the harbor murders, Seal's death, white slavery, the whole nine yards. Anyway he said, quote-unquote, a 'responsible person' has been appointed in each of the countries in the region to address the problem. Could you find out all you can about who they are, what's being done, perhaps talk to them? You comfortable with taking that on? Tomorrow, if possible?"

"Certainly. I'll speak with Fedor to begin with. I can even bring in the Yard to help locate them."

"Excellent. And the next thing. Fedor also mentioned a guy named Mugur in Bucharest. We're going to meet with him tomorrow. Fedor says Mugur signs up young girls for cruise ship jobs and many of them end up disappearing."

"Oh, boy," George said flippantly.

"Exactly."

"Mugur the mogul," Karl said. No one acknowledged the comment.

"So it occurred to me," Henry continued, "Gail, could you contact several cruise lines and find out what predominant native country or countries their female employees come from? What the turnover rate is, and what the main reason is if they leave their jobs?"

"Will do."

"Now, as I said, Ed and I will fly to Bucharest tomorrow—it's not that far. But before that, I'll be interviewing Vasilakis. Jay, you've had some experience in customs work—why not join us in the Stellar Room at nine?"

"I'll be there."

"And that's it, I guess," Henry said, scratching the back of his head. "We shouldn't take long in Bucharest. Let's reassemble in the Stellar

Room at about four. That means you two . . . ," he regarded George and Karl directly, ". . . will have some free time on your hands."

"Oh, good," George said. "We can either nap or go check out the hot spots." His face reflected fabricated joy.

Henry was about to depart for the reception when Fedor stopped by to deliver a pair of .45s in shoulder rigs. "And more ammo," he said, handing over a small box. "Pray God you will not need it." The commander acknowledged Henry's gratitude and left. Henry removed his blazer, slipped into the rig, and put several rounds in his pocket. A minute later he watched as Ed repeated the process.

In terms of people and decibels, the reception in the annex to the grand ballroom was like a neighborhood cocktail party magnified twenty times. Cigar and cigarette smoke hovered over the guests like a fog. Pretty hostesses picked their way through the crowd carrying trays of chicken canapés, olive pinwheels, and cheese and sausage hors d'oeuvres. A string quartet held to its collective smile but could not be heard. All the GIFT members were in the room. Henry nursed a glass of plum wine and stood in a corner comparing observations with Ed. He also exchanged pleasantries with an occasional American official who recognized him. He noticed George glad-handing at one end of the room and Karl drawing diagrams of who-knows-what at the other.

The dinner in the ballroom was less noisy. GIFT sat at the same table along with Fedor and a gentleman introduced as Nicolae from his staff. When asked, Fedor indicated that Basil Vasilakis was not in attendance. Jay sat expressionless while George and Gail—their laughter lusty, near bawdy—had cornered the wine bottles. For Henry, ten o'clock arrived in glacier time; he wished he had skipped both events and gone to bed early.

Back in his room, he bemoaned the cigarette odor on his clothes and wondered about the value of the preceding three hours. He had been impressed by only two things: the guns he received from Fedor and Gail's outfit. She wore a taupe jacket detailed with leopard-print accents. Her black knit skirt ended well above the knees and had a side slit. Henry swore she had raised the hemline and slit on her own.

And he was *not* happily impressed with one thing: her overindulgence in alcohol. He followed as Jay steadied her to the elevator and down the hall to her door. Henry helped with the key card.

Ten minutes later there was a knock on the door connecting the two rooms. Though weary, Henry thought Gail might have become sick, so he opened it. Barefooted, she stood before him in a skimpy red silk nightgown. She staggered past him toward the bed, turned, and said, "Pardon me, Henry. Sorry . . . so sorry . . . to b-burst in like this—that's what I did—but I've got to get . . . to get . . . you know . . . I got to get somethin' straight. I mean . . . if you don't mind. Why are we here . . . for chrissake . . . if they have it . . . you know . . . all wrapped up? Nice and pretty like."

"First of all, Gail, please sit down."

She sat on the bed, nearly missing the edge.

"Second, as Fedor pointed out, the Hungarian government wants to validate their conclusion worldwide or at least in the United States. Because of the setting of so many dignitaries, they want to prevent the death from becoming an international incident."

Gail wrinkled her nose as if trying to sniff the essence of what she had just heard. "I get it," she said. "Now it makes sense."

She rose and put her hand on his shoulder. "Well," she said, "we are here . . . I mean . . . here we are. I feel funny, you know . . . but nice. Don't you, Henry . . . I mean . . . feel nice?" She tugged at his tie, and tried to unloosen it.

"Not exactly," he answered, moving back.

Gail, on her toes, stretched to wrap both arms around his neck. "Aw, c'mon," she whimpered, "it wouldn't be so bad . . . promise . . . I promise . . . not so bad."

"That's what I'm afraid of."

"Whee . . . I'm dizzy . . . here . . . I hope . . ." she moaned and collapsed onto the bed.

Henry checked her pulse and respirations. Confident that her condition would wear off after a night's sleep, he carried her to her own bed, returned to his room, and closed the door.

He blamed the incident on a combination of jet lag and overindulgence. But he wondered if he should have changed the room back after she had rearranged the details.

WEDNESDAY, OCTOBER 23
BUDAPEST TIME

At seven the next morning Henry slipped down to the coffee shop without Ed. The .45 felt snug at his shoulder. The last person he expected to see at that hour was Gail, but she was sitting alone at a corner table looking about blankly. He joined her.

"Good morning," he said.

"I've forgotten the derivation of that phrase, but from what I recall, it doesn't apply to me and my surroundings right now."

She wore no makeup and had the countenance of one who needed an ice bag applied to her forehead.

"Some affair last night, wasn't it?" he asked.

"I don't remember a thing."

"Nothing?"

"Nothing after the tiny hot dogs."

"They didn't *serve* tiny hot dogs. Maybe the sausages?"

"The sausages then."

"You don't remember what you ate for dinner?"

"I ate dinner?"

"Or my room?"

"Your room where?"

"Next to yours."

"No. Was I drunk?"

"In a manner of speaking."

"Did I make a fool of myself?"

"You ask as if you have before."

"I hope not."

"Well, you didn't—not in front of anyone else at least."

"At least? At least? You mean you?"

"I'm not telling."

She blanched.

"Don't worry," he assured her, "nothing happened."

As she regained her composure, Henry shifted to another subject. "Can you still tackle what we talked about yesterday? Are you up to it?" he asked. "You know, the prostitution thing, the cruise ships?"

"It's not a problem. I can handle it." She drained the last of her black coffee and wandered off.

Before going to the counter for a cup of tea, Henry sat engrossed in thought. A great actress? Too convincing. A drinking problem? Doubtful. Too valuable an asset to press her on sexual improprieties? One should feel flattered. A professional asset, but not a personal one.

At nine o'clock, Henry and Ed walked into the Stellar Room. Jay was already there.

Without a greeting Jay said, "I never saw Gail like that before."

"Jet lag," Henry said.

"We all have some of it," Jay said with authority.

"But we didn't drink as much."

"True. I've never seen her drink like that either. Strange."

Basil Vasilakis stepped through the door followed by Fedor. The customs official was dressed in a dark suit and tie. Unlike before, his hair was slicked down. Eyes downcast, there was no cigar odor this time. His shoulders drooped and his spinal curve appeared more pronounced.

Jay and Ed shook his hand and gave their condolences, but before Henry had his opportunity, Fedor said to him, "I will leave you alone but may I speak to you in private outside?"

In the corridor, Fedor closed the door behind them and said, "Before your meeting, I think you should be aware. No Basil Vasilakis on invitation list."

Flabbergasted, Henry silently assessed whether or not to bring up the subject with Vasilakis. His decision was made easier by Fedor's parting remark: "You must deal with it in there."

Back in the room, Henry embraced Vasilakis and expressed his sorrow. The four men took seats at the table.

"Basil," Henry began, "I realize this is a difficult time for you, and I appreciate your coming here today."

"Thank you, but it's quite all right." Then, in nearly inaudible tones, he added, "I wish we had never made the trip though."

"I understand," Henry said, index cards in hand. "If I might, I'd like to interview you as part of the overall investigation. I'm sure the Budapest police have already put you through some of this and I hope there isn't too much overlap. In any case, I have only a couple of questions. Okay?"

"Okay."

"First of all, I believe you and Helen are not on the invitation roster for the conference." Henry wanted the first issue to appear as a statement and not a question.

"Really? Probably an oversight." Vasilakis perked up. "But come to think of it, why should we be listed when the official US attendees are from the Department of State? I'm from Homeland Security . . . Wait! Of course. That's why. I was invited mainly to give my talk."

"I heard about that. Well received I'm sure."

There was no return comment.

After a complete review of time lines, Henry said—again as a statement—"So you obviously never got to the opening ceremony."

"No."

"And after your talk, you planned on returning to the States?"

"Not immediately. We weren't exactly certain about this, but we thought as long as we were in the area we might visit with some of my counterparts around here. Our countries all have problems with contraband and it's getting worse since 9/11. Not necessarily with the amount of contraband but with how to beef up border security."

"And by contraband you mean?"

"Smuggling. Anything illegal. Drugs, explosive devices, biological weapons."

"People?"

"Yes, people. Terrorists, illegal aliens."

"I see." Henry recorded a brief note. "Thank you." He turned around to the others. "Does anyone else have a question?"

"I hope you might touch on a couple of points, Mr. Vasilakis," Jay said. "I'm especially interested in border protection. In fact, I'm a consultant to the US/Canada NEXUS program. How did you get involved in Homeland Security?"

"Nothing spectacular really—or glamorous. I was in the coast guard for a number of years, then joined Treasury. After 9/11 when Customs and Border Protection became part of Homeland Security, I went with it. Guess I was born to be a border snoop."

"And so," Henry interjected, "it was a natural progression for you to get into antiterrorism?"

"Yes, I would say so."

"The second point," Jay said, "and it's in the form of a question. Did you have any drinks yesterday or last night?"

"No."

"They found a significant amount of alcohol in your wife's system. Can you explain it?"

"No, unless whoever killed her—and the police told me that someone did—unless whoever killed her had a bottle with him. So either she had to know him, which is ridiculous. Or he forced her to drink, which seems even more ridiculous. I still think it was an accident though. I can't help but believe that."

Fedor drove Henry and Ed to a small airport for their private flight to Bucharest. Before they boarded, he handed them a map and a thin magazine, *Romania*. Its subtitle was *Transylvania, Moldova, Maramures, Dobrogea, Valahia*. During the fifty-minute trip, Henry skimmed through the magazine and read of Romania's history as a cross section of cultures; of its capital, Bucharest, which acquired its name in part from an early shepherd named Bucar; of Transylvania, which was ceded to Romania after World War I. The article mentioned that rancor remained between Hungary and Romania over Romania's acquisition of Transylvania. It explained that Transylvania was home to Dracula's Castle, but that one could get the flavor of the castle without ever leaving Bucharest. The city's Count Dracula Club was a popular restaurant with piped-in background organ music and animal trophies displayed on every wall. The legendary character—with "blood" painted at the corner of his lips—would rise from his casket each night, candelabra in hand, and would mingle with startled guests and declare, "I would like to join you, but I have already dined!"

But Henry's interest was most piqued by a different section. While reading, he had some difficulty understanding the awkwardly written piece.

DRACULA

FACT: Prince Vlad Dracula, named after his father, spent his first four years in Sighisoara, one of the German fortress cities in Transylvania. When his father became king of Valahia in the fifteenth century, young Vlad was sent to Istanbul as warranty for his father's good faith. There he was kept hostage at the sultan's court. He received an Ottoman military education, which was believed to contribute to his later military genius.

Because of his successful battles against the Turks, the father became part of the *Dragon* knighthood order as *defender of Christianity* and was awarded the Symbol of the Dragon Knights. In the Romanian language, *Dracul* means Devil and *ula* means *son of*. Later when Vlad himself became ruler of Valahia, he received the nickname *Tepes* (the impaler) because of his penchant for dining while watching Turkish captives being impaled alive on wooden stakes.

FICTION: Irish writer Bram Stoker made the name of "Dracula" and "Transylvania" famous around the world. He was, together with George Bernard Shaw and other writers of his time, part of a club that studied the occult. Stoker chose an unusual theme for that period; hence a new gothic novel about vampires was born. He based the novel on research not only in the field of vampirism but also on historical fact. Thus the real-life female character he used for inspiration was Elizabeth Battory, a Hungarian countess who became notorious for her crimes. It was rumored she would bathe in maidens' blood because she believed it would preserve her youth. Although she was very cruel, Stoker decided he also needed a male character for his book and created Count Dracula, a corpse that returned to life at night, attacked innocent people, and, like any vampire, sucked their blood. According to folklore, a vampire must obtain a constant supply of fresh blood by biting the necks of victims, who in turn die and become vampires themselves.

Reading this made Henry want to see the Dracula movie again. The story weighed on his mind even as the plane landed and as they were whisked away in a police car.

At the Count Dracula Club, the officer hopped out of the car, knocked at a door with a round hole in its center, and spoke to the lower half of a face in a kind of code. The thick door opened slowly and the officer drove off. A plump middle-aged lady in a black apron greeted Henry and Ed with a nod and a smile; she said nothing but pointed in a down and left direction with dramatic flair.

The club was tucked into a remote cobblestone alleyway and from the outside appeared to occupy a single story as opposed to its reputed three. Inside, however, one immediately grasped its multilevel, mostly underground layout with compact dining areas separated not by hallways but by passageways. It was no effort for both Henry and Ed to touch ceilings as they navigated their way past a sign—MUGUR POPA—toward the back of the building. Wolf, bear, and wild boar trophies draped the walls; pelts lay scattered on some floors. A handful of patrons were having lunch; many more waitresses moved about aimlessly. Henry was struck by the women's remarkable similarity: black dress, dour expression, gray bobbed hair. They reflected the mood of the club, as did its pockets of dank air. Were it not for the aroma of food, he wondered what the prevailing odor would be.

Henry rapped on the door at the end of the passageway.

"Please enter, Dr. Liu." The voice was deep and resonant, like one in a cave.

They stepped into a cluttered, underheated, underlighted room with no windows. A small fan hummed on a corner chair. Real dust and cobwebs were conspicuous, not the theatrical kind. Henry expected to brush away a spider any second. On the far wall, chains of all shapes, colors, and lengths were suspended on hooks. The furniture—what there was of it—reminded Henry of his first rental in college. Seated at a desk, a hulk of a man swung around in his chair, leaned on a cane, and rose stiffly. He put out a beefy hand; Henry and Ed shook it.

"I was expecting you, doctor. I am Mugur Popa. Please call me Mugur; everybody else does. I own this little place."

Henry introduced Ed and said, "Thank you for meeting with us.

You should know right from the start that my interest in Dracula goes back a long way. This is a special privilege for me."

"Thank you, but it is I who is privileged."

"Your English is fluent."

"Well, I was educated in England."

Mugur was slightly taller than Henry. He also appeared to be at least a decade older, with jet black hair too perfectly trimmed to be real and eyebrows that met in a deep V, giving him a fierce expression. Clean shaven, his facial skin was dry and splotchy as if it had existed longer than he had. Wrinkles terraced his forehead, and his teeth hardly showed when he spoke. He looked like a man beleaguered by an unfulfilled promise; regardless, it took Henry less than an instant to appreciate that Mugur was a smothering presence.

"I notice you have more waitresses than patrons," Henry said.

"But of course. We do most of our business at night—just like Count Dracula." He flashed a menacing smile.

The more Henry considered it, the more he thought that if Ed resembled Clint Eastwood, then Mugur resembled and sounded like Bela Lugosi. And he told him so.

"Thank you," Mugur said. "I take that as a compliment."

Henry wanted to get the small talk out of the way. He looked around and said, "You like chains, I see."

Mugur sat heavily in his chair and pulled down on a black sweater that was too tight and did little to hide an ample belly. "But please sit and I'll explain about chains. We have at least two more chairs in here I believe. There, there's one. Put the fan on the floor and drag over the other one."

Henry and Ed positioned themselves opposite him and took out cards.

"Okay to take notes, Mugur?" Henry asked.

"Good, you're using my name."

"I shouldn't?"

"No—please. It's just that you didn't until now. I thought maybe you'd forgotten it."

"Why would I forget it?"

"I thought you'd remember 'Popa' and not 'Mugur.' But, see, I think of 'Mugur' as my first and last names. To answer your question, notes are not a problem. However, pictures are a different matter; as you can see, I eat too much." He leaned back in a thunderous laugh, his shoulders shaking.

Henry improvised a grin.

"Now, the chains," Mugur said. "Throughout history, their worth has been underestimated and I don't mean as a method of bondage and torture." He went on to describe the nomenclature of chains, listing a variety of links and dwelling on each one: roller, twisted, straight, and stud. He spoke of different sizes—from small ones used in jewelry to huge ones used in heavy machinery—and included a discourse on the iron, brass, steel, or plastics used in their manufacture. He turned to face the wall of chains.

"There's even one—there, the big one on the left—that was handed down from a distant relative. It was used to chain down people who didn't want to hear about their future."

"I don't understand," Henry said.

"There were well-known soothsayers in those days who were paid good money to predict bad futures for certain debtors. Like loan sharks using enforcers in modern society. You have them in America; we have them here. Way back then, instead of having their bones broken, a soothsayer was sent to the debtor. He knew what it meant and didn't want to hear terrifying news, like 'I see your head falling off,' so, to keep him from running away, he was chained while the prediction was pronounced."

Mugur twisted and untwisted a paper clip. "The debt was always paid off within a few hours," he added.

"Do you believe in that hocus-pocus?" Henry asked.

"Soothsaying? Clairvoyance? I do."

Henry crossed his legs. A recollection of Felicia Phillips and her clairvoyant pursuits was instantaneous. "Don't tell me you practice it?" he inquired.

"Practice? No. Receive? On occasion."

"Are there such clairvoyants in these parts?"

"Yes. We have many Gypsy groups—Rom Tribes—in Eastern Europe. They do their fortune-telling for a living. And they're proud of their metalworking—have been for many centuries. Perhaps that's what led to their fascination with chains."

"So you consult fortune-tellers, clairvoyants?"

"I don't trust Gypsies. There are reliable clairvoyants in your country, however."

Henry's chance. "Do you know any personally?"

The paper clip snapped. "One or two," Mugur replied.

Henry thought it civil to pencil in a note on his card although his mind was elsewhere. Before he had a chance to bring up another subject, Mugur preempted him. "But you came here, I understand, from Budapest and wish to ask me some other kinds of questions. Not on subjects I bring up. I rather enjoy questioning, you know—makes me think. At my age, that's important."

"May I cover a range of topics? It won't take long, I assure you."

"Yes—please. And take as long as you wish."

"Thank you. To begin with, have you heard of the triple murder in New York recently? Three lovely young girls?"

"No, I haven't. But that's not unusual with the kind of press we have here. This isn't London. Although it's getting better, I suppose. At least it's freer than before."

Henry detailed the harbor deaths, stressing the positioning of the bodies, the nudity. He cited Vernon Seal's killing as well.

"Nasty," Mugur said.

"You certainly heard though about the woman who plunged seven stories at the Marriott in Budapest the night before last."

"Yes, I read about it. Wife of a US diplomat or something. Attending that conference. Bad timing . . . bad *any* time, really."

"May I ask a personal question or two?"

"Sure. I haven't much to hide. Everyone has something, you know—I mean to hide. Skeletons in closets, that sort of thing. I love lines like that, by the way. 'Don't hide your light under a basket' is another one."

"I hear you're a descendant of Vlad the Impaler. Is that right?"

"Yes, unfortunately. A part of my family tree I'm not proud of."

"Was Dracula real?"

"It depends on how you approach the question." Mugur then gave a concise history of the count, much the same as Henry had read an hour before.

"Do you visit Transylvania often?"

"Very often. I went to school there; still have boyhood friends around."

"Schooling in Transylvania also?"

"Yes. Elementary there. University in London."

"I see." Henry thought it was time to go for the jugular. "This may seem out of the blue, Mugur, but do you have any friends in the cruise business?"

Mugur rolled his neck a few times and responded. "I don't understand what you mean by 'cruise.'"

"You know: ocean liners. Travel on the high seas."

"No, I don't have friends in that business and, as a matter of fact, I never took a cruise myself. Not even around the corner on the Danube. Isn't it funny? I understand there are citizens in your country—living in Philadelphia, Pennsylvania—who never saw your Liberty Bell."

"That's true, I'm afraid. Now, one last question, Mugur, and if it's too invasive, don't answer. Why aren't there any *young* waitresses here?"

"Oh, that? They were young when they were hired. They've all been with me over twenty-five, thirty years."

For more minutes than Henry wanted, they conversed about the political situation in Eastern Europe. Finally Mugur said, "I must admit, Dr. Liu. I have a bone to pick with your government."

"Oh?"

"Yes. Forty-four and a half years ago, I was refused admission to the School for Hotel Management at Cornell University."

"I'm sorry to hear that, but we're not a communist country."

"What do you mean by that?"

"The bone should be picked with that private university, not with our government."

Mugur thought a moment and bellowed another laugh.

On the way out Henry located the woman in the black apron. "Do . . . you . . . understand . . . English?" he asked.

"Little bit," she replied.

"How . . . many . . . years . . . have . . . you . . . worked . . . here?"

The lady held up two fingers.

Once alone in their seats on the private plane, Henry turned to Ed and said, "So?"

"That place gave me the creeps."

"That's what it's supposed to do. But aside from that?"

"My impression of Mr. Dracula look-alike?"

"Yes."

"Lies through his teeth. I wouldn't trust him with a pet snake."

Henry gave him a bewildered glance. "Where did *that* come from?"

"What?"

"Snake."

"Who knows? Mugur—snake? Snake—Mugur? What did you think?"

"That's he's eminently capable of doing the things Fedor says he does. That he's eerie. Frightening."

"How about evil?"

"I wouldn't bet against it."

"You thought of Felicia I assume?"

"Naturally."

"Think there's a connection?"

"We'll come right out and ask her. For a minute I wanted to ask him, but something told me not to, at least not then."

Until they landed, Henry shuffled cards, pausing now and then to fill one out or to enter a single, one-line thought.

Outside the Marriott at midafternoon, a Budapest police car stopped to let them out at the junction of the hotel's circular drive and the main thoroughfare. Henry, who, with Ed, was returning from the airport, sat behind the driver. He could either wait for the congestion of cars to clear from the circular drive or get out there. He opted not to wait. He so informed the officer and indicated that, rather than slide over, he would leave through his own side door—toward traffic—and that the officer should stay put. He would open the door himself.

Henry got out when a panel truck unexpectedly was barreling toward him from behind his left side. He knew an imminent sideswipe when he saw one, even at a distance of sixty feet. But he was caught between twin instincts: spin to the right and run around the front of the car, or somehow propel himself forward out of the truck's lane but into the lane of other vehicles. Knowing he couldn't make it to the front of the car in time, he ignored Ed's scream to "Run, Henry, run!" So, in a whip-fast maneuver, Henry dove into a somersault, landing on his feet in the center of the one-way thoroughfare. The truck swished by, snapping the police car's side-view mirror in the process.

All the traffic had stopped or swerved to different lanes to avoid Henry's hurtling body, possibly alerted by the officer who dashed from the front seat waving his hands.

Ed rushed up. "Y—you okay?"

"It was nothing," Henry gasped.

"Nothing? Then why pull your gun?"

Henry stared at his right hand as if the .45 it held wasn't his. His look changed from blank to pained as he tucked in his bum shoulder.

"And how in hell do you yank it out in the middle of a somersault?" Ed added.

"Training, training, and concentration."

The officer redirected traffic.

Henry returned the gun to its rig and dusted off his trousers. *Even here in Budapest?* He wiped away a mustache of sweat. It dawned on him that the forty-eight-hour warning at Seal's wake was—now. But he didn't want to remind Ed.

The regrouping of GIFT members was yet an hour away, so Henry and Ed stayed in their respective rooms. Henry opened the liquor cabinet and thought of downing the mini whiskey bottle, or the Hungarian Bull's Blood wine he'd heard so much about. But, with the meeting coming up, his reason prevailed. He decided to unwind in a hot tub instead.

There, ready thoughts came to mind. He questioned GIFT's effectiveness this past week. Had another brush with death not just occurred, he doubted the subject would have arisen. But the words of a popular New York City mayor rang in his ears. In the 1980s, the mayor would start many news conferences asking reporters, "How am I doin'?" Henry asked himself the same question.

He pictured George, Karl, Gail, and Jay and tried to attach a sliver of animus to their faces, words, or actions. He couldn't. There were only George's hugs and sarcasm, Karl's formality and joking, Jay's careful choice of expression, and, on a professional level, Gail's valuable insights. Still, their current heightened participation was a good sign. Their promise to implement background checks back home was another. Yet Henry couldn't avoid a new thought muscling into his consciousness: the business of danger. *Shouldn't they share in it?* Who else among them has been lethally threatened, tranquilized, or nearly squashed by a truck? He could have added, seduced by one of their own, but he didn't believe that qualified as a danger. He answered the question forthwith. He was the lead investigator and whoever was after him knew it.

All along, Henry had automatically applied his sequence of reaction-analysis-decision-action to the unfolding phases of the investigation—from the harbor murders through the dart gun experience, to Seal's murder, to the many interviews, to the inn fire, to Fedor and his revelations, to the fatal plunge of Mrs. Vasilakis, to the meeting with Mugur. He reviewed each issue as he soaked, fashioning implications, beginning to form links. Through the muddle, it seemed slowly to become a little clearer. But then, there was yet this new attack on his life. This ratcheted up his resolve to identify Mr. or Ms. Big. Whether the Mafia, the Triads, the Yakuza, or any other denizens of gangland be damned, he would not rest until this case was solved.

In the Stellar Room, Gail was decked out in a lavender silk blouse with tight white slacks and pumps; Jay wore a turtleneck sweater; George a jacket and shirt with open collar; Henry, Karl and Fedor a jacket and tie. They sat around the table.

Henry led off by apprising the group of his and Ed's impressions of Mugur. Henry gave a systematic account of the chains, the Dracula story, and Mugur's experience with clairvoyance. With raised eyebrows, each of the others uttered Felicia's name practically on cue.

Jay, asked by Henry to give his report, summarized the meeting with Basil Vasilakis.

Gail gave hers by first citing her two assignments and following with: "Regarding the heads of the committees looking into the prostitution problem, I really didn't need Scotland Yard. Fedor here helped me a great deal and I thank him for it. I contacted Romania, Bulgaria, the Czech Republic, and, of course, Hungary. I spoke with the subordinates of each person he identified as the leader of the prostitution investigation in each country. They vouched for each other and their superiors."

"Are their committees active?" Henry asked, "or just some sort of window dressing?"

"*Very* active, and I learned more than I suppose I actually wanted to hear. About the young girls, I mean. The sordid lives they must pursue. The way their spirits get dashed. We are a fragile people on a fragile earth, aren't we?"

Henry thought he'd heard that before.

"We take turns on earth," Karl said.

"Meaning?" Henry asked.

"He doesn't know," George said. "It just sounds good. I hear him say it at every convention, no matter what the topic."

Karl started to make an obscene gesture, glanced at Gail, and stopped.

"Regarding the cruise lines," Gail said, "I checked with four of the largest. Their stories were amazingly consistent. They wouldn't elaborate but said they did hardly any advertising for help because they deal with an employment agency in Bucharest. I couldn't get the name of the agency out of any of them, but there was something astonishing. Three of them claimed there's a woman in the US who's involved in all transactions of employment."

"How?" Henry asked.

"I couldn't get it quite straight—try as I did—but apparently there's some connection between her and the Bucharest agency. They kept referring to that as the employment agency and the woman as the placement agency. She's a sort of go-between, I would imagine."

"And no names were given?" Karl asked.

"None."

"Did you cover the question of how long they would work on a ship?"

"Yes, indeed. Again, rather vague replies. They wouldn't supply definite durations, only that the turnover was uniformly more than desirable."

They traded brief stares, shaking their heads.

After writing several words on a card, Henry said, "Good work, Gail. Excellent. Now, doctors, the autopsy. Was what we were told accurate?"

"Hardly," Karl said. He met George's gaze. "You want to do this or should I?" Karl asked him.

"No, you go ahead, I'm too pissed . . . sorry Gail."

"First of all," Karl said, "the whole thing was sloppy—a lot of cut corners, estimates instead of true measurements, and many other things that I won't go into. Suffice it to say it was amateurish. Forgive me, Fedor, but I must be honest, okay?"

Fedor answered, "It is understood. That is not my field anyway."

"To be practical," Karl continued, "I can summarize our own important findings in two sentences: first, one eye was glued open, one glued shut. Second, the middle finger of the right hand was cleanly severed at the second joint. And if you were to ask me, I can't think of any reason why a pathologist would do that; so somebody else did."

"Why someone else would," George said, "we have no idea."

Henry's sigh was loudest. "Talk about fouling things up," he said. "Basil Vasilakis returns as a suspect. I'd eliminated him because of the time line, but now we have to ask whether or not he hired someone to kill her." Henry reconsidered. "I shouldn't be so blunt about it. Let's say, instead, that he should remain on the list. Motive. Opportunity. Means. The means were there; he didn't need the opportunity if someone else did it; and the motive would be unknown at this point."

"But the eye sign?" Gail said.

"It could have been a mix-up in communication, but it sure implicates the Triads again. Or one of their subgroups such as the Wah Cing or the Hip Sing. Even the Ghost Shadows or the Flying Dragons. But as I think of it, it could be the work of the Fuk Ching, and I'll tell you why. Some of the early followers of the Triads, including the Fuk Ching, wanted to strike out on their own, develop their own way of doing things. They copied the idea of cutting off fingers from the Japanese samurai. In the beginning they used it to extort money, sending fingers to relatives in exchange for cash. Soon it became their calling card for any 'hit.' It became a vicious subculture that was both organized and seething with jealousies and turf wars and payoffs. Animals at best. Some of them would just as soon lop off your ear as look at you."

Gail shifted in her chair. "It's not clear, Henry," she said. "Why the extortion?"

"I didn't say that was their intention. What I *am* saying, and it's just a guess, is that possibly some offshoot of the Triads got its signals crossed, treated Helen Vasilakis as one of the prostitutes, and gave her the eye sign. In fact, they may have been so confused they cut off her finger."

"So they did what they sometimes do to uncooperative prostitutes," Gail said. "Exactly."

"But she was old compared with the other victims," Jay said.

"As I said, a botched-up contract," Henry said. "Anyway, great job, men. Did you point out the omissions to the pathologist?"

"Hell no," George said. "He didn't even show up. We dealt with an assistant."

Henry checked his watch and said, "We'd better move along."

Over the next five minutes, Fedor indicated that the stunt coordinator, who based his analysis on the falls of a human dummy, believed

Helen's death was consistent with murder. Henry then informed the group of Paul Mitroi's message regarding the Hungarian twins. Next, the five GIFT members agreed on where and when to hold their first post-Budapest meeting: Connecticut's Forensic Center on Thursday morning at nine, Eastern Standard Time. Henry insisted that future daily meetings should take place in a location more convenient for the group as a whole, perhaps in Fairfield County. They would decide on Thursday.

Karl asked if they should consider a Felicia-Mugur connection.

"Let's keep that for tomorrow," Henry said.

They disbanded, and Fedor led Henry and Ed to a rear room crammed with modern electronic equipment. Fedor contacted his central office, to which Henry dictated a final report. He made no mention of the prostitution issue.

Henry and Ed handed over their .45s, the rigs, and the extra ammo.

At the main entrance, the three men embraced warmly.

"On behalf of Hungarian government and me personally, thank you very much," Fedor said.

"The thanks go to you, my friend," Henry said. "Much appreciate it."

Fedor walked out the door into a waiting police car. At the same time, Henry wondered why the police hadn't informed the commander about the truck incident, and, if they had, why Fedor hadn't mentioned it.

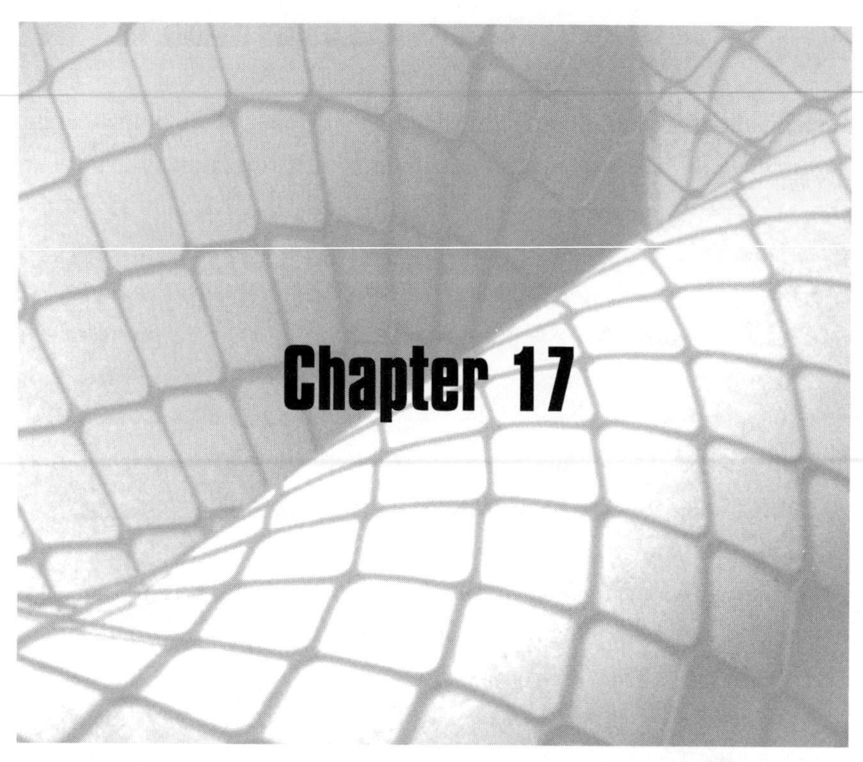

Chapter 17

CONNECTICUT, THURSDAY, OCTOBER 24

The walls of Henry's favorite conference room at the Center were plastered with illustrations of "trees" of logic for various types of crime scenes and investigations:

DEATH SCENES
RAPE / SEXUAL ASSAULT
SHOOTING SCENES
BOMBING / EXPLOSION
FIRE /ARSON
DRUGS / POISONING

POLITICAL ASSASSINATIONS PATTERN RECONSTRUCTION

Shortly after 9 AM, the last member of GIFT—George—joined the others around a long table. Ed had decided to skip the meeting in favor of tending to some administrative problems that had arisen while they were gone.

"For openers," Henry said as if he couldn't wait to get started, "here's the thing that's so ironic. We're embroiled in this nightmare of a case—let's label it 'White Slavery' for now. Then we get a call from Eastern Europe. No big deal under ordinary circumstances—we respond to any request from all over the globe—but this time what we discover is directly related to our own case, to white slavery."

"Related in more ways than one," Karl said.

"By that you mean . . . ?"

"I mean all the stuff you learned about what's his name . . . Mugur . . . yes, Mugur. Maybe tied in with trapping girls here and there under the cover of cruise ship work. Plus . . ."

"Wait a minute," George said.

Karl kept on. "Plus, the murder we're asked about has as its victim the wife of a guy who may or may not have been invited to the conference. Why specifically was he there anyway?"

"Specifically to give a lecture," Henry said.

"Aw, c'mon," Karl said. "A European could have given a talk like that. Terrorism's a hot topic, and there are plenty of experts around nowadays. Even *I'm* better qualified than he is."

Henry steepled his fingers across his mouth for a few seconds. "You were about to say, George?"

"I'm interested in Mugur and the Dracula connection. The Dracula legend was based on fact. One of the book's characters was a gal named Elizabeth who apparently was a Hungarian countess in real life. She was the one, if you remember, who took baths in maidens' blood, but it was whispered that she also may have engaged in some form of prostitution."

"You're an expert on history, too?" Karl said.

"I happen to read a lot—but particularly anything in relation to this case."

"What are you driving at, George?" Henry asked.

"I'm not sure. It's just that I'm disturbed by—he counted on his fingers—Mugur . . . Dracula . . . Elizabeth . . . prostitution . . . vampires . . . blood sucking. Doesn't it strike all of you as strange?"

They looked at one another like moviegoers leaving a horror show.

"Let's move on," Henry said. "Now before we left for Budapest, we agreed on some individual tasks—finding out whatever you can about some key players in this . . . in what's turning out to be a saga with more ramifications every hour." He was about to pull out a card but realized he knew the assignments by heart. "Karl, you'll cover Mitroi; George, you've got Maxwell Pierce and Vasilakis; Jay—Paddy McClure and buddy boy, Augie; and Gail—Roscoe Fern, Cliff Carpenter, and Felicia. And given our new information, whatever you can find out about our female Lothario becomes extremely important."

"Speaking of that, Henry," Karl said, "tell us again what she's like."

"I'd say Felicia's in her midsixties. Attractive. Stylish clothes but overly made up. Been around the track more than a few times. I'd call her . . . ah . . . worldly. Yes, worldly."

"I'm jumping to conclusions," Jay said, "but do you think she's capable of heading up a prostitution ring?"

"I *know* she is. She told me she did."

"I mean the whole ball of wax."

"Ms. Big, right?" Karl inquired.

"Precisely," Jay said.

"With no hesitation in ordering executions when required?" Karl added.

"Right."

Four sets of eyes homed in on Henry.

"Well?" George said.

"Capable?" Henry said. "There's no doubt in my mind."

"Oh, wonderful, gentlemen," Gail said. "Now my task becomes pivotal. We're talking the whole white slavery issue here. Madams, mayhem, and market sex."

"Great alliteration, Gail," George said, "but you left out murder."

"Murder, too," Gail responded. "So suddenly I'm a point man."

"You *can't* be a point man," George said.

Gail asked why not.

George teased out a lecherous smile and said, "Take off your clothes and I'll show you."

"George!"

"You asked, didn't you?"

"You men all think the same way," she shot back.

They continued the meeting for another half hour, raising questions about Vasilakis, Mugur, and Felicia. Even Fedor. Each offered interpretations of interpretations. They deferred comment on the other people they would be researching, like Mitroi, McClure, and Augie.

Before breaking up. Henry wanted to clarify where each would live during their intensified collaboration in the States.

"Karl," he said gleefully, "George will take you in like a stray cat."

Karl cast a nasty look. "Go ahead, Henry," he retorted. "I'm keeping count."

"And Jay," Henry said, "you'll be staying where?"

"New York City."

Henry didn't want to ask if that meant Gail's place.

The group also decided to gather at the Center one more time, then move to a new location beginning Saturday—the Fassett House in Greenwich, equidistant from Manhattan and Henry's home.

Henry walked them to the front entrance. Karl and Jay shook his hand, Gail barely missed his lips during a kiss, and George gave him a big bear hug.

Henry returned to his desk. Lori walked in, pad and pencil in hand.

"You haven't missed a beat, have you?" he asked.

"Well, you've got messages and I've got to know what to do about them."

Henry thought she was wearing more than her usual complement of jewelry: earrings, necklace, brooch, bracelets on both wrists, and rings on four fingers. All in gold.

"What's with all the jewelry?" he asked.

"I'm celebrating your return. Now are you going to brief me on Budapest?"

He did, emphasizing the issue of the murder victim's identity, the botched autopsy, the interviews of Vasilakis and Mugur, the reference to clairvoyance, and Gail's investigation of the cruise lines and their link to an unknown woman in the United States.

"Felicia?" she asked.

"I'm sure of it. In fact, get her on the phone, please. The messages can wait."

"Okay, talk to her but then you'd better contact—of all people—Augie."

"The hood?"

"The hood."

"What's he want?"

"Didn't say but he's called twice."

"He left his number?"

"Yes. At his winery. And you'd better check out this AP story that ran two days ago." She handed him a short newspaper clipping with the headline: "Reputed Mobster Attends Seal Wake and Funeral."

Henry read the article. It stated that Augustine "Augie" Minotti had been seen chatting with several mourners, then quickly slipped away from both events. One paragraph described the Cayuga Vineyards and Winery in Upstate New York. The concluding sentence was: "Famed forensic scientist Dr. Henry Liu also paid his respects."

"Get me Felicia before I call this guy," Henry said.

"Before you talk to either one of them, two other items. There was a short wire service piece in the paper about the Vasilakis death. They reported it as a definite murder."

"Doesn't take long, does it?"

"And the other is this call from a fellow in Chinatown. Said it's urgent."

"Chinatown in Manhattan or Flushing?"

"Manhattan."

Henry called the number and identified himself.

"Thank you so much, Dr. Liu," a man said timidly. "My name is Shilin Han—Hugh Mo's brother-in-law—and I run a liquor store in Chinatown. My wife and I bought it two years ago. I read the article about Augie Minotti and I want to share something with you. We get fifty percent of our wine from his place. Until I read the article, I didn't realize he had such a bad reputation. I called him yesterday to cancel any further business with him." The man's breathing became heavier. "He said I better reconsider if I value my health."

"Then what?"

"I said I'd reconsider and let him know. He hung up. We decided to try getting in touch with you. At first we were going to call the police, but we agreed that might not be the right move yet . . . you know . . . with what he said . . . the cops would plow ahead . . . and we couldn't stop the complaint if we got cold feet . . . it's hard to explain. Then my wife mentioned you."

"Why me?"

"We've been reading about the terrible Brooklyn murders and that you're investigating them. With your reputation and all, maybe you could tell us where to go from here. We don't want anything to do with the Mafia, but honestly we're a little scared. One other thing that bothers us, Dr. Liu. We didn't pay much attention to it before, but we should have known better. Augie Minotti's been seen down here in Chinatown quite a bit lately. Been in our little place a couple of times. Said he was in the vicinity and just wanted to say hello."

"Go on."

"I can talk to you this way, Dr. Liu, and I don't want to cause any trouble but all of us know about the Triads. They say there's a lot of them hanging out here. My brother-in-law saw Augie drinking with them at a local bar."

Henry advised the man to do nothing more for the time being, thanked him for the call, and moved on to Felicia.

"Felicia? Henry Liu here. I won't keep you. You're at work?"

"Just getting ready to go in. How have you been?"

"Fine. A simple question: Do you know Mugur Popa?"

"Mugur in Bucharest? Of course. Everyone knows Mugur."

"I didn't."

"But you were never there, were you? Now you do."

"You knew I was in Bucharest? How?"

"Mugur told me. He's impressed with you."

"He called you?"

"Yes. I'll tell you why, so you won't have to pussyfoot around trying to find out why. He wanted to know exactly when I was coming to Bucharest. Clairvoyance, you know."

"So *you're* the one he was referring to."

"Did he say nice things?"

"They weren't bad."

"Then I'm the one."

"You go there often?"

"For the kind of cash he doles out, about once a month."

Henry quickly sized up different scenarios he had to pursue. "Listen," he said, "someday soon, I'd like to meet again."

"Your place or mine? There was a time when I'd say, 'honey.'"

Henry left it that he would contact her before the weekend to arrange another meeting.

He referred to the message note that Lori had given him, punched in the phone number, and didn't mince words with a guttural male voice at the other end: "Your boss there?"

"Who's this?"

"Dr. Henry Liu."

"You got it."

"Dr. Liu," Augie said. "You and me gotta talk in person again."

"About what?"

"A deal. You'll see. I can't come there . . . you know, they put the heat on . . . can't even do a goddamn funeral anymore. And you don't want to be seen with me anyway, right?"

Even though Henry believed the question wasn't worth an answer, he said, "That's not my problem right now. My problem is, can I afford the time to make the trip? Ithaca area—that would be how far time-wise?"

"Five hours, tops. I think it would be wise for you to drop everything and come up here. And if you're worried that we might bop you . . . the girl I talked to yesterday . . . she there?"

"Yes."

"Good. Put her on a line. Go ahead, have her listen in."

Henry had no idea where Augie was going with the idea but covered the receiver and shouted out for Lori to pick up.

"Two of you there now?" Augie asked.

After positive responses he said, "Now you must have good equipment in a place like that, right? If you want to record this talk, be my guest. I'll wait and you tell me when. Then I say I have a business deal to talk with you about, Dr. Liu, and if you think this is a setup, let this recording tell that I'm Augustine Minotti. I'll say the date and that's that, okay?"

"It won't be necessary," Henry replied. He figured anyone willing to be recorded could be trusted on the matter, even a hood. Especially a hood. "But are you sure we can't cover the whole thing over the phone?"

"Sorry, doctor, I never make propositions by phone. That's a real bad way to do business, know what I mean?"

"No, but to each his own." Henry waited for a response. When none was forthcoming, he added, mockingly, "Know what I mean?"

"Look, doc. Let's cut the bullshit. You comin' or not?"

"I'll be there at three or four."

Augie gave directions to the winery and said he hoped the traffic would be light.

Henry left at 10:30. Ed drove and Jake—two cars behind in an unmarked cruiser—had a companion: State Trooper Mike Flanagan.

Ed had the window down, his elbow partly out. The morning smelled cool and fresh. There was little conversation; the radio was tuned into a pop music station. At about noon, both cars stopped at a Burger King for takeouts.

On the near fringe of Ithaca, past sylvan valleys and dozens of vintage inns, Ed said, "You know your wines?"

"Not very well."

"But you know your teas."

"I'm glad you asked."

"I didn't."

"Didn't what?"

"Ask about tea," Ed said, then adding under his breath, "Here we go."

"What was that?"

"Nothing. What about tea?"

Henry turned off the radio. "Well to begin with," he started, "tea is the world's most popular beverage, second only to water in total consumption. Did you know that?"

"I do now."

Henry categorized tea into its three main types: untreated green, roasted black, and half-treated, such as oolong.

"What about herbal?" Ed asked

"That's not even a tea. It's an 'infusion' made from flowers, spices, and herbs. Only Caucasians enjoy it."

Henry next gave a brief history of tea, its possible health benefits, and its relationship to key tea-drinking countries. China: "Most of the tea served there is half-treated." Japan: "It has tea schools that teach the 'way of tea.'" India: "Chai tea is boiled in milk and fruits." USA: "You know the 'Boston Tea Party?' It probably led to the Declaration of Independence. Ed, you want to learn about reading tea leaves?"

"Look!" Ed said, with relief. "There it is up ahead. See the sign?" He took a left-hand turn onto a dirt road and through a vine-laden stone arch that read:

Cayuga Vineyards and Winery
Jewel of the Finger Lakes

Jake followed along.

Ed said, "I can make out a building up ahead. He said the road was a quarter mile long?"

"Yes."

The road angled by vast expanses of water interspersed with dry islands just as vast. Instead of what one might expect around damp air, it smelled clean and raw and invigorating as if everything could start over.

"Check out all this wasted land," Ed said. "Both sides. Flat. Looks fertile. You'd think they'd be growing grapes right here."

"They probably have it earmarked for future expansion."

"But getting back to tea," Ed said, "how can you calmly talk about it at a time like this?"

"Because tea is really more important than we are or what we do."

"Tea?"

"Sure. When we're long gone, it will still be around," Henry deadpanned.

Ed looked over, all comprehension gone out of his face, his features flat.

"What's the matter?" Henry asked.

"We're in wine country. Why are we even *discussing* tea?"

"You asked."

"Now I'm really confused. I did?"

"In a roundabout way."

Ed speeded up, and when he applied the brakes in a designated parking area, a cloud of dust shrouded the cruiser. An elongated dark-stained building bisected the area. Ed had pulled onto the left side. Jake drove to the right and parked more gently. Eight to ten black sedans occupied other spaces.

Behind the building an enormous plantation of vines was arranged in neat rows that swept away from the eye and disappeared to a single distant point. The wilted brownish vines clung to tilted stakes, but a few grapes remained—reminders of days before the recent harvest.

A large pyramid of oak casks sat in front of the building. On either side of it was a glass-covered display of wine bottles of diverse colors. A central entryway was marked OFFICE.

Henry and Ed got out, and as they strolled toward the office, Ed signaled to Jake to stay put. Trooper Flanagan emerged from the front seat and entered the back one, sliding to the rear of Jake.

The office door swung open and Augie, smiling, said, "I saw you guys pull in. Welcome to Cayuga." He was dressed in a black shirt, black pants, brown pointed shoes—and needed a shave. A bulky, pockmarked man stood behind him, chewing gum. His chin bore a dimple as large as a navel. Only Henry and Augie shook hands.

They passed through a small room of benches smothered by cardboard cartons and packing supplies. Cigar smoke trickled from the doorway of an adjoining room. Ed coughed. Augie led the way down a corridor with walls that featured photographs of racing horses. Henry was reminded of Vernon Seal's apartment. One particular photo caught Henry's attention. It depicted Augie standing by a horse on which another man was mounted. The man was grinning broadly with unmistakable Asian features.

Henry called Augie back, pointed to the photo, and said: "Who's your friend, a Triad?"

"Him? Yeah, he's the one I know the most. Not a bad guy. Not what they call . . . like a . . . like an enforcer. You know, the guys who do the . . . the zappin'."

"Don't they all zap sooner or later?"

"Maybe, maybe not. Right now he's their business manager—takes care of the books."

"Like the consigliere in one of your families."

"Yeah, a Chinese consigliere," Augie sniffed. "You got off a good one, doc."

The corridor widened at its end. Two doorways appeared before them. More cigar smoke oozed from the right one, its door cracked open. They walked through the left door into an unimpressive space. It was an enclosed storage area, the kind seen in warehouses with high ceilings, exposed steel beams, dangling fluorescent light fixtures, stacked crates, tables and chairs piled on one another, dollies lined up. There was a messy desk near the far wall and several battered wooden chairs nearby. Augie sat behind the desk; the other three took chairs in front of him.

"First off," Augie said, "glass of wine?"

Before he could receive an answer, he followed with, "Thank you for making the trip, Dr. Liu. It was the wise thing to do, and I think you will see it's worth your while. I always say worthwhile things are wise to do. We here at Cayuga give—what percent, Tony, maybe five?—yeah, five percent of our wine supply to charity so they can raise some dough for scholarships. Know what I mean? That's a wise thing to do. I mean for us and for them." Tony, cleaning his nails, never looked up.

"Next," Augie said. "Your pal there? He stays in the hall, okay?"

Impassive, Henry answered, "He stays with me."

"In the hall."

"Only if your pal goes with him"

Augie's eyes darted about. "Tony, you go with him," he said.

Ed glanced back and Henry nodded.

"Now, doctor, number three. You're not wired by any chance?"

"Wired?"

"Yeah. You know, bugged."

"No."

"Can I check?"

"What do you mean check?"

"Could you take off your jacket?"

Henry complied, then put his blazer back on.

"I see you're packing lead," Augie said.

"Under no conditions does *that* get delivered to the hall," Henry said with determination.

Augie gave his throaty laugh, hardly able to get the words out: "Who knows, I could have a little protection myself somewhere." He lifted his arms like stationary wings.

"Then we're even, aren't we?" Henry said.

"You win on this one. You're not really the law, you know."

"How do you mean?"

"It's what I said at the wake. You think I'd talk to a real cop? Get nailed?"

"You might. I don't know."

"Well, I'm not nuts. But the trouble is—is you're smarter and you sneak around much *more* than the cops, see, and that could get unhealthy."

"You already told me that once. You dragged me all the way up here to tell me again?"

"I'm telling you to stick with the small stuff, whether I told you before or not. Don't get too greedy. And keep your fuckin' pants on—I'll get to why I let you in my place."

"You mean what you do is big? That's how it sounds by inference."

"Look, doc, don't get fancy with me. You know what I'm sayin', right?"

"Right."

"Okay. I gotta level wicha. I gotta problem . . . for a little while anyway. You read the papers, seen the TV. The heat's kinda on so I can't do my client's request until the heat dies down. Stupid cops'll forget seein' me where they see me. So I have a deal for you. You accept it, and we call everything fair and square."

"I'm waiting with baited breath."

"Case you don't figure on it, I know what that means. So here it is: I can arrange to hand you a million in cash each year for five years if you pull out of the case . . . you know the one I mean . . . and, like I say, if you turn around and do the small stuff."

"You're trying to buy me off!"

"I'm makin' a deal wicha."

There was no way Henry would cooperate, but he wanted to prevent an incident. And, dirty people always think everyone else is dirty. Henry answered, "I need a little time to think about it," adding, "Augie" for good measure.

"How much time?"

"Forty-eight hours seems to be a favorite for you."

Augie leaned over the desk and extended a hand. "It's a deal," he said.

Henry shook it while wanting to cross his fingers behind him. "As part of it, and since I'm here, you willing to answer a few questions? Just for the record."

"What record?"

"Mine. Before I close the books."

"Shoot. If I don't like the question, goo'bye question."

"Do you get to the city much?"

"What city?"

"New York. Do you visit there often?"

"Enough."

"Harlem?"

"I seen it."

"The Bowery?"

"Seen it."

"Chinatown?"

"Seen it. Look, I already told you before that I know some Triads. So what you drivin' at?"

"Just closing the books, that's all. Next then: you also mentioned you know Paddy McClure and Felicia Phillips from the Flotilla bars. How about Mugur Popa? You know him?"

"Yeah, I know him. Small peanuts."

"How do you know him?"

"Through Felicia."

"What's small peanuts mean?"

"He thinks he's a big shot, but his territory . . . ah . . . his friends don't go past his country. What is it? Romania or somethin'?"

"Yes. And a 'big shot' in what?"

"In whatever he does. He acts that way."

"You've met him then?"

"Not in person. That's enough of that question."

Henry sensed his window of opportunity was closing fast. "Do you know Paul Mitroi, Basil Vasilakis, or Cliff Carpenter?"

"Say 'em one more time."

"Mitroi, Vasilakis, Carpenter."

"Those Meter and Vas guys? Never heard of 'em. I heard of Carpenter. His place burned down, I hear."

"You heard right. How do you know him?"

"Through Felicia."

"Everybody knows Felicia."

"She's good. Lotsa guys know her. I'm getting tired, doc. Thanks again for comin' up. You got my card. Call me before Sunday, right?"

"Right."

"You give me the smart answer, and I hand over the cash. One of my boys can drive down."

Once again on the road, Ed asked about the meeting.

"He made me an offer he thought I couldn't refuse: a hefty payout. Millions. I said I'd think about it for forty-eight hours. He must think I'm stupid. Or, Ed, this whole trip and the offer were just a ruse to get us to let our guard down for a couple of days—to throw us off track. But if you don't mind, I'll elaborate tomorrow at the meeting. I hope you'll sit in."

"I can wait. You look bushed. Why not close your eyes for a while?"

Instead, Henry shuffled blank index cards on and off for over two hundred miles southeast, and it wasn't until they crossed the Connecticut state line that he filled out four of them. Despite the multimillion-dollar offer, the focus of his notes was on Felicia: her honesty with him and her popularity. But most important, was she Ms. Big?

He was dropped off in his driveway at 9 PM, saluted Jake who parked across the street, thanked Mike Flanagan who joined Ed for a ride home, and praised Ed for asking about tea. By 9:20 Henry had taken a hot shower and dropped into bed. He felt a sense of dread, but he couldn't put a finger on why.

FRIDAY, OCTOBER 25

The next meeting of GIFT began promptly at 9 AM. Henry wasted little time giving a blow-by-blow account of the Cayuga visit—including Augie's "offer." Their faces registered the kind of bewilderment reserved for children gawking at a circus act.

"I'd like to hear your individual reactions," Henry said, "but with your indulgence, can we postpone them and move on to what you did or didn't learn yesterday? Also with your indulgence, I'll write the tasks on the board and then we can proceed from there."

He rose, referred to a card for a moment, and printed on the blackboard:

KARL—MITROI
GEORGE—VASILAKIS, MAXWELL PIERCE
GAIL—FELICIA, ROSCOE FERN, CLIFF CARPENTER
JAY—PADDY, AUGIE

"Now from my perspective," he said, "a review of these players serves a dual purpose: first, to keep you all involved, which is extremely important as I've pointed out before. In a nutshell: to draw on your expertise. And second—although there may be overlap and repetition for some of us—to ascertain even the slightest bit of new information, maybe something none of us thought of before."

"Karl," Henry said, "why not start us off? And incidentally folks, forget wasting time telling how you got your information. We're all familiar with the sources to consult, the numbers to call, the departments, the bureaus, phone records, law enforcers, the NCIC, NSPIN—you know the drill. If what you found out is extensive, fine. If it's only a snapshot, that's fine, too. I realize you've only had twenty-four hours for this, which reminds me, do you all get the sense of urgency here, or is it just me? It's like hurry up in order to hurry up."

The others nodded while George declared: "None of us wants another bad incident to happen. I think we *all* sense it."

"I didn't plan to get into this," Henry continued, "but do you also get the feeling that so many things are coalescing? *There are so many links?*"

"That's a good way to put it," Karl said. "Now we have to try to decipher the meaning of the links."

He opened a pad he'd been fingering. "Paul Mitroi," he said, "was born in Bucharest, Romania. Two years ago he and his wife moved to Paterson, New Jersey, where they still live. He was apparently a well-respected member of the Romanian Chamber of Deputies. His day job was that of an elementary school teacher over there. Interestingly, he's a school custodian here. But the most relevant thing is that their daughter was found dead in Atlantic City three years ago; in fact, that's why they moved here to the States."

George interrupted. "She's the one whose autopsy results I checked."

"I remember that," Jay said. "Another case of one eye open, one eye closed."

"Correct."

"Just a couple of other items," Karl said. "After his daughter's murder, he became a kind of crusader against prostitution, especially if it involves young girls forced into it. I mean he's *really* immersed in the subject on a worldwide scale. Has a database and everything. One of my sources told me that Mitroi understands why his daughter's on the list." He flipped through his pad. "I've got some other leads to follow up on, but that's all for now," he said, "except that he seems to do an enormous amount of traveling. Mainly to Central and Eastern Europe."

"Where else?" George asked. "The same with one of the people I researched. I wouldn't be surprised if we have a pattern here."

"I agree," Gail said. She looked at the blackboard. "But I'll wait my turn."

"Before we leave Mitroi," Henry said, "let me elaborate on the database. He's organized a group—kind of a citizens' action group—covering four or five continents. They've put together a list of over a thousand names—young girls found murdered in the last five years . . . the same way . . . shot in the head. He sent me their current list. Those Budapest twins I briefed you on before? They're on it." He thanked Karl and motioned for George to speak.

"I had two individuals to check on," the pathologist said, "and I can dispose of one right off the bat. Maxwell Pierce, the editor? He seems clean. Respected. Been at the *Sentinel* for years and years. Well liked there. Stable family life. No trouble with the law. As far as I can tell, his only travel out of the country was to Paris and Rome." He spoke without notes. "But the other one—Vasilakis? That's a different story. We know about him and his wife in Budapest and I don't have anything else to add to that. But he's a *strange* guy. Everyone implied that without saying it in so many words. Born in Budapest. Moved to the States with parents when he was in grade school. He now lives in Alexandria, Virginia. No children. Funny thing about his wife—he had her body cremated in Budapest, but they'll ship her ashes here. I couldn't find out whether he's definitely back yet. Certainly he's not back at Homeland Security. I talked to a couple of different people there. They said he mouthed off a lot about terrorist cartels—that young women posing as prostitutes were really couriers for them. He has the reputation of a skirt chaser even though he doesn't look the part."

"I'll vouch for that," Henry said.

"What about all this counterterrorism expertise?" Jay asked. "Is it legit?"

"Apparently," George said, "but some of his colleagues resent it. He's off lecturing weeks at a time, away from the office. Not pulling his weight, they say. Except for that, he's generally well liked. Thought of as competent."

"Has he written on the subject?" Karl asked.

George shrugged.

"Taught a course on the matter?" Gail chimed in.

No one responded.

"It's the similar travel that stands out with these two," Jay said. "*And* with where the conference was held. *And* with the countries Fedor spoke about. *And* with the ones you've listed several times, Henry. The destinations are like a Central and Eastern European League of Nations."

"I'll add to it when I'm on," Gail said.

"You're on now," Henry said. "Unless you have more, George."

"Tune in tomorrow," George said.

"I have three," Gail said, opening a loose-leaf notebook, "and I'll save the juiciest for last. Our arsonist, the late Roscoe Fern, checked into the Hollings Sheraton the night before the fire at the inn. There was an exchange of four phone calls between his room and Cayuga, New York—two that night and two the next morning. I assume that would be your friend at the vineyard, Henry. Fern was born and lived most of his life in Natchez, Mississippi. Worked at the Flotilla in Westport for the last five or six years—at a Natchez explosives factory for twenty years before that. Obviously must have known Paddy McClure very well. Dabbled in antique cars, as did Felicia. I'll get to her in a minute. Then we have Cliff Carpenter. He was tough to get inside information on. He has a lot of longtime workers at the inn, and I couldn't readily tell whether they were still in shock over the fire or just plain protective of him, but they didn't open up much. I'm fairly certain, though, that he's never been to Eastern Europe!"

Gail paused for laughs and received them.

"Apparently the inn was built around 1910 and for many years was a favorite hangout for sexual mischief. One of the employees said, 'until Cliff came along thirty years ago and cleaned the place up.' I must say the man wasn't very convincing."

"What's our feeling about why the fire was set?" Karl asked. "Certainly not to dispose of Henry. There are easier ways to achieve that."

"Thank you very much," Henry said, holding up his thumb.

"To teach Carpenter a lesson?" George said. "But over what? Maybe he knows too much."

"Frankly," Gail said, "I think Helen Vasilakis knew too much." She turned to another page. "Now to Felicia Phillips. To begin with, that's not her real name. It's Olga Tomich. She was born in Leningrad—and, as you know, it's now St. Petersburg. Family moved here—Providence, Rhode Island—right after World War II. Somehow, she ended up in Natchez as a teenager, then in Hempstead, Long Island, about six years ago when she started working for Paddy McClure. She took the name Felicia Phillips in 1960 and that's when she became a part-time porn queen and full-time call girl. Evidently all of it is still well known in certain circles. She had three husbands along the way but is currently unmarried. No children. Like her fellow Natchez citizen, she dabbles in antique cars. And finally, gentlemen . . . what am I going to say?"

Henry beat the others to the punch. "She's traveled extensively throughout Eastern Europe."

"Well, Hungary and Romania anyway. So if we take the tidbit about a woman in the United States who may be connected to cruise ship companies—and if we couple that with what I've just said, I believe we could make a substantial case for a link between our sex goddess and white slavery. End of presentation."

"There's that word 'link' again," Henry said, "but I'm afraid we don't have quite enough evidence yet. Strong, but not enough."

"If you want my opinion, we could make a case for all of them so far," Karl said.

"Jay," Henry said, "you're on."

"We're well acquainted with Augie and his probable role in this improbable saga," Jay said. "I'd only add what I learned from some of the RCMP's most trusted informants—from Buffalo, actually. Augie's not a top boss, but a middle manager—a capo. They said that for a few years he was on his way up until those higher in the chain of command suspected he had his own agenda. Skimming, that sort of thing. Word on the street is that he's a renegade mafioso who had better shape up or he might be bumped off himself."

Jay's reference material was a single sheet of paper. He drew a line through the upper half. "Next, Paddy McClure. He's had a rags-to-riches career, I guess you'd call it. Navy man to begin with; after he got out, tended bar for a time; and finally ten years ago began putting together what's become a very successful bar and grille franchise. Speaking of the navy, need I say that he, too, spent some time stationed in and around Eastern and Southeastern Europe? Let's see . . . Felicia manages one of his bars . . . Roscoe Fern was one of his bartenders . . . his establishments do a thriving business . . . no evidence of hanky-panky going on in them, at least not in an obvious, organized way.

Never married." He folded the paper and put it in his pocket. "There's much, much more to run down," he continued, "but I think I can wrap up my part tomorrow."

The others echoed the sentiment before Henry said, "You were all great. Excellent. If I had some of my little gold deputy badges or my O. J. rulers with me . . ." Ed shielded his eyes. "I'd give each of you one of them." The rest shielded their eyes.

"Am I to understand," Jay asked, "that this represents a consensus suspect list?"

"Unless you can think of any more," Henry answered. "I would say it's reasonable to conclude that none of them is involved, or maybe one of them is."

"Or more than one," Gail said.

"That's more like it," Henry said. "In my judgment, there's an international prostitution ring out there, but there's also a leadership network running it. It's too large for one person. There may or may not be a Mr. or Ms. Big, but considering the links among different people and countries and commercial businesses, there's got to be a network."

"Anyone interested in taking a straw vote on the top dog?" George asked.

"Are we ready for that?" Henry said, even as he began handing out index cards.

"Good idea," Karl said. "It doesn't necessarily hold us to how we should proceed tomorrow."

"Why not just say our choice out loud?" Gail asked.

"Because," George said, "you know *us*. We'll start defending our choice and all of that. We'll be here all morning. This is cleaner. I'd suggest printing the name and not even signing the card. It's only a hint of where GIFT stands at this moment in time."

Each person wrote down a name, turned the card over, and handed it back to Henry. He shuffled the cards a few times, looked at each one, and announced: "All four votes for Felicia."

"Wait!" Karl exclaimed, "Henry, you didn't vote."

Henry spread the four cards on the table for all to see. "I only break ties," he said. Before anyone could speak, he added, "You all did the tough work—I know what background checks can be like. Now would any of you be averse to my contacting some of the suspects directly? Unless you already have, and I assume you haven't."

"But Henry, how about the vote," George said. "How do you come down on it?"

"On a vote on this subject, at this time, at this place, at . . ."

"What's your answer?" Karl demanded.

"I agree with the vote." Henry took out a blank card, penciled in Felicia's name, and underlined it with a flourish. "Unanimous," he said and returned to his own question. "Okay for me to contact them directly?"

Each nodded in consent.

"Which ones?" Gail asked.

"Mitroi . . . Paddy . . . Vasilakis, if he's back. I'll simply phone them. Felicia's a different story. I may run down and see her in person. It's not much more than an hour away."

"Careful of her," Gail said.

He thought she sounded jealous. "I'll be on my guard," he replied.

Gail let out a humpf.

Henry looked at the others as if pleading for mercy.

"Pierce and Carpenter?" Jay asked.

"Back burner for now," Henry replied. "Good luck today, guys."

The meeting broke up with the understanding that they would regroup for breakfast at eight the next morning in Greenwich.

Chapter 19

It occurred to Henry that he hadn't informed Lori of his Cayuga experience. When he came to the attempted bribe, she said with obvious mock sincerity, "Maybe you should refuse, see. Then, I offer to take half the amount with the promise to convince you to back away."

"Thanks, Lori. I'll keep that in mind," he said. There were other things concerning him, not the least of which was a troubling matter he'd never encountered before. He indicated he'd soon need her assistance in placing several phone calls, but in the meantime, he wanted to be left alone at his desk.

Whenever Henry empathized with a victim's family and showed his emotion outwardly, it was always a mere shadow of what he felt inside. Concern . . . sorrow . . . compassion? Yes, but only as played out against a scientific detachment required in the sometimes grisly world of forensics. And he couldn't recall ever having any positive feeling toward the perpetrator, only repulsion. But this case—on a much grander scale, with unique twists and subplots and links—was an exception. It had gradually evolved into a drama not only of criminality but also of far-reaching social, economic, and political import. A many-headed monster. Henry was well beyond the stage of questioning his capacity to deal with it. The question now was how someone could turn such a monster loose upon society. Was the perpetrator deranged? Was the motive more than money or power or control? All of which fell under the umbrella of *greed*, in Henry's mind. More to the point, if Felicia were such a person, how could she have used the same sexual enticements she herself had relied on for so long to damage a world through authorized force, degradation, and murder? It was hard to believe she could be that cruel. Not to mention the age of her prey and the grief of their family members. Henry slowed down his breathing. Was his barrier of scientific detachment leaving him?

He eyed the four prompts on the framed card at the corner of his desk. What he had just pondered represented REACTION and ANALYSIS. Next came DECISION and ACTION. He felt stuck on the idea of greed as opposed to another dynamic he wasn't entirely sure of, but had heard about: a form of *displacement*. He continued to dwell on Felicia. Over time, did she develop any guilt or anxiety stemming from the conduct of her life prior to the "age of white slavery"? Did she transfer her own transgressions as a commodity to an international commercial operation with widespread appeal and, by so doing, confer on her past an acceptance? Thus, was her anxiety relieved and was greed a secondary consideration? He decided to take action by first seeking the opinion of an old friend, Dr. Sam Corliss, chairman of the Center for Behavioral Health at Hollings General Hospital. He was psychiatric consultant to the twelve police departments of the greater Hollings area and former president of the State Psychiatric Society. Henry had last conferred with him three weeks before on a case of dismemberment. He now wanted an expert's view on the dynamics of Felicia's career. It wasn't a matter of curiosity, rather one of potential reward: armed with the psychiatrist's insights, perhaps he would have the wherewithal to extract a confession from Felicia. Though highly unlikely, an approach worth exploring.

Second, he would confront Felicia, preferably in person, beginning with the question of guilt, remorse, and anxiety over a career of turning tricks. He recalled she had spoken to him freely about those years. If her answers fit the script, he would next ease into whatever he might glean from Dr. Corliss.

Despite the straw vote result, and having the permission he'd sought from his GIFT colleagues, Henry still wanted to speak to the other consensus suspects. He laid out his personal agenda for the remainder of the day. In addition to a visit to the psychiatrist's office and a call to Felicia, he would phone Mitroi, Vasilakis, and Paddy McClure. He considered such systematic follow-up calls a necessity, hoping to gauge the truthfulness of answers to simple questions that he wanted to pose. And before the day was out and bedtime arrived in Budapest, he had a few questions for Fedor as well.

When Henry phoned Dr. Sam Corliss, he was informed that, if their meeting were brief, he could come right over; a patient had canceled her appointment.

The office in the hospital's Rosen Hall was simply furnished with two recliners, a leather couch, a maple desk, a high-back chair, and two pastel filing cabinets. Its ivory sidewalls were sprinkled with diplomas, photographs of class reunions, and certificates of achievement. Paintings of Sigmund Freud and Karl Menninger hung on the wall behind the desk, framing Corliss as he sat.

He was a caricature of a psychiatrist: white beard, pince-nez, frumpy brown suit. Tall and stooped, a star key medallion dangled from his neck. Some patients wondered if he used it as a metronome in hypnosis.

They had their usual discussion about confidentiality in psychiatry.

"Who knows?" Corliss said. "I may be treating one of your fellow scientists at the forensic center, but I'm ethically and morally bound not to divulge his or her identity."

Henry wanted to yawn but responded, "And who knows, Sam? We may be doing a DNA analysis on someone in your department because he or she is suspected of being a serial killer—but I can't say anything about it yet."

"Aha! 'Yet' is the key word, my friend. In psychiatry it doesn't make any difference. Even a simple visit here must be kept under wraps. People hate to deliver the mail; interoffice memos never arrive; patients sneak in with their collars turned up. I'm like the plague. It's not easy being a psychiatrist."

"Why not build a secret entrance out back, maybe underground," Henry said.

A variation of such a theme had been commonplace for over twenty years. Then, as now, they would pump each other's hand to near pain, the equivalent of a coded handshake between fraternity brothers.

"So what brings you here, Henry? Anything to do with what I've been reading lately?"

"Exactly that," Henry said, "but first, thanks for squeezing me in on such short notice." He sketched the story of international white slavery and the possible role of a former prostitute and madam as the supreme leader. "And here's what I'm wondering. Understand I may be all wet, but can this sort of person, if she's had periods of remorse . . . her father had been a minister . . . can she transfer that emotion to a situation she creates . . . that has the same sordid characteristics only with thousands of participants? In other words, could a longtime prostitute cope with guilt by establishing prostitution rings all over the world, thus deluding herself into thinking it's more acceptable behavior because of the number of people and cultures involved? Or is this too simplified, too much of a stretch?"

"Not in the least," Corliss said, his eye twitching. "What you say is quite astute and quite possible, particularly given her father was a man of the cloth."

From past experience, Henry felt that everything was possible to Corliss's way of thinking and every action had a psychological explanation—even actions that could never take place. He waited for more.

"But I'd be remiss, Henry, if I didn't point out that money is likely part of the equation here—however, that's okay. Though that is still compatible with the psychological principles we're discussing. The idea of remuneration—even in exchange for prurient activity—fucking privileges, let's say—makes it a worthwhile endeavor in her mind, which in turn makes *her* feel worthwhile. When she was an ordinary hooker, she may have thought of it as a livelihood, but that rationalization wears thin. Now if you compound her role, multiply what she's done manyfold . . . that is, in terms of becoming a ring leader . . . then one can reason that, in helping many others make a living, she's bolstering her self-esteem all over again."

"What if she condones murder to achieve that goal?"

"It depends on her degree of anxiety or guilt as you call it. Anxiety is the substrate here. I don't mean for the murder but as a result of her errant sexual activity over the years. Sometimes the anxiety is so strong—so dominant—the individual stops at nothing to reach the goal and thereby alleviate her pain. Betrayal. Larceny. Suicide. Murder. But I must elaborate some. You see, we're skirting all around the issue we call *displacement*. It's a defense mechanism that helps reduce anxiety. In the case of this woman, she might direct an anxiety-coated response away from herself and attach it to someone or something else—such as the groups of other women or the enterprise as viewed as a business. The latter becomes invested with the emotional significance originally associated with the former. This displacement of emphasis shifts the traumatic emotion—anxiety—away from her conscious awareness. She now has a defense against anxiety. The stronger the anxiety, the stronger the defense must be. Could it include murder? Given the right circumstances, most certainly."

Henry considered asking about the "right circumstances," but determined he had more than enough ammunition to face Felicia.

Chapter 20

Outside, Ed and Jake were waiting for Henry in the cruiser. Jake left for his own vehicle and drifted behind as they drove back to the Center.

"Psychiatric gobbledygook?" Ed asked.

"You've got to listen carefully," Henry said.

At his desk Henry called out for Lori.

She stood before him and commented that his yell was softer than usual. "How come?" she asked.

"I didn't want to raise your anxiety level."

"Oh brother," she replied. "The new Dr. Liu."

He gave her a list of names—Mitroi, Vasilakis, McClure, and Fedor—and indicated he wanted to speak to each one. He would let her know when to begin the process—sometime after he placed a call to Felicia.

A gentleman answered the phone at Flotilla Two. Henry could barely understand him over the loud chatter. It took awhile before Felicia came to the phone.

"You sound busy there," he said.

"No more than usual. Lunchtime crowd."

"I'd better call back later," Henry said. "I want to cover some things with you."

"Why not come down to my place again? I'll be there by 3:30. We can relax."

It was exactly what Henry wanted, but not for the same reason she undoubtedly had in mind. He said he'd arrive around 4:00.

He printed some words on a card and positioned it before him:

YOU KNOW OTHERS?
YOU TAKE CRUISES?
SHORT AND SWEET—IN & OUT

He went to the small refrigerator behind the curtain, returned with a prepackaged meal of chicken, rice, and water chestnuts, and wolfed it down. Sipping on green tea, he spread out several blank cards for note taking and shouted for Lori to start. Within three minutes Paul Mitroi was on the line.

"I haven't had a chance to thank you for the list you sent," Henry said. "It may prove to be very useful."

"How's the investigation going?"

"We're making progress; let's put it that way. May I again ask you a question or two? It will take only a minute. You've been so helpful in the past."

"Certainly. Whatever I can do to help."

Henry's intent was to lead with an innocuous question. "The list. You said it arrives regularly at your home?"

"Yes, every single day I get a merged list."

"And the merged list is from all the countries where you have chapters?"

"Yes, that's right."

"Okay. Now we're trying to find out what we can about certain people. Please understand this in no way is meant to implicate anyone. It's just routine investigation work. Do you know Basil Vasilakis, Paddy McClure, or Felicia Phillips?"

"No, I don't."

"How about Augie Minotti? He owns a vineyard in New York."

"No. Wait a minute—that Vasilakis? Isn't he the guy I just read about? I mean I read about his wife. She was killed in Budapest? Fell off a balcony or something?"

"That's the one. You know him?"

"No, but his wife's death was reported as a murder. I feel sorry for him."

"Does the name Mugur Popa mean anything to you?"

"Mugur? Yes, of course. Anyone who's ever been to Bucharest knows about Mugur and Dracula."

"Have you ever met him or talked to him?"

"No, I haven't—but it would be interesting."

"Last question, and this is a shorty. Have you ever taken a cruise?"

"An ocean cruise?"

"Ocean or river."

"My wife and I took a cruise down the Rhine some years ago."

Short and sweet—in and out.

"That's all, Mr. Mitroi. Much appreciate it. May I call you in the future if we need your input?"

"Absolutely. Anytime."

Getting Vasilakis on the phone took longer than expected. Lori said that he hadn't appeared at his Homeland Security office, but that he had called there stating he'd arrived back from Budapest. He informed them he would take the next week off because of his wife's death. She tried his home phone and left a message on his answering machine; he returned the call shortly thereafter. During the track down, Henry scrawled in notes about the Mitroi conversation and reviewed some old notes on Vasilakis.

"First of all, Basil, I feel I didn't thank you enough for cooperating with us during a most difficult time for you in Budapest."

"It's still difficult, doctor."

"I'm sure. You must be exhausted and preoccupied on top of it. I won't keep you long. Can you manage a few more questions that have cropped up since our return?"

"That would be fine."

"Good. Our investigators know how you got attached to Homeland Security, but how did you become an expert in counterterrorism?"

"Actually I sort of stumbled on it, and I'm not so sure I'm an expert. The Bureau of Customs and Border Protection, which is really where I work—it's now under Homeland Security—they carved out a new role for me. I now divide my time between what I'm supposed to do and what I like to do."

"Which is?"

"Give talks on the subject. It's no secret that since 9/11 people have been screaming for us to increase border protection activities—national security in general. At the same time, calls were pouring in for someone to lecture about effective ways to prevent future terrorist attacks. It's a long story, but somehow I got roped into representing the bureau in this area. I can tell you one thing though: the more I travel around and speak, the more I learn."

"You mean about the subject?"

"About how underprotected borders are everywhere. It's really frightening."

"On your trips, did your wife usually go with you?"

"Many times, I'd say. Perhaps about half. I wish she refused . . . Budapest . . ." His voice trailed.

"I'm sorry for that question, Basil."

"No, it's okay. Please go on."

"The last time we talked, we brought up contraband, and I asked if that applied to people, too. You said yes and gave illegal aliens and terrorists as examples."

"I remember that."

"Do you have any thoughts on white slavery?"

"As applied to contraband?"

"Yes."

"Plenty of thoughts. The trafficking of women is a very serious problem—no question about it. And the reason is the laxity—or I *should* say—the laxity and the corruption of government officials. Those in the know tell me that officials in every single country participate in human trafficking to one degree or another—that there's a clear link between white slavery and government corruption. Immigration officials have been at it for years. Then there's the missing persons rate. It's escalating in many countries. Bosnia, for example."

"Bosnia? How do you know that?"

"It was in Vernon Seal's articles, and he was one of the best damn reporters around."

Henry wrote a brief note before asking the next question.

"I'd like to move on. A couple of quickies. We're trying to find out what we can about certain people and, believe me, this isn't meant to implicate anyone. Do you know Paul Mitroi or Paddy McClure or Felicia Phillips or Augie Minotti?"

"No, I can't say that I do."

"Mugur Popa?"

"If you've ever traveled to Romania . . ."

"I know, I know: everyone's heard of Mugur . . . and Dracula."

"They're living legends there. At least Mugur is. Dracula's dead . . . but I wonder."

Henry thought he heard a laugh, and he was glad. It was the first lighthearted verbal exchange they'd had since before the balcony murder.

"Finally, Basil—and this might sound off the wall—have you ever taken ocean or river cruises?"

"Hell no. I spent too much time in the coast guard, seen enough of water. I'll spend my vacations on land, thank you."

"Have you gotten to know anyone in the cruise ship business through your border experiences?"

"No. We don't deal at that level. Only with their security detail."

Henry thanked him for his time. Vasilakis, like Mitroi, stressed his willingness to answer future questions.

Henry's watch read 1:45. Two more calls and he would head off to Hempstead. He alerted Ed.

Lori indicated that Paddy McClure was on the line. Henry picked up.

"Dr. Liu," he said, "good to hear from you. Felicia tells me you're driving down to see her." The background chatter wasn't as loud as at Flotilla Two.

"She called you?"

"No. I called her at work. Flotilla stuff. She mentioned it."

"That reminds me, I have to leave soon. Strictly business—let's make that clear."

"With Felicia I never wonder about nothin'."

"Hmm, I'm not sure how to interpret that."

"I mean there ain't anything impossible with her. In her lifetime, she's done it all."

Henry didn't know how to interpret that either but, pressed for time, went ahead with his protocol. "Paddy," he said, "as part of the overall investigation, okay to bother you again with a couple of questions?"

"Be my guest."

"About your former bartender, Roscoe Fern. You knew of course that it's all but certain he torched the Clemensville inn?"

"Yeah, sure looks that way. I couldn't guess that in a million years."

"There was nothing in his past that we should know about?"

"Not that I could tell. He came and went, did his job, never complained. Sometimes you never know."

"He was reliable?"

"Reliable."

"Now switching. You told me and we've heard from many sources that all of your establishments do not encourage anything illegal. Let me be honest—I'm talking prostitution. Nothing like that, right?"

"Like I said once before, if people want to meet here, have a drink, or a bite to eat, and then go off and screw or whatever, that's their business. We don't promote it, let's say. But we'd be nuts to think it doesn't happen. It happens here, at all my other bars, at the swanky places in the city, out in the boondocks, you name it. Can anybody stop it? I doubt it."

"I see. It's hard to argue with that. Now switching again. We're trying to learn whatever we can about certain people. Obviously you know Felicia, but what about a fellow named Paul Mitroi?"

"Never heard of him."

"Basil Vasilakis?"

"Him? I think it was him. No, not him, his wife. Wasn't she killed at that political thing not too long ago?"

"That's the one."

"I never heard of him except I heard everybody puttin' their two cents in about the wife. I hardly read the papers anymore. No kiddin.' I learn all I want to learn just by keepin' my ears open here. And you know, doc, the customer's never wrong."

"You said you were in Romania some time ago. I assume you heard of Mugur Popa? Was he around then?"

"Mugur? He's been around forever—just like his buddy, Dracula. I used to think that Mugur was one of them zombies or—what is it—vampires? Yeah, I met him. Went to his place more than once. I get a kick outa the joint."

"But you never formed a friendship, a relationship?"

"You mean the kind where you keep in touch? Nah."

"Last question, Paddy. Do you ever take cruises?"

"Are you kiddin'? First off, I ain't married, so why go alone, unless I wanna get some . . . If I wanna get some, there's plenty around here. Know what I mean? Nah, I don't need no cruise."

"And second?"

"What?"

"You said 'first off,' so there must be a second."

"Yeah. Time. Don't have time for a cruise even if I wanted one—which I don't."

"Oh, I forgot," Henry said. "Augie Minotti. You know him? Has a vineyard in New York."

"Never been there, never met the guy."

"You ever hear of him?"

"Never."

Henry rushed through the usual ending and asked Lori to contact Fedor.

Surprisingly, they were connected before Henry had a chance to bring his notes up-to-date, although he did arrive at a decision about the calls as a whole. He concluded that, in each instance, the responses were given without a hint of contrivance—that if each phone call were a lie-detector test, the stylus would indicate no failure.

"Henry! You made it back safe. The flight was good?"

"Yes. No problems. A little bumpy, but it was probably your Hungarian gods giving us hell for leaving. I've got only one thing to clear up, Fedor—real quick. You may have covered it, but I forgot. You said the missing persons rate in your part of the world has increased significantly, right?"

"Right."

"Since when?"

"Big jump after tragedy in your country. Trade Center."

"The first or second incident?"

"The big one. The airplane crashes."

"That's all I have to bother you with this time, old friend. Thanks."

"It is never a bother. And never worry about time difference. You call *any* time, and I hope I can do the same."

"Day or night. Oh, and by the way—in all the years we've been friends, you'd think I'd know this. Have you ever visited the United States?"

"Two times. Both for pleasure. I like New York and Chicago, but San Francisco is best one."

2:30 PM
LEAVE FOR HEMPSTEAD

During more tea, Henry skimmed through his collection of filled index cards and other materials that were stuffed into five folders.

He summoned Ed and they walked through a cold light drizzle when they took off for Felicia's compound. Henry shared his opinion about the phone calls and what he had learned from them—little in the way of new information and even less in terms of incriminating responses.

Time seemed to drag, punctuated by Henry's stabs at humor, which uncharacteristically fell short of the mark. Ed, in turn, remained solemn. Both made frequent checks of Jake through their side mirrors.

Henry was once again bemused by the pace of the moment as it applied to what he called the "quotidian factor," a term he had originated. "There can be slow-moving events that recur frequently," he might say to a graduate class, "or there can be quick events that occur infrequently. Individual events occur during a specific time span. But the duration of the event and the duration of the time span are independent of one another."

He thought of it all in the context of rare lulls in an otherwise frenetic nine days—he had them counted. His life had become an unbroken continuum of travel, meetings, phone calls, laboratory work, consultations, interviews, and death threats. Whatever happened to cozy dinners and concerts and forensic seminars and teaching sessions? Not to mention crime scene reconstructions. Where did the laughter with social friends and the banter with students go? He popped a third candy in his mouth.

4:05 PM
ARRIVE AT COMPOUND

Both cruisers stopped out front. Henry asked Ed to accompany him. Jake remained outside.

Henry rang the doorbell several times. There was no response.

"Did you hear the ring?" he asked.

"I heard it fine," Ed said.

Henry guessed Felicia had been held up in traffic. He tried the door. It was not locked. He opened it a crack.

"Felicia," he shouted. "It's me, Dr. Liu. Are you home?" There was no answer.

Henry withdrew his .45 and saw that Ed had done the same. They assumed positions on either side of the door and crouched down. Henry inched the door open with the butt of his gun.

"Uh-oh," he said.

"Son-of-a-bitch," Ed exclaimed.

At the far edge of the foyer, Felicia lay spread-eagled on the floor—fully clothed, her head twisted to one side, a thin strip of wire set into a deep furrow around her neck.

They stood frozen for a moment, gaping in stunned silence.

The foyer was in disarray. Furniture pieces and bamboo plants were overturned; the miniature cars were scattered about the base of the display table.

"She put up a struggle," Henry whispered. He gave Ed his gun and asked him to stand guard while he inspected the body.

The skin of her deep purple face had a translucent look. Both eyes were open; there were numerous tiny hemorrhages in and around them. He pressed two fingers against her cheek. It felt warm and did not blanch.

Looking at his watch, Henry knew she had to have been garroted within the past half hour and his findings confirmed it.

His voice still lowered, he said, "Ed, you and Jake check out back. Include the side buildings. I'll cover the other rooms in here. We're looking for ambushers not physical evidence—first things first."

"But there aren't any cars outside."

"Do you think they'd leave cars if they're lying in wait for us? The way things are happening, who knows if they were aware of our coming here? Maybe Felicia even told them. Maybe they talked before she was killed. So let's get started. Then either you or I can notify the locals." Henry apologized for his brusque remarks but believed there was no time to mince words.

Ed said he understood and disappeared out the front door. Henry began a methodical and stealthy search of each room and closet in the house, ending in the basement. There he found a full-sized but dismantled antique car and wondered whether repairs and upgrades were part of her automotive hobby. Or had someone else been helping out?

Regrouping, they assured one another that no one was lurking about the compound. Henry phoned the local authorities, then asked Ed to go for the camera in the cruiser and snap several pictures of the crime scene. Awaiting the arrival of the police, Henry took out a magnifying glass and searched for trace evidence.

Two teams of detectives from the Hempstead Police Department arrived quickly. Henry knew the lead detective and spoke briefly with him, explaining how Felicia fitted into the overall investigation and why he, Ed, and Jake happened to be there.

The crime scene was cordoned off and the detective said, "You're welcome to stay and contribute, Dr. Liu."

"No, we'd better run along—you have your own forensics team. If you need any assistance from me later, let me know."

5:10 PM
LEAVE FOR CONNECTICUT

The Merritt Parkway was congested and the light drizzle had changed to a violent downpour. Henry thought the weather symbolized the dramatic shift in the investigation's focus.

He put in a call to Lori's home and informed her of Felicia's murder. Her initial silence said it all.

"Do me a favor," he said. "Phone Karl and the others and tell them. You're better at tracking them down than I am. You have their URGENT numbers with you?"

"A set at the office, a set in my purse."

"Good. Do that, would you? And say I'll be in touch."

Henry hung up and ran his hand over his brow as if it were pounding.

"Now what?" Ed asked.

"Back to the drawing board. 'And then there was one.'"

"What?"

"I had it down to two and, like my GIFT colleagues, I had her listed as number one. Who's left? I don't dare pick him out yet. Look what happened—the straw vote. Everyone—but *everyone*—selected Felicia and then, wham! I have a good idea about who our Mr. Big is. But we need a little more proof, and I know where to get it. Can we let it go at that? Is that okay, Ed? I mean if I don't mention his name right now? Call it superstition if you like."

Ed looked wounded but said, "No problem. Let's do it right."

A minute before, Henry had been asked a simple "What" and now realized he had answered with a mini sermon. But he couldn't help it. The murder of the madam-turned-clairvoyant had put a new spin on everything—the suspect list, the next move, Henry's mind-set.

6:40 PM
ARRIVE HOME AT 17 ARROW PLACE

The rain had stopped. Henry and Ed entered the house and the phone rang. Paddy McClure was on the line.

"Look, doc," he said, his breathing labored. "I know about Felicia's death. I had nothin' to do with it, but I got to warn you. They're on a rampage. You gotta be prepared and . . ."

"Hold it! Who's 'they'?"

"We don't have time for that. My watch says 6:40. No one's shown up yet?"

"No. I just got here."

"Well they were supposed to see you at 6:30. I tell you what. You better have some cops with you. Only keep 'em under wraps."

"I have."

"How many?"

"Two."

"Right with you?"

"One with me. One outside."

"Send the outside one away or bring him inside. They might change their mind if they see him. Here's a chance to nab 'em while you can."

"Paddy, this is all stupid. You tell me you know about a murder. Then you warn me to watch out for unidentified people who might stop by . . . *I suppose to dispose of me, too.* Is that what you're telling me?"

"You got it."

"But why should I trust you?"

"You're smarter than that. Why would I tell you to round up a gang of cops? Figure it out, doc . . . only don't figure too long." McClure hung up.

Henry thought he still had a twenty-four-hour reprieve and now surmised that Augie didn't share the news with his cronies.

He and Ed raced outside to brief Jake on the call; they asked him to park around the corner and join them indoors. Back in the house, Henry contacted Detective Kathy Dupre, explained the situation, and was told that a contingent of unmarked police cars would soon be secreted nearby, ready to roll at a moment's notice.

"You need some kind of signal?" he asked.

"No, we'll handle it." She assured him they had experience with these kinds of operations.

"Arrow Place, right?" she asked.

"Yes. Seventeen."

"Hang tough, Henry. Our men are fast when they have to be. We'll be there before you know it."

Chapter 22

6:52 PM

Guns drawn, Henry, Ed, and Jake had peered through the front window a full ten minutes before Henry reached down to make certain the .22 snubby was handy at his ankle. He wiped a sticky palm along his pants leg as he straightened.

They looked at one another as a sedan made a second pass around the block. Each time it had slowed to a crawl before the house. A third time it eased to a halt at the curb.

The sedan was long, black, and shiny—a touring car, the kind government dignitaries were chauffeured around in. It had tinted windows and three radio antennas. Henry guessed it was custom made, probably a Lincoln.

No one got out. He could hear the engine idling, not a smooth noise, one with a skip, a carburetor glitch. The waiting, the anticipation, the motor noise—the combination triggered a feeling of déjà vu for a time when a dignitary *did* appear: a United States president. A more joyous occasion, to say the least.

Without even thinking, he flicked his head to dislodge the memory, for this was something of a different order, potentially cataclysmic. Lethal. He was afraid Kathy hadn't been able to round up help in time. Were the officers in place? Or not, at this crucial moment. Where *were* they?

Then without warning, two units of police squad cars swooped in out of nowhere and converged on the sedan, front and back—eight cars in all—funneling to a stop within inches of the vehicle. Close behind, a smaller white car with flashing lights pulled up. A woman in a blue raincoat emerged and sidestepped her way to a position behind one of the squad cars. More than a score of police officers swarmed toward the sedan; most brandished handguns, some aimed shotguns at the windows. The helmeted officers appeared barrel-chested; Henry would have bet they wore bulletproof vests. One shouted orders while others yanked the doors open.

"Get out! Now! I said *now*! And hands up! Hands up or you're dead!"

Four burly Asian men piled out and, following instructions, leaned over the hood, legs spread. While they were frisked, an officer used his gun to direct a fifth man from the far side of the sedan out onto the sidewalk.

The man's face was pale in the twilight. Henry flinched and mouthed his name: "Vasilakis!"

Henry, Ed, and Jake dashed out. The woman met them halfway.

"Stay with him there, Bart," the woman instructed the officer.

"Kathy," Henry said. "Thanks for this. Your men are fast all right."

"SWAT teams have nothing on us," she said proudly.

Detective Kathy Dupre was short and petite, but had the swagger of someone larger. Henry often needled her with words like "spunk" or "pluckiness," and, more often than not, had questioned her choice of profession.

One time he said, "Why a cop, Kath? You're too sweet and pretty."

"Don't give me that line, Henry," she replied. "Remember I'm engaged."

Now he'd never again question her choice of profession.

"You know," she said, "if it wouldn't sound so foolish at a time like this, I'd say, 'What's the good word'?"

"The good word is I think we have our man, but it's not definitive."

"Definitive?"

"I have to double check. You can have your men take away the Asians and question them, book them—probable cause—whatever. I'm sure they're Triads. But the white one there, I'd like a minute with him inside. Care to join us?"

"No, better not. I left something hanging at the PD. But I'll have two officers stay behind with you. I'll go with the others. Catch you there later?"

"Maybe. We'll be in touch. You know the scope of this thing, and I've got to act fast in some other areas. Your men will take notes?"

"I'll tell them to." She turned to leave. When she reached her car, he called out: "Kathy?"

"Yes?"

"Much appreciate it."

Ed approached him and pointed in Vasilakis's direction.

"He's the one you figured?"

"He's the one. We'll see definitely in a minute or two. I was just thinking though. Fortunately, they all stayed in the car, no doubt listening to this guy, planning their course of action. Dumb, real dumb. But it probably saved their lives because if they'd gotten out, there would have been gunfire."

"The way they came in? Bloodshed big time," Ed said.

"If our counterterrorism expert *is* Mr. Big," Henry said, "the bastard must get some jollies over being at murder scenes. He was at the harbor one, at Vernon Seal's, maybe at Felicia's—probably would have watched his own wife being dumped off the balcony if he weren't giving his little talk. And, come to think of it, he wanted to be at mine."

"Why say he was at the others'?"

"You'll see, I hope. Let's take him inside."

A coffee table separated Vasilakis from Henry, Ed, and the two Hollings police officers. Jake had gone to retrieve his cruiser. Ed took out an index card; both officers took out writing pads.

"Well, here you are," Henry said, his fingers steepled, "at the end of the road."

Vasilakis crossed one leg over the other.

"In case you plan to claim that riding in the same car as some lowlife Triads doesn't prove a thing," Henry said, "let's go a few steps further. Number one: how long have you been wearing that orthopedic shoe?"

"That? Since I was a kid—and it's not an orthopedic shoe. It's a shoe with a heel lift. What business is it of yours?"

"Three-quarter inch?"

"An inch."

"You realize of course that in lifting that side of your body, it increases the pressure on your other side?"

"So what? If it helps straighten me, it helps straighten me."

"I want to show you something." Henry left for the den and returned with a manila envelope. He withdrew several photographs and spread them on the table before Vasilakis, who picked them up grudgingly and perused them.

"What do *they* prove?" he asked.

"The enhanced shoe prints clearly show one deeper than the other.

In case you're wondering, the photos were taken at the harbor crime scene. These together with a shoe print found on more compact ground at the recycling center—just enough pressure for a solitary print of the shoe *opposite* the one with your heel lift—together they place you at both crime scenes—Brooklyn and here in Hollings."

"But . . ."

"Listen to me!" Henry rubbed his bum shoulder. "Number two. Earlier today, you said the missing persons rate was escalating in Bosnia—you specified that country—and that you knew about it because Vernon Seal cited it in a *Sentinel* article. But I remember all the articles, and there was no mention of Bosnia. I submit to you, sir, that you had personal experience with such an escalation. *You were responsible.*"

Vasilakis readjusted himself in his chair. Henry's face took on an austere glaze, his lips moving just enough to form words. The other men wrote without stopping.

"Number three. Human trafficking in countless European countries—countries you visited on a regular basis—suddenly spiked when you started your speaking tour. As did white slavery all over the world. Quite a cover. Quite a clever way to move around. Check on your supply. Meet with your contacts. Like Mugur the Magnificent. Sure . . . magnificent in throwing young women your way. You devised an ingenious scheme, Mr. Basil Vasilakis, and you ordered killings to make it work, even your own wife's. Believe me, we'll lay out an ironclad case against you in due course." One of the police officers read him his Miranda rights.

"So are you ready to fess up now or wait till you're brought downtown?" Henry asked.

"I'm innocent."

Henry jumped up, fists clenched at his sides. "That's bullshit!" he exclaimed. He jerked his head in the direction of the other three and demanded, "Write it as I said it!"

He turned back to Vasilakis, shot him a fierce look, and said in a restrained tone: "You—make—me—sick."

"I want an attorney," Vasilakis said.

After everyone left, the first thing Henry did was drain a Dewar's. The second was to call each of the GIFT members and fill them in on the day's events. Each man indicated he would return to his individual schedule but asked to be kept informed. Gail, however, stated it differently.

"If you care to come to New York tomorrow, Henry, just think, you could give me the details personally, and then we could celebrate any way you want."

Henry said he'd let her know.

"By when?"

"If you don't hear by tomorrow, I'd better take a rain check."

"Okay. If that turns out to be the case, I'll be returning to London. If you change your mind after that, you'll call me?"

"I promise. If I do, then what?"

"I'll take the first flight back. Maybe."

After being brought into custody, Basil Vasilakis was soon charged with masterminding the prostitution of young women and the murder of those who resisted. Henry was relieved to hear that. The United States District Court judge ruled that the case would be prosecuted at the federal level for three reasons: one, the defendant's position in Homeland Security; two, the fact that the case involved parties from different states; and three, the case's international reach and ramifications.

Search and seizure warrants were issued, which resulted in incriminating documents and photographs being found in the Vasilakis home. The media predicted he faced a certain death sentence, so he elected to sign a Cooperation Agreement. In exchange for a sentence less than execution, his lawyer struck a deal with the US Attorney's office stating his client would "come clean" on all matters involving the prostitution operation and murders, both at home and abroad. This included fingering others involved. Accordingly, arrest warrants were issued for Augustine Minotti, Paddy McClure, Cliff Carpenter and—with the assistance of Budapest's Fedor Kocyk—Mugur Popa. They, along with thirty-five others from an array of countries, were cited for varying degrees of complicity.

Weeks of legal wrangling ensued, during which time Henry returned to full-time forensics and teaching. He kept his GIFT colleagues apprised of further developments.

Eventually he was pleased to learn that the Cooperation Agreement would direct a transcribed deposition of Vasilakis. If he were found guilty, his level of cooperation and the forthright nature of his responses would influence the length of his sentence. The court would not participate per se but would be available for consultation during a process involving defense counsel and the prosecuting attorney. The process took two afternoons. A day later, Henry was given a copy of the proceedings. He asked for and received permission to reproduce it in quadruplicate, one for each other member of GIFT. In making copies, Henry trimmed them, leaving only the questions and answers relevant to GIFT's role in the investigation.

On December 6, GIFT members met at their usual spot, Baderro's in Manhattan. Before both dinner and a discussion of upcoming hot and cold cases, they decided to read through the questions posed to Vasilakis and his recorded answers. Gail had the honor of reading the document aloud as the others followed along:

Question: Mr. Vasilakis, you call the operation your "network"?
Answer: Yes.
Question: And you were its founder and leader?
Answer: Yes.
Question: Who was second in command?
Answer: Augie Minotti and Paddy McClure. They were on equal footing. Felicia Phillips was slightly below them.

Question: Was Vernon Seal part of the network?

Answer: No, but he knew about it and wanted in. At least he wanted a piece of the action.

Question: Is that why you had him killed?

Answer: Yes. He wrote those articles to show the power of the pen but then he went too far with his mouth. He threatened to expose everything unless he was allowed in. He should have been satisfied with the payments we gave him.

Question: Sometime before his death, we understand that Mr. Seal contacted Dr. Liu. Do you have any knowledge of why?

Answer: No. He probably feared for his life because he should have.

Question: We also understand that you personally went to see Dr. Liu shortly after the three young women were found murdered on the Brooklyn pier. Is that correct?

Answer: Yes, I did.

Question: Why?

Answer: To see what he knew. It was reported he was in on the investigation.

Question: And you ordered those women killed? If so, why?

Answer: Yes. They stopped cooperating. We wanted to send a message.

Question: So if other women in your employ—and we use the term loosely—if they chose not to cooperate, they would also be killed?

Answer: Yes.

Question: While we're on the subject of the three women, why were their eyes treated the way they were?

Answer: It's a sign the Triads use. We decided to use it to notify our girls that they better behave. It's well known.

Question: But why was it used in the case of your wife?

Answer: The Triads botched it. Got things mixed up. They should have just taken care of her and left the eyes alone.

Question: You ordered her killed also?

Answer: Yes.

Question: Why?

Answer: She knew too much. She kept quiet for some time, but after she caught me with this last girl I was seeing, she swore she would pull a Vernon Seal and sing like a canary.

Question: Did the Triads do the actual killing of the three women, Seal, and your wife? We'll get to Felicia Phillips later.

Answer: Just Seal and my wife. Augie's men took care of the three girls.

Question: The Mafia?

Answer: Yes.

Question: Would you explain the relationship of the Mafia, the Triads, and your network? In detail please.

Answer: Augie is a different kind of mafioso. I call him a renegade, not a capo. I never used capos because they're too expensive. He worked well with the Triads. They're the cheapest and ask the fewest questions. Augie was good at keeping the girls in line—and also the coyotes . . .

Question: One moment please. What is a coyote?

Answer: A people smuggler. They worked in cooperation with local hoteliers and bar owners.

Question: Go on. What else can you tell us about Augie and how the network operated?

Answer: He was our enforcer and also our manager. Not the business manager—that was Felicia's job. Let's say he was our operations manager. We owned the girls and our customers would make a down payment and lease them from us for a monthly fee.

Question: And for Augie's services, he was part owner of the business?

Answer: Yes. I got forty percent. He and Paddy got twenty-five each, and Felicia got ten.

Question: For all his muscle, why didn't Augie run the whole show alone?

Answer: Because I had greater reach—all the connections.

Question: Through Homeland Security and your travels on behalf of counterterrorism?

Answer: Yes.

Question: Could you tell us about the extent of your operation?

Answer: Yes. The best way to put it is that the girls get used up and then they're replaced by new recruits who arrive monthly. So it became a massive operation with many people in all quarters of the globe getting paid off if they only looked the other way.

Question: Let's get to Felicia. You ordered her killed?

Answer: Yes.

Question: Why?

Answer: She wanted more money. She said she would pull out her senior girls, which would have had a bad effect on the system, especially overseas. A mixture of seniors and raw recruits was our winning combination.

Question: And she handled the business end of things?

Answer: Yes. You know . . . computers, credit cards, sophisticated technology. She was good at it.

Question: We understand she was a kind of go-between with Mugur Popa from Bucharest.

Answer: Yes. When it came to cruise ship lines, he was the best. He routed many of our girls through them before they got to their final destination. She oversaw that phase.

Question: About a couple of other people, Mr. Vasilakis. The owner of the Clemensville inn, Clifford Carpenter. Was he in on anything?

Answer: No, but he knew quite a bit, probably through Felicia.

Question: You hired Roscoe Fern to set the fire?

Answer: Yes.

Question: Why?

Answer: Carpenter also wanted a piece of the action. Said in return he would open up his place to more activity. I didn't think that was such a good idea and told him. But he kept insisting so I decided to teach him a lesson.

Question: Paul Mitroi?

Answer: I didn't know him personally, but I believe his daughter was taken care of some time ago.

Question: Paddy McClure. He turned on you. Called to warn Dr. Liu on the day you were apprehended. Why would he have done that?

Answer: He was upset that we took care of Felicia. They were great friends. We should have taken care of him at the same time.

Question: As part of our agreement, you will supply us with the names of all those involved in your network. Is that correct?

Answer: Correct.

George's reaction was immediate. He indicated that not every single question had been answered by the document, but it was sufficient to provide some measure of closure.

Jay summoned the wine steward and ordered champagne. Glasses raised, each gave a different version of the same sentiment—a combination of thanks and relief. Henry felt his cell phone vibrating. He took the call. It was Paul Mitroi. He said he wanted to thank Henry and his team for what they had done on behalf of his daughter and the other victims. He hoped that many girls in the future would be spared a similar fate.

"Thank you, Dr. Liu," Mitroi said, his voice reduced to a whisper.

"Our pleasure," Henry said. "And thank you for all your help in solving this case."

Karl stood up with a glass in each hand and declared, "We haven't stamped out 'voluntary' prostitution by any means, but we certainly made a dent in white slavery. Hail to our GIFT!"

Dan, the owner of Baderro's, walked in. "Hey, where you docs been?" he asked.

"On a cruise ship," Henry replied.